Praise for the Ma

WITH VICS YC

"A sense of danger and mena   is
lightened by Mad's genuine   ιs
crafted an extremely unique mystery series with an intelligent
heroine whose appeal will never go out of style."

— *Kings River Life Magazine*

"If you love Doris Day, you'll love Madison Night, decorator
extraordinaire. She specializes in restoring mid-century homes and
designs, and her latest project involves abductions, murder and
vengeance!"

— *Books for Avid Readers*

"A well-constructed tale with solid characters and page after page of
interesting, intelligent dialogue. Diane Vallere delivers a cunning
plot as well as humor and romance."

— *ReadertoReader.com*

THAT TOUCH OF INK (#2)

"A terrific mystery is always in fashion—and this one is sleek, chic
and constantly surprising. Vallere's smart styling and wry humor
combine for a fresh and original page-turner—it'll have you eagerly
awaiting her next appealing adventure. I'm a fan!"

— Hank Phillippi Ryan,
Agatha, Anthony, and Mary Higgins Clark Award-Winning Author

"Diane Vallere...has a wonderful touch, bringing in the design
elements and influences of the '50s and '60s era many of us hold
dear while keeping a strong focus on what it means in modern
times to be a woman in business for herself, starting over."

— *Fresh Fiction*

"All of us who fell in love with Madison Night in *Pillow Stalk* will be rooting for her when the past comes back to haunt her in *That Touch of Ink*. The suspense is intense, the plot is hot and the style is to die for. A thoroughly entertaining entry in this enjoyable series."

— Catriona McPherson,
Agatha Award-Winning Author of the Dandy Gilver Mystery Series

PILLOW STALK (#1)

"A humorous yet adventurous read of mystery, very much worth considering."

— *Midwest Book Review*

"Make room for Vallere's tremendously fun homage. Imbuing her story with plenty of mid-century modern decorating and fashion tips...Her disarmingly honest lead and two hunky sidekicks will appeal to all fashionistas and antiques types and have romance crossover appeal."

— *Library Journal*

"A multifaceted story...plenty of surprises...And what an ending!"

— *New York Journal of Books*

"If you are looking for an unconventional mystery with a snarky, no-nonsense main character, this is it...Instead of clashing, humor and danger meld perfectly, and there's a cliffhanger that will make your jaw drop."

— *RT Book Reviews*

"A charming modern tribute to Doris Day movies and the retro era of the '50s, including murders, escalating danger, romance...and a puppy!"

— Linda O. Johnston,
Author of the Pet Rescue Mysteries

WITH VICS YOU GET EGGROLL

**The Madison Night Mystery Series
by Diane Vallere**

<u>Novels</u>

PILLOW STALK (#1)
THAT TOUCH OF INK (#2)
WITH VICS YOU GET EGGROLL (#3)

<u>Novellas</u>

MIDNIGHT ICE
(in OTHER PEOPLE'S BAGGAGE)

WITH VICS YOU GET EGGROLL

A Madison Night Mystery

Diane Vallere

HENERY PRESS

WITH VICS YOU GET EGGROLL
A Madison Night Mystery
Part of the Henery Press Mystery Collection

First Edition
Trade paperback edition | April 2015

Henery Press
www.henerypress.com

Copyright © 2014 by Diane Vallere
Cover art by Stephanie Chontos

This is a work of fiction. Any references to historical events, real people, or real locales are used fictitiously. Other names, characters, places, and incidents are the product of the author's imagination, and any resemblance to actual events or locales or persons, living or dead, is entirely coincidental. No affiliation with Doris Day or Paramount is claimed or implied.

ISBN-13: 978-1-941962-43-5

Printed in the United States of America

For Deenie

ACKNOWLEDGMENTS

It is always a joy to reflect on a completed book and think about who was a part of the journey with me. As always, I'm grateful to Sisters in Crime, the Guppies, and the Mysteristas, and to Josh Hickman, who introduced me to Lakewood, Texas, and to the world that became Madison's.

I owe much of this book to the influence of three women who I am proud to call my friends:

Cynthia Kuhn, for suggesting that the Mysteristas sign up for NaNoWriMo in 2013. I started this manuscript that November to support your own efforts. I did not finish it (nor did I hit the NaNo 50K challenge), but I set out enough of the story that I was eager to revisit it in May 2014.

Thank you Nancy Golub, who may be the nicest woman in Dallas, for your hospitality. From our fun-filled, mid-century modern weekend to a feast of Chinese food! And especially for suggesting that morning walk through the Greenville Cemetery.

Thank you to Kendel Lynn, who has been a strong advocate for Madison since *Other People's Baggage*. Writing this book made me laugh and cry, and I was nervous to send it to you. Your reaction helped me feel like I'd done something right. Both Madison and I love having a home at Henery Press.

ONE

The flashing red and blue lights remained visible in my rearview mirror far longer than I would have liked. I accelerated through the twists and turns of Gaston Avenue's residential streets, almost lost control and swung wide when the road cut to the right, but kept going. If the police officer behind me wanted to catch up with my zippy Alfa Romeo, he was going to have to put pedal to the metal.

He'd been pursuing me for over a mile. Up ahead, the tall parking lot lights of the Whole Foods grocery store loomed. It was after ten and the neighboring businesses had long since been closed. I put on my signal, turned into the vacant lot, and parked under a row of streetlamps by the store's east-facing exit.

The royal blue Dallas police car pulled up behind me. The glass of the car's windows were tinted, telling me nothing. I double-checked that my doors were locked and kept my engine running. My heart sped like a leaky faucet with a rapid drip.

A gloved hand tapped the window. I cranked the lever until there was a two-inch opening and looked up at the officer. He shone a flashlight into my car. His expression changed from serious to concerned, probably as he noted the smudges of concrete and dirt from the construction site I'd been at all day. His eyes dropped to the navy blue coveralls I wore, and then moved to the yellow hardhat that had fallen from the passenger side seat onto the floor.

"License and Registration, ma'am," the officer said.

"May I see your identification first, officer?" I asked.

He held what looked like a small black wallet in front of the window. One side displayed his police badge. The other had a photo identification. I cranked the window down another turn so I could read his credentials more clearly.

Officer Brian Iverson. Lakewood Police Department. That was Lt. Tex Allen's precinct. I reached into my bag and pulled out my wallet. My hands shook. I fumbled while trying to get the license out of the plastic sleeve. When I finally did, I handed it to him.

"Madison Night," he read. "Wait here."

He strode back to his car. I waited until he was seated before reaching for my phone, flipping it over twice before making the call.

"Lt. Allen? This is Madison. I just got pulled over."

"Where are you?" he asked, a trace of panic in his voice.

"The Whole Foods parking lot by the Lakewood Theater."

"Did you get a badge number?"

"I saw his badge. Officer Iverson. Blond, fit. Looks to be in his forties or fifties."

"Brian Iverson. He turned thirty last month. Lives a hard life. Not sure what the job is going to do to him in the long run, but he's a good cop. You're safe with him."

I tipped my head back against the head rest and closed my eyes, imagining the tension leaving my body. It was okay. Tex knew the police officer who had pulled me over. He wasn't the Lakewood Abductor.

"What did he get you on?" he asked, the tone of his voice shifting from concern to flirtation.

"I don't know yet."

"You should have told him you know me. Might have saved you from a ticket."

"I don't like using our relationship like that."

"It's not like you're using it for anything else. One of these days you'll see me for the prince I am."

"And until then I'll see you as a frog."

"It's not easy being green. Remember that."

Officer Iverson returned to my window. "I have to go," I said to Tex.

"Call me when you're home." We hung up.

I took the paperwork from Officer Iverson, slid my license back into my wallet, put the registration inside the front cover of the Alfa Romeo car manual, and put the manual back into the glove box.

"Do you know why I pulled you over?" Iverson asked.

"No."

"Broken tail light." He tapped the end of his pen against a metal clipboard that held a form I sincerely hoped wasn't a citation.

"Doesn't Lt. Allen work in your precinct?" I asked.

He tipped his head to the side and smiled. "That's how I knew your name. Madison Night. You were there when Lt. Allen got shot."

"Yes."

He tapped his pen a few more times and looked at the form in front of him. "I sure wish you'd told me that when I first pulled you over. I already wrote up this ticket." He looked torn between protocol and doing me a favor. "Tell you what. I'll make this a warning. Get the tail light fixed in the next five days and take this paperwork to the courthouse." He pulled a piece of the multi-layered form off and handed it to me. "I couldn't help noticing that you gave me a little chase before you pulled over."

I took the form. "The only thing on the news these days is about the missing women and the Lakewood Abductor. The reports say we shouldn't pull over for anybody unless we're in a public parking space or a crowded area."

"That's right. Glad you're paying attention. Are you headed home now?"

I nodded.

"Your address says Gaston Avenue. Home's close?"

"A couple of blocks."

"Good. Be careful, Ms. Night."

I waited until Officer Iverson was back in his car before I backed out of my space. It was true that I was only a couple of blocks from my apartment, but I'd lied when I called it home. There was a time when it had been the place where I felt most comfortable, but I hadn't been staying there lately. Nobody had.

I drove down Gaston Avenue, past my apartment building, and then took a side street to Greenville, double-checking the rearview and side mirrors frequently. My heart still raced.

From Greenville I turned left on Monticello and slowed when I reached the house I'd inherited a few months ago. I parked the car in the detached garage, hustled past the tomato plants to the porch and let myself in. This was where Rocky waited for me, and in my book, home is where you keep your puppy.

Now two years old, his hyper nature came and went in spurts. Anybody entering the house was cause for an outburst. He bounced around my feet and stood on his hind legs, paws on the back of mine, while I set a plastic milk crate filled with files on the dining room table. I put the hardhat next to the files and stepped out of the dirty blue coveralls.

Ah, the glamorous life.

I scooped Rocky up. "Hey there, cutie! Are you happy that I'm home?" He licked my cheek and nuzzled his face into the side of my neck. I locked the front door behind me and locked the door between the front door and the kitchen. After turning on the TV in the living room, I carried Rocky upstairs. I set him on his dog bed, a custom-made, heavily padded circle with a one-foot high border. The whole thing was covered in turquoise bar cloth printed with black radials and white squigglies, all reminiscent of the atomic era I specialized in with Mad for Mod Decorating. The dog bed had arrived as a very large package delivered to my studio a few weeks ago. *To Rock, From Hudson.* It was the only gift to mark the occasion of my forty-eighth birthday, and even though it was clearly for my Shih Tzu, I found the timing pleasantly suspicious.

The bedroom was hot. I kept a window AC unit ready to roll at bedtime, but otherwise preferred to spend my time on the first floor of the house. Under the coveralls I'd worn a belted light blue tunic and matching blue cotton trousers from my latest estate sale bid. I made a habit of making offers on estates of people I learned about from the obituaries, and while most of the time it was the wife who outlived the husband, in this case, the husband had been the one to maintain their mid-century modern ranch after his wife had passed away. Her closet had been filled with clothes from the late sixties—a large portion still with the tags on them. They were slightly groovier than my usual early to mid sixties wardrobe, but I wasn't one to look a gift horse—in this case, in the form of forty-five-year-old new-with-tags merchandise—in the mouth. The dirty clothes went into the wicker hamper in the corner. I showered and dressed in a paisley caftan and went downstairs. Rocky followed. I made a salad from the lettuce in the crisper and the half chicken breast leftover from last night, and carried it to the living room, and then doubled back to the kitchen for a glass of white wine.

"We have breaking news on the identity of the Lakewood Abductor," a female reporter said as I took my seat on the sofa. She stood at the end of a parking lot, an empty field behind her. I speared a chunk of iceberg and crunched on it. The photo of a woman flashed onto the upper right-hand side of the screen.

"The body of Kate Morrow was found by two Lakewood residents who were hiking by Lockwood Park earlier this evening. Kate, a pre-med student at Loyola University, was in town visiting family. Her family reported her missing, and the police have been looking for leads. A witness from the Organic Foods Market in the Casa Linda shopping center said he saw a woman matching Ms. Morrow's description get into a black sedan last week. According to the police, evidence found near her body confirms that the abductor was impersonating a police officer. She has been dead for several hours."

The report was chilling. Kate's rental car was found abandoned in the parking lot of the Casa Linda shopping center last month, only a few miles from where I lived. Her handbag and keys were on the passenger side floor. The two security cameras in the parking lot of the organic food store had malfunctioned so no video had been recorded.

I knew the Casa Linda shopping center well. It was so named because of the old theater that occupied one of the corners of the lot. After closing its doors in the early nineties, the theater had passed through a number of hands, eventually falling into a state of disrepair. A group of movie historians invested in it, renaming it The Mummy Theater, where I was a regular volunteer. We put together a calendar of events featuring classic movies to be shown on the big screen. Even though the theater had been renamed, the shopping center had kept the Casa Linda marquis, and residents of the Lakewood area continued to refer to it as such.

In addition to the theater and the organic foods market, there was a comic book store, a pet store, a paint store, and a takeout Chinese restaurant.

Images of three other women joined that of Kate Morrow on the TV screen. Below each image was the victim's name. "We are still on the search for the two other women who have been reported missing in the past two weeks. The Dallas Police have reason to suspect that the perpetrator being referred to as the 'Lakewood Abductor' may be driving what appears to be an unmarked police car." The blond reporter turned to the police chief. "Chief Washington, what can you tell us about your findings today?"

Chief Washington looked like a linebacker in a black made-to-measure business suit. He leaned toward the microphone, but didn't take it from the reporter. "Initial reports from the medical examiner state that Ms. Morrow has been dead for less than a day. We found ligature marks on her wrists that were consistent with marks made by handcuffs. The recent rain washed away any evidence of footprints, but we're still combing the immediate area for something that will give us a lead on the guy behind this."

"Are you any closer to revealing a profile of her attacker?"

"Since the first abductions, we suspected he was impersonating a security officer or a law enforcement officer. New evidence supports this theory."

"What is this evidence?"

"We're not releasing that information yet. Maybe this man met her before she was abducted or maybe they had a previous relationship. We have identified a person of interest and are in the process of finding out what his connection to her—to *all* of the women—is."

A sixty-something woman in jeans and a white button down shirt screamed behind the police chief. "I want him locked up! I want him arrested! He killed my girl!" she yelled hysterically. "He was a cop. He was supposed to protect her and you let him kill her!"

The reporter kept the microphone in front of the chief. "Is that true? Is your suspect a member of the police force?"

The chief looked uncomfortable. "Right now he is not a suspect, but until we have a chance to understand the nature of his relationship to Kate Morrow, he is a person of interest. We are pursuing this lead with all of our resources. If one of our officers is involved in the abduction and murder of Lakewood residents, we will show no leniency."

I thought about how Tex's world would change if one of his fellow officers was responsible for these heinous crimes. It would be an uphill battle that would severely damage the reputation of the Lakewood Police Department, possibly long term.

The mother of the victim stood off to the side of the crowd, her hysterics subdued by her sobs. The reporter raised the microphone and spoke directly to the camera.

"Tonight, a murder victim provides a clue to the possible identity of the man terrorizing the Lakewood/White Rock Lake area. What that means to the residents of Lakewood is unclear. Chief Washington is still urging everyone to be careful. Chief?"

This time the chief took the microphone. "We encourage everyone to follow these safety tips: If you see a police vehicle behind you, do not pull over until you reach a crowded or well-lit parking lot. Do not turn off your engine. Ask to see his badge. If he is a legitimate officer, he will be aware of these safety issues and will act accordingly. If he does not, call 911 and head to the nearest police station. You will be safe there."

Suddenly the hysterical woman broke away from the crowd and charged the police chief. She grabbed the microphone from him. "You don't protect the citizens of Lakewood, you protect your own! I know you found a badge by my daughter's body and I know whose it is. I want Lt. Tex Allen arrested for murder!"

TWO

I dropped my glass and wine splashed onto the throw rug. Instead of cleaning it up, I grabbed the remote and turned up the volume. The reporter, initially stunned, regained her composure and took the microphone from the hysterical woman. She thrust it at Chief Washington. "Is there any truth to her accusation, Chief? Do you have evidence linking one of your homicide detectives to the murder of Kate Morrow?"

Chief Washington's face colored. "This interview is over," he said to the reporter. He turned away and walked past a row of uniformed officers. The camera followed them to a parking lot filled with royal blue police vehicles. The officers surrounded their chief, but the audio was a recap by the reporter who had conducted the interview moments before.

"Possible new evidence in the abduction and murder of Kate Morrow points to the Lakewood Police Department. Can any of us feel safe? The hunt for the Lakewood Abductor continues. Anyone with information on Kate Morrow, or any of the missing women, is urged to call the number on the screen." A phone number appeared.

The abductions had started about a month ago. Kate Morrow had been in Dallas visiting her family. She'd rented a car at the airport and driven herself to their house. The visit had been cut short when Kate went out for groceries and didn't return. Her mother called the police after four hours, but she wasn't treated as a missing person until twenty more had passed. It took the police a while to connect her to a rental car found abandoned in the Casa

Linda Shopping Center, but once they did, there'd been a heightened sense of concern. A store employee came forward and said he'd seen a woman matching Kate's description leaving the parking lot with a man in uniform. He hadn't thought much about it until reports of a second missing woman came in, and then a third. Employees of local businesses had been questioned, but no one had seen anything out of the ordinary.

Like other residents of Lakewood, I'd held out hope that the women were alive, though the longer they were missing, the scarier that hope became. If they were alive, where were they? And what was someone doing to them to keep them detained?

Warnings had been issued, general advice to people heading out alone, but the victims had been out-of-towners, people who may not have been tuned to our local news. Kate Morrow's car was a rental. The next two bore out-of-state plates. They'd found the vehicles abandoned in public parking lots around town, the occupants missing. Nobody knew how the women were being targeted or what was happening to them.

Until now.

Kate Morrow had been wearing the clothes she was last seen in, and according to the police, she'd been dead for less than a day. Marks on her wrists and ankles indicated that she'd been physically restrained wherever it was she'd been held, but her cause of death had been a slit throat.

And now—my stomach churned with nausea at the thought of the mother's accusation. I went to the kitchen for a towel to mop up the wine and then dropped down on all fours to scrub at the spill, my hand shaking as I pushed the towel back and forth over the wet spot. Did Tex have a history with Kate Morrow? What was his connection to her? When I'd called him from the parking lot outside of Whole Foods, had he known he was a person of interest in these abductions? If so, why hadn't he said anything?

* * *

I was at Crestwood pool by six the next morning. I wore my bathing suit under a white terrycloth dress that zipped up the front. Rocky led me past the locker rooms and the lifeguard's tower to the benches that lined the pool. I was the youngest of the early morning lap swimmers. I wasn't much for ageism, but I liked how my fellow swimmers, themselves octogenarians, treated me like a youngster.

I waved at the lifeguard on duty and pulled a bottle of sport strength sunscreen from my tote. Each day it took a healthy amount of SPF 75 on my arms and shoulders to protect my fair skin from the aging rays of the sun.

"Bobby, do you mind keeping an eye on Rocky while I swim?" I asked.

"Hey Madison," he said. "No problem."

I looped Rocky's leash around the base of the lifeguard stand and carried my cap and goggles to the end of the lane. There were only a handful of us today, Mary Elizabeth and her friend Grace at the end lane designated for the slow swimmers, and Carole in the lane next to her. The pool had six lanes, so I was able to have my own. I waved to the ladies, tucked my hair under my cap, and pulled the goggles on top. I ran my toes through the water to check the temperature. It was cool. Still, I jumped in, letting my knees collapse under me until I was completely submerged. When I floated back up to the surface, I pushed off the wall and started swimming.

One of the reasons I like swimming early in the morning was the beauty of the landscape, uninterrupted by the noise of a crowd, the fumes of exhaust, the rudeness of people on their cell phones. Everything faded away and the only thing left was the feeling of my arms slicing through the water, propelling me forward. Two laps was all it took to find that Zen place.

That's why I didn't notice Tex until my fifth lap. It wasn't so much that I saw the lieutenant standing in the shadows of the bleachers, it was that I saw something that interrupted the idyllic scene I'd come to expect every third stroke when I breathed to my right.

I stopped at the deep end of the pool and raised my goggles. My body was just starting to get into a groove, where the water temperature is comfortable and my muscles feel loose. My heart rate was at the point I tried to maintain over the next forty-five minutes, but now that I'd seen Tex hovering to the side of where I'd left my belongings, I didn't think maintaining my heart rate would be much of a problem.

I let go of the wall and treaded water. Tex hadn't moved. He wore a white polo shirt with the Lakewood PD logo on it and khaki pants. His arms were crossed, and the sun flashed off his silver Swiss Army watch, shooting a beam of blindness in my direction. At the other end of the pool, Grace and Mary Elizabeth jumped up and down, raising foam noodles over their heads. Carol was in the middle of a lap.

I pulled myself out of the water and walked to the bin of kickboards. Tex rounded the side of the bleachers and met me.

"Swimming again?" he said.

"Swimming again."

"Trying to get your life back to normal."

"Trying."

"So...you heard."

"I heard."

I tossed the first two kickboards back into the white metal bin as if they weren't exactly what I was looking for and reached for a third.

"Night, I didn't have anything to do with the abductions."

"You don't have to defend yourself to me."

I'd met Lt. Tex Allen about a year ago when I was planning a Doris Day film festival and happened upon some evidence in an unsolved murder. He had been convinced that I was in danger. I hadn't wanted to believe him. Turned out he was right.

Since then, I'd gotten to know him a little better. What I saw at a glance—bachelor, playboy, flirt, womanizer—turned out all to be true. But he was also insightful, protective, insistent, and honest. Lt. Tex Allen was a lot of things, but a killer? No.

I pulled an orange kickboard from the stack. He grabbed my wrist. I flinched. His grip relaxed. "You're not going to hear from me for a while. Okay? Don't call me. Don't try to find me."

"After everything we've been through, you're going to start playing hard to get?" I asked, keeping my voice light.

His eyes shifted from my face to the top of my head. I'd forgotten that I was wearing a swim cap. "I would have expected you to wear one of those caps with the big colorful flowers all over it."

I shook my head. "You are so predictable."

"Really? You're standing in front of me in a wet bathing suit and I'm talking about your swim cap. I thought you'd give me points for that." He dropped my arm and stepped back. "I need to find out what the police know. I'll be in touch when I can."

"Let me know if I can help," I called behind him. I wasn't really sure what kind of help an interior decorator could offer a police lieutenant suspected of murder even if he did take me up on my offer, which I knew he wouldn't.

For the first time in longer than I could remember, my mind wandered while I swam and I lost track of the distance I'd logged. Forty-five minutes later, I stopped by the side of the pool. Tex was gone. I pulled off my cap and goggles and climbed out, and then showered and changed into a white shirt, orange vest, and khaki pants.

I first fell in love with the mid-century decorating style through the movies of Doris Day, who shared a birthday with me. From watching those movies over and over, developing an eye for decorating in that sunshiny style, I also became a fan of the way she dressed. A lot of people laughed at the image of the smiling, freckled actress, especially since her most popular movies took place in a time when entertainment was changing from lighthearted fare to more politically driven subjects. Doris Day's last movie, *With Six You Get Eggroll*, had been in 1968, the same year Bobby Kennedy and Martin Luther King, Jr. had been assassinated. The world was changing. The look of the late sixties was far from the beginning.

People who weren't fans of the actress didn't understand that through much of the sixties, Doris Day played independent women, characters who owned their own businesses, ran households, and often didn't need a man. The irony was, she usually ended up with a pretty good one: Rock Hudson, James Garner, and Cary Grant, to name a few.

My secret strategy when first starting my own decorating business was to read the obituaries and contact the next of kin of women who'd been in their twilight years. It wasn't the kind of strategy I fleshed out on the loan application I turned into the bank, but I'd learned that women in their eighties and nineties tended not to renovate with the more current interior decorating trends. Aside from the creepy factor, it worked.

With a little effort and an "early bird gets the worm" mentality, I'd amassed a decent amount of inventory to use in decorating jobs that came into Mad for Mod. The signs of age and wear were easily minimized with TLC and the talents of Hudson James, my most trusted handyman and creator of Rocky's custom dog bed. More often than not I'd beat the auction houses to the punch and get my pick of an estate.

My studio came with a storage locker behind it, and I filled the space with all sorts of accumulated objects to decorate a room in an authentic manner, instead of going the reproduction route. Fortunately, making an offer on an estate often included the contents of the deceased's closet. Most baby boomer children had no interest in dealing with a closet of polyester shift dresses and hats with tassels. Score for me.

Recently I'd finished an atomic kitchen for Connie and Ned Duncan, clients who had become friends. I'd outfitted their kitchen with turquoise metal cabinets from 1963 and a set of Starburst by

Franciscan dinnerware service for ten that I'd found in a warehouse in Denton, and we'd recessed top of the line appliances below the counter to mimic Rod Taylor's atomic kitchen in *The Glass Bottom Boat*. We'd even installed an original Sputnik lamp over the dining table—all for five thousand and three dollars. I would have rounded it off, but five grand had become something of a bad omen for me. Connie and Ned had been so happy with the final reveal that they extended a standing Friday night dinner invite, until last week when they took off for a month-long vacation in Palm Springs, California.

After getting dressed, I slathered a tinted sunscreen over my fair skin and applied a rosy lip gloss. I didn't spend much time on my hair since it would be under a hardhat in a matter of hours, instead finger-combing the snarls out and securing it behind my head in a low ponytail. I collected Rocky from the lifeguard and left.

I drove to Sweetwater Drive with the sound of the air naturally drying my wet hair keeping me from hearing anything else. My vintage Alfa Romeo was my second in five years. The first had been involved in an unfortunate accident, and the insurance company had determined that the cost of repairs outweighed the value. I took their check and put out feelers with every used car dealer in a two hundred mile radius.

After months of waiting, I got a call from a guy in Louisiana who turned up a blue one almost identical to the one that had been totaled. The cost of travelling to Louisiana to get it wiped out any profit I might have made from the insurance check, so I had to pass on the offer of installing a sound system like I did with my last one. Repairs to the broken gas gauge and dashboard clock were going to have to wait too. For now, I wore a watch and topped off the tank every Monday.

I parked in the shade of a pink dogwood tree in front of a rundown ranch house. The property now belonged to Cleo and Dan Tyler, a married couple who owned a movie development studio in Los Angeles. They'd purchased the property for a song thanks to its rundown condition and hired me to make it livable. Despite the condition, I immediately recognized the hallmarks of the original Cliff May, even before they showed me the floor plans they found in the attic.

Rocky circled around in the passenger seat, eager to get out and run. "Ready to play with Daisy?" I asked. Rocky stood up and looked at me like playing with Daisy was the greatest thing in the world. Aside from peanut butter in a rubber toy. Nothing beat that.

"Remember to behave yourself. I have work to do. Okay?" I said to him. He sniffed my hand and charged across the center console to my lap.

I clipped his leash on, and we got out of the car. With my spare hand, I grabbed my milk crate, coveralls, and hardhat. Cleo met us on the front stairs. She wore a gold one-piece bathing suit under a long white robe and held a tiny tan and white Chihuahua.

For the past few weeks I spent Tuesdays, Wednesdays, and Thursdays here. From the initial conversations we'd had when they hired me, I'd learned that they bought the house sight unseen. After closing escrow, they discovered their mid-century jewel was more of a diamond in the rough thanks to the unfortunate eighties remodel the previous owners had taken on. Enter Mad for Mod and my enviable skills with a chisel, a sledgehammer, and a vision.

"You are a trooper, coming to work on our house every day."

"This is what I do," I reminded her. "When you hired me to work on your home, I explained the process of deconstructing the eighties remodel before I could restore the mid-century interiors."

"I *know*. I just didn't expect you to be the one doing it yourself. I almost feel bad. It's so unfeminine."

The tiny dog wriggled around in her arms and Rocky picked up the pace when he spied his friend.

"Rocky!" I called.

Cleo set the Chihuahua on the porch. "It's okay. They're such good friends by now." Rocky extended his leash the full distance and jutted out his head trying to get to Daisy.

"I'm going to be working with chemicals today and I have to ask that the dogs be kept away from the house."

"Of course. I'll take them to the backyard with me." She stooped down and ruffled Rocky's fur.

I handed over the leash and we went separate directions. In a couple of seconds I heard the mingling barks of Rocky and Daisy coming from the backyard.

Whatever had brought Cleo and Dan Tyler to Dallas, Texas for their home away from home was a mystery to me, but I wasn't going to complain. They'd loved my proposed renovation and paid me a sizeable deposit up front to bump them to the top of the job queue.

I stepped into the coveralls and pulled the sleeves over my arms one at a time. With the hardhat tucked under my elbow, I headed through the house. I wouldn't need it until I started deconstructing the wall of glass bricks that divided the living room and dining room, and truth was, I hoped Hudson would be available to oversee that part of the job. If only I knew where he had gone when he left Lakewood, and if he was planning to return.

Cleo returned to the living room. "What's on the agenda today?"

"I thought I'd work in the bathroom. I ran a test on the sink yesterday and it's not really a white fixture. Once I strip it down to the porcelain, you'll have an original Mamie Eisenhower pink bathroom."

"A pink bathroom! Very of-the-era. Are you sure you don't want to rip out the fixtures and start over?"

"Then it wouldn't be original." Not for the first time I wondered about this renovation and why Cleo and Dan had come to me to perform it. When I found out the apartment building I owned had pink fixtures hidden under industrial paint, Hudson and I spent the weekend stripping each and every one of them. The next morning I added a description of the pink bathrooms to the rental listing. Cleo seemed somewhat confused by the meaning of "mid-century" and the excitement of exposing it.

I rooted through the bag of stripper, gloves, sponges, and wooden spatulas that I'd brought. Four paint chips littered the bottom of the bag. Paintin' Place, a local paint store, had become my destination of choice for supplies. The store sat in the corner of the Casa Linda shopping center where Kate Morrow had been abducted. The owner, Mitchell Moore, ran his store with personalized service and offered residents of Lakewood products you couldn't find at Lowe's or Home Depot. After I'd exposed a counterfeiting ring and become something of a local celebrity, he'd invited me to endorse a capsule collection of mid-century modern paint colors. We'd poured over hundreds of swatches, finally agreeing on shades of red, yellow, aqua, and taupe. The only thing left was for me to name them. The job with Cleo and Dan Tyler had taken over my life and I'd back-burnered the task. Mitchell had called a few days ago, saying he wanted to advertise the paints in his end-of-month mailer. That gave me a week to be clever.

My fingers closed on two of the swatches. Daisy Yellow? Malt Shoppe Taupe?

No. And nope. I tossed the swatches back into the bag. "I'm leaving the windows open while I work. The chemicals are strong and I'll need the ventilation."

"Let me call Dan. He'll buy you a fan while he's out."

I tied a pink and white bandana around my head and set to work. A mild breeze pushed the curtains into the bathroom. I started working on the sink, pouring epoxy remover into the basin and using my gloved fingertips to smooth the gunk over the paint. It took a few minutes for the chemicals to react, and then the smooth surface bubbled up and separated from the sink like a layer of cheap rubber. I used a wooden spatula to ease the temporary coating from the original pink surface. Long ago I'd found wooden spatulas from the dollar store to be a good bet when it came to stripping porcelain. The rounded tip was more forgiving at delicate junctures, and the size of the tool was perfect for the size of my hands. What I couldn't do with a spatula I did with a chopstick. I bought them in bulk from the local Thai market.

By the time the paint was stripped, the noxious fumes had left me lightheaded. I peeled off my gloves and tossed them into the trash, and then went through the great room to the sliding doors that exited to the pool out back. Cleo lounged on a turquoise and white chaise, sipping from a glass of tea, watching a sizeable television set that sat on a small cart.

"I hope you don't mind some company. I needed some fresh air," I said.

"Oh, my," she said, fanning her hand back and forth past her nose. "Honey, that's not Chanel No. 5. Is that what the chemicals smell like?"

"Can you smell them? I must be immune."

"Sit down for a second. Let me get you a glass of tea."

I glanced at the empty chaise next to hers, but couldn't picture myself stretching out in my coveralls next to her in her Grecian poolside ensemble. On the TV, the show she was watching was interrupted by a news brief. Chief Washington stood behind the podium on a stage. Blue curtains hung down on either side. A row of uniformed officers stood next to flags of the United States and Texas. The chief shuffled a few papers and cleared his throat. I fumbled around the buttons of the remote and turned up the volume.

"Based on evidence found at the crime scene of Kate Morrow, we have linked one of our officers to the crimes of the Lakewood Killer."

A chill swept over me from head to toe, despite the heat and humidity. I stepped backward once, then again, and bumped into Cleo. I whirled around and tea sloshed out of the plastic tumbler she carried. "Hold on, there, honey," she said.

"I have to leave."

"What happened?" She looked behind me to the TV. "Did they catch the guy who killed those women?"

"I don't think so," I said.

"Yes, they did. Look, he's right there." She pointed at the screen and I followed the extension of her finger. Next to Chief Washington stood Tex, and he didn't look happy.

THREE

A press conference was underway. Chief Washington greeted the audience and thanked them for coming. He made brief statements about what he would discuss and what he would not, and finished by saying when he was done, he would not be taking questions. He paused, looked at Tex, who nodded. The chief picked up his statement and spoke.

"Because of circumstances relating to the recent abduction and murder of Kate Morrow, it is my belief that Lt. Thomas Allen's presence may cause distractions to the ongoing investigation and the operation of the police department. At my request, Lt. Allen has agreed to take a voluntary leave of absence. This is not an accusation, nor is it an admission of guilt. Lt. Allen has served the city of Lakewood for twenty-four years and is looking forward to the matter being resolved so he can return to his job of protecting our community."

Tex stood next to the chief, his hands in front of him. His jawline was rigid and his blue eyes were troubled. When Tex had left me at the pool that morning, he said he needed to find out what the police knew. He had told me not to look for him. I couldn't imagine what had happened in the next couple of hours to lead to him being asked to take voluntary leave.

I gulped for fresh air but only took in the sticky humidity that surrounded me. The lightheaded feeling from working with the chemicals in the bathroom returned, and I reached out for something to stabilize myself.

"You don't look so hot, sugar," Cleo said. She took my elbow and led me to her chaise. This time I had no compunctions about dropping into it. "Drink this," she said. I took the glass and guzzled the tea until it was gone.

Cleo sat next to me and put her hand on my back. I stared ahead at the expanse of blue swimming pool. "That man didn't do it. He didn't commit those crimes," I said.

"The police lieutenant? Do you know him?"

"He's a friend. A close friend."

"Well, normally I would think having a police lieutenant friend would be a good thing, but now I don't know what to say." She patted my thigh. "Sure is handsome," she added.

"If you don't mind, I'm going to have to cut my day short so I can find out what happened."

"I don't think that's such a good idea," said a voice from the back door.

Cleo and I looked up at the same time. Her husband, Dan, stood in front of us, holding an oscillating fan in one hand. He was shorter than Cleo and had the solid build that came from lifting weights. His hairline receded, and what was left of his hair was combed straight back over the top. Razor sunglasses covered his eyes, but I felt them piercing me all the same.

"Did I overhear you say you know that guy?" he asked.

"Yes. He's a friend. He helped me out in the past—"

He held up a hand. "He might be the type to help old ladies with their groceries for all I know. He looks to be about, what, late forties?"

"That's right."

"Police lieutenant. You know much about the psychology of cops?"

"I never really thought about it."

"What do you think it takes to get someone to sign up for that kind of life? Thrill seeker. Thrives on chaos and danger. Pushes boundaries. Does any of this sound familiar?"

I hated that he was talking about Tex, a man who had entered my life with just about every cliché you could think of and had become one of the few people who I trusted. I hated that everything he said was dead on.

"Do you know why cops have the highest suicide rate of any job? The stress gets to them and they gotta find an outlet. Physical expressions of violence are one. Working out, firing guns. Abusing women. High rate of alcoholism among them too. It's another way to blow off steam."

"How do you know all this?" I asked.

Cleo put her hand on my arm. When she spoke, her voice was steady. "Dan's brother was a cop for twenty years. He died in a drunk driving accident."

"I'm so sorry," I said, looking back and forth between their faces.

Dan pulled the glasses off his face. His expression hardened into a mask. "Don't be sorry. My brother's blood alcohol level was 1.9. He was on his way home from a cop bar. He lost control of his car and killed two girls in a head-on collision. The whole precinct knew what happened, but they buried the story. They didn't want to tarnish the reputation of one of their own. It's bad enough knowing my brother was responsible for the death of those girls, but to know that the police department was so corrupt they'd hide the truth was even worse. That's what kind of moral fiber you're referring to as a friend."

He turned and went back into the house, leaving Cleo and me alone.

"It's going to take Dan a long time to reconcile his brother's death. They were close as kids but lost touch shortly after George went to the police academy. I think Dan saw signs of George's aggression manifest early on and tried to do something about it. George didn't like it—his younger brother telling him what to do."

"When was this?"

"Right around the time Dan and I got married. George was best man at our wedding."

"And when was the accident?"

"Five years ago. George had been on the force for twenty years.

If he was alive, he'd be retiring this year."

She looked away from me and stared at the grass at the edge of the concrete pool deck. I sensed she had gone into her head at the memory of her wedding, but judging by the look on her face, the memory wasn't all sunshine and roses.

"I think maybe you were right. You should cut your day short. I need to talk to my husband."

We both stood. I picked up the empty plastic tumbler and Cleo took it from my hand and set it back on the table. "Leave it. Molly, our housekeeper, will be here shortly and she'll clean up."

Something about having a housekeeper come while her house was mid-renovation seemed ridiculously indulgent, but my mind was too far from our conversation to ask her about it.

"Thank you. I don't know if I'll be here tomorrow. I'll call in the morning to let you know."

She nodded her understanding and slid the back door open. I followed her through the great room to the bathroom and peeked in. The Mamie-pink fixtures looked close to brand new, a whimsical note completely anachronistic to the news about Tex. I pulled the door shut, collected Rocky, and headed to my apartment building.

Without Hudson, I'd had to fall back on the list of contacts I had to complete small repairs in the apartment building, a problem that seemed to matter less and less as my tenants moved away. I considered putting the building up for sale, but I knew I'd get a fraction of what it would be worth without the necessary upgrades.

I cut through a series of residential streets to get there as fast as possible. I parked behind the building, bypassed the four security measures I'd had installed on the back, and went down the hall to the front door. A pile of newspapers had been fed through the mail slot. I scooped up as many as I could and climbed the in-need-of-replacement royal blue Berber carpeting that covered the staircase to the second floor. The corners had pulled away from the wall and were frayed, spiking out plastic threads. It was one more sign of neglect, of tasks I couldn't handle on my own.

One of the reasons I didn't like spending time here was the

almost complete silence. About two and a half months ago, I'd turned my apartment over to the police to search for evidence in a counterfeiting operation. Their search had destroyed the floor: pulling up planks of the hardwood, leaving subflooring exposed. The incident caused most of my tenants to move out and look for new housing. I'd spent my forty-eighth birthday alone in the building, doing what I could to minimize the damage.

The police search had also done a number on my role as anonymous landlord. My tenants had come to view me as a friend. A friend who occasionally got mixed up in some trouble, but a friend, nonetheless. Once they'd learned that I'd been the one collecting their rent—the same person who had first brought a killer to the building, and then a counterfeiter—things changed. Lease renewals went ignored. New units weren't rented. Several assured me it had nothing to do with me, per se, but more with the idea that someone they considered a friend had lied to them. There were no words for me to offer to undo that particular violation of their trust.

Truth was, any coziness and sense of home I'd once had at my apartment had been shattered by a series of unpredictable events and violations of my own trust. I now equated this building with lies I had been told and the lives that had been taken. It didn't matter much that I owned the place. I'd added additional locks to the front and back doors, a coded gate to the entrance to the parking lot in the back, and an emergency phone in the hallway. No matter what I did, I didn't feel safe.

Now that ten of the eleven other residents of the building had moved out, the small two-floor structure felt like an abandoned fallout shelter. The lack of white noise that accompanied aloneness was what threatened my way of life the most.

I unclipped Rocky's leash and turned the TV to the local news. I'd been spending more and more time at Thelma Johnson's house, but kept enough food that, if I chose to be here, I wouldn't starve. While a commercial tried to sell me on the latest antidepressant to hit the market, I microwaved a Tupperware of leftover paella and filled Rocky's bowls with fresh food and water. He buried his nose in the food and I carried my own to the living room and set it on the desk by the computer. The act of eating was more out of habit than necessity; after hearing that Tex was on voluntary leave, I wasn't really hungry.

Impatient for news, I cued up the internet and searched for something on the Lakewood Abductor. I found several links to articles that repeated the same bits of general information: Based on evidence found on the body of Kate Morrow, Lt. Thomas Rexford Allen of the Lakewood Police Department had been brought in for questioning. None of the articles mentioned what the evidence was.

I divided my attention between the internet and the television behind me. The information became a blur—what came from where?—but I pieced together what the police knew about Kate.

Her car had been reported as abandoned by a maintenance worker at the Casa Linda shopping center. In the back seat was a shopping bag from the grocery store and a receipt time-stamped for two days earlier at 6:30 p.m. Her body had been found by two hikers in the field by Lockwood Park. She hadn't been sexually assaulted. The police pulled the security feed from inside the store and recorded every person they saw enter and exit. Once they identified Kate, they requested the security tape for the parking lot, which was when they learned the camera didn't work.

A witness, one of the store's cashiers, claimed to have seen a man in uniform approach a young woman in the parking lot and offer to help her with her packages. Her description of the man was light on details, save for the fact that he was fit. They'd walked to her car together, and then the cashier went back to work. That had been the last time anyone had seen Kate Morrow alive.

Ever since the first abduction, the police had been warning Dallas residents to take extra care when driving alone. After the second missing person's report, the police focused their warning toward women. No one knew who the killer was or what was driving him. He didn't send cryptic notes taunting the police like criminals do in the movies. He didn't drop a calling card or follow up with the media and take credit for his crimes. Weeks went by, then a month. Police beefed up their presence on the streets, but no new evidence turned up.

And now, one of the missing women had been found dead and a witness linked her to the very people who had sworn to protect us. It seemed even with additional police presence in public areas, there was no way to protect yourself anymore.

I moved to the chair in front of the TV and listened to what they were saying. Phrases like "based on what we know," and "voluntarily turned himself in," told me things were far from open and shut.

Suddenly, Rocky raced to the door of the apartment and barked. His shrill yaps were meant to alert me that we were no longer the only people in the building. I double-checked the locks on the front door and moved to the bedroom where I could see the parking lot through my windows.

Right now the building was mostly empty; the only two occupied apartments were mine and Effie Jones, a soon-to-be college graduate. She was looking for a job and didn't want to take on the added stress of finding a new place to live. Plus, she had a thing for Rocky. Effie's MINI Cooper was parked in a haphazard manner across two spaces. The door to the car was open but the young woman wasn't there.

I left Rocky in the bedroom and shut the door behind him, grabbed a can of pepper spray, and unlocked the front door. I crept down the carpeted stairs. Effie's terrified face stared through the glass pane at the center of the back door. Her eyes connected with me. I couldn't hear her through the window, but I read her lips. "Help me," she said.

I unlocked the door from the inside. She came in and slammed the door shut behind her, throwing deadbolts and securing the lone padlock. She threw her arms around me.

"Madison, I didn't think I was going to get away. He was after me! I thought I was going to be the next victim!"

She shook like an electric toothbrush. "It's okay. You're here.

He's not going to get you," I said.

"But it's not okay! He's still out there!" She pulled away from me and looked behind her. "He knows where I live, Madison. He knows where you live too."

"Who?"

"Lt. Allen—he tried to kill me!"

FOUR

Moments ago, I'd been watching a live report on TV. Tex had stood next to Chief Washington, who updated the press on the state of the investigation. There were very few things that I was certain of at the moment, but one of those things was the knowledge that Tex had not been Effie's attacker.

"Come upstairs with me. We can talk."

"But Madison, you don't understand," she said.

"I think I do. Come with me and we'll call the police."

"No!" She jumped back, fear filling her wide eyes.

In the background, Rocky barked. Effie looked up. "Rocky's here?"

"Yes."

"C-c-can I see him?"

"Of course." I kept one arm around the young woman's shoulder as we scaled the stairs side by side. I had questions, lots and lots of questions, but I knew not to ask them. An idea was forming in my mind and, as much as I hated what the idea would involve, I knew it might be the best thing for everyone involved.

When we reached the second floor landing, I turned to Effie. "Do you want to go to your apartment first?"

"No, I don't want to be alone."

"Okay." I unlocked the front door and held it open for her, locking it behind us. I led her to the sofa and asked her to sit, and then went down the short hallway to the bedroom and opened the door. Rocky charged out like he'd been released from a slingshot. He flew to Effie and jumped onto the sofa and into her lap. Her tears of fear turned to tears of happiness, morphing her from woman on the cusp of adulthood to girlishness. She wrapped her arms around his neck and buried her face in his fur.

I went to the kitchen and pulled two stemmed glasses out of the cabinet. Effie had turned twenty-two a month before I'd turned forty-eight. I figured we could both use a glass of wine. When I returned, she was staring at the TV. I picked up the remote and clicked it off.

"That was him, wasn't it? On the news. It said it was live. How could that be?"

"Lt. Allen has been at the police station all day today. He's been working this case, trying to find answers. I don't know details, but something linked him to the woman they found yesterday. He went in voluntarily. There's no way he could have been your attacker, don't you see?"

She nodded, but I could tell she didn't believe me. "Effie, listen to me. I think we need to call the police and—"

"I'm afraid of them!"

I took a deep breath. "What if we call a woman? Someone you know?"

"The police lady who used to live here?"

"I wish I could call her, but she doesn't live in Dallas anymore. What about Officer Nast?"

Officer Nast—or Officer Nasty as I and half of the police department called her behind her back—was the last person I wanted to willingly call. She was a late twenties bombshell with long brown hair, curves in all the right places, and the kind of complexion that needs no tanning bed to maintain its glow. She and Tex had an on-again/off-again history. My own involvement with Tex had brought on at least one of the off-agains, and I figured that didn't make me very popular in the world of Nasty. She was the only woman I knew who could put on a standard issue navy blue polyester police uniform and make it look like it came from Fredericks of Hollywood's costume section.

Conversely, if anybody else out there believed in Tex's

innocence the way I did, it would be her. And since she was on the force, she'd be privy to information I couldn't otherwise access.

I waited for Effie to consider my offer. "She helped you out with your ex, didn't she?" she asked.

"In a manner of speaking."

"Yes, okay. I'll talk to her."

I didn't leave time for either one of us to change our minds. I reached for my cell phone and flipped through my contacts until I found hers. The only reason it was there was because she and Tex had spent a short amount of time living together, and when Tex called me from her phone, I'd programmed it in, labeled In Case of Emergency.

Indeed.

She answered on the first ring. "Madison?"

"Donna?"

"Shit. Things really are this bad, aren't they?"

"I know we could spend hours catching up on old times, but I have a young woman at my apartment who claims Lt. Allen tried to assault her earlier this evening."

"That's not possible."

"I know that and you know that but she's pretty shaken up. I think she should talk to someone on the force. She's afraid of anybody in a uniform, but she agreed to talk to you."

There was a slight pause, where I assumed Nasty was checking to see if hell had frozen over. "Where are you calling from?"

"My apartment building on Gaston. The gate code is four-oh-three. Park in the back."

"I'll be there in ten minutes."

Effie, Rocky, and I waited in silence. I hoped Effie would be ready to talk when Nasty arrived, but I couldn't count on it. Closing in on ten minutes later, I heard tires on gravel to the east of my windows. When I glanced outside, I spotted a dingy green Saab pull through the gate and park in the lot.

"I have to let her in. I'll be right back," I said to Effie. She hugged Rocky close and nodded. I pulled the door shut behind me and heard the locks being turned before I was halfway down the staircase.

Nasty was waiting for me outside the door when I reached the bottom of the stairs. She stood back and looked at my legs. "You're getting around pretty well," she said. "Almost can't tell you were injured."

Physical therapy had done wonders in healing my formerly twice torn ACL, but frequent trips up and down the stairs still left me with a soreness that only went away with plenty of ice and anti-inflammatories. It was a constant reminder of what could go wrong when you let down your guard.

"I'm working toward a full recovery. I don't like having a reminder of my past."

"You and me both."

Nasty wore a white sleeveless ribbed man's undershirt over a black bra. Through the sheer cotton of the undershirt I made out the outline of a silver belt buckle by her waist. Red platform stilettos were on her feet. Clearly, she'd been off-duty.

"Thank you for coming. I know this is weird."

She came inside and pushed the door shut behind her. "I'm here to help Lt. Allen. Now, who is this girl?"

"Her name is Effie Jones. She lives in the building. She's the only person who lives here besides me right now, and I only live here half of the time. She didn't say much about what happened tonight except that Lt. Allen tried to attack her. But when we got inside and she saw him on the TV, she knew something was wrong."

We'd reached the top step. "Which is yours?"

"This one," I said, pointing at my door.

Nasty tipped her head toward it. "You should go in first."

I fed the key into the lock and unlocked the deadbolt above it. When I opened the door it caught on the chain.

"Effie? It's Madison and Officer Nast."

"Just a minute," she said. The door closed, the chain rattled, and the door reopened to let us in. "I'm sorry," she started.

"No need to apologize. I'm Donna. I understand you had a scary night?" Nasty said. She led Effie to the sofa and sat next to her. I sat in the chair across from them.

"I was out with my friends. We like to go to the happy hour at the Landing, but my friend's sister just got a job she really, really wanted, so we stayed later to keep celebrating."

"How many people were you with?"

"Let's see, Angie, Allison, Terri, Nancy, Olivia." She ticked the names off on her fingers. "And Barbie, Angie's sister. So six."

"Seven counting you," Nasty said. "Did you stay until closing?"

"No." Effie's eyes moved to the glass of wine on the table. "I left early. I have an interview tomorrow and didn't want to be out too late."

Nasty kept her eyes on Effie. "That was smart." She kicked off her shoes and tucked one foot underneath her. Her body language was as far from threatening as it could be, more like that of an older sister or friend who was just hanging out.

"We were having lots of fun until Barbie realized her necklace was missing. It's a gold chain with the profile of a trucker girl on it. She freaked out until somebody found it by the jukebox. I left the bar after that. A police officer approached me and I thought he was going to give me a hard time for drinking, so I rolled down the window to tell him I was fine. He stayed back from the car so I didn't seem him real well. He told me I had a tail light out and asked if I wanted to see it."

A broken tail light. That's what Officer Iverson had pulled me over for. With the news about Tex, I'd forgotten to take care of it. But now, it didn't feel like coincidence.

Nasty sat forward. I could tell she was absorbing Effie's story, but I was surprised by how easily she related to the recent college grad. There was no police power play coming from her. No sense of "I'm in charge" like I'd seen in the past.

"Did you get out of the car?" Nasty asked.

"I swore, and then I apologized for swearing. I didn't want him to think I was cursing at him. I asked which tail light it was. Instead of answering, he asked why I wanted to know, which seemed strange. He stepped closer to the car and I read his nametag. It said Lt. Tex Allen. I was going to mention you," she gestured to me, "but then I saw something in his hand. It looked like some kind of hook. I threw the car into reverse and I think I hit him when I backed out of the space."

"Did you stop to check?"

"No, I was too scared. I took off and drove straight here."

"Did anyone follow you?"

"I don't think so."

"Effie, how well do you know Lt. Allen?"

"I've met him a couple of times, once or twice when he was here to visit Madison."

"And you're sure the man who approached you was Lt. Allen?"

"I don't think it could have been him if what I saw on the TV was true."

"That's not what I'm asking. You've seen Lt. Allen face to face. Did the man who stopped you tonight look like the man you've met?"

She looked at me, pleading me to help her. "Effie, it's okay," I said. "Officer Nast is trying to help."

"I don't know. It was dark and I didn't see his face. He could have been Madison's lieutenant."

I cringed. Nasty scored even more points for not reacting.

"Can you describe him?"

"He was tall, at least I think he was. I was in the car so it's hard to tell. He wore a hat so I couldn't see his hair, and he had on mirrored sunglasses even though it was dark."

"Effie, why are you so sure it was Lt. Allen?"

"His name was right there on his uniform. 'Lt. Tex Allen.'"

I looked at Nasty to see if she was thinking what I was thinking. We both knew Tex was a nickname. Besides that, Tex was a detective. He didn't wear a uniform. They were little things, but they meant a lot.

Nasty kept her eyes focused on Effie. "Can you describe the

uniform?"

Effie's forehead scrunched up while she thought. "I think it was black or navy. Short sleeved shirt that buttoned up the front. I think it had epaulettes. The pants were the same color. He had stuff attached to his belt...a radio, a pair of handcuffs, and a club. There was a patch on his sleeve. It was dark with red edges and gold and white words in the middle."

"What about a car? Did you see one?" I asked.

"I don't know. I didn't see a car. He walked up to my window."

"Is there anything else you can remember?"

Effie shook her head.

"You did a good job, Effie. You were smart. You did exactly what you should have done. Do you want to call your friends and make sure they're okay?"

"I called them when Madison went to let you in."

Nasty put a comforting hand on Effie's arm. "Good. Are you going to stay in your apartment tonight?"

"Can I stay here with you, Madison?" she asked. She kept her arm wrapped around Rocky's neck, like Linus with his security blanket.

I hadn't been planning on spending the night at the apartment, but the last twenty minutes had been a schooling in things I hadn't planned on doing. "Yes, you can stay here with me. Let me get a pillow and some sheets for the sofa."

I went to the hall closet and pulled out a yellow sheet set. I added a pillow and pillowcase to the pile, and a pale yellow blanket trimmed in satin. In the background, Effie and Nasty exchanged information. The truth was, Nasty's presence had been oddly calming. Unlike my own encounters with the law and threatening situations, there had been something different tonight. I didn't know what it was, but for Effie and Tex's sake, I would do nothing to upset the apple cart.

When I returned to the living room, Nasty stood up and looked at me with a funny expression. "Can I talk to you?"

"Sure."

"Wait," Effie said. "Madison, I hope you're not mad, but I asked Officer Nast if she'd stay here too."

Nasty looked at me. I looked at Effie.

It was turning into a freakin' slumber party.

FIVE

My mouth tightened, paralyzed with numbness. I put a hand on the arm of the sofa for balance. "Is that something you feel comfortable doing?" I asked Nasty.

She raised an eyebrow at me. "I don't want to impose."

"It's no imposition."

An awkward vibration of tension filled the air. "Okay then, it's settled." I looked around the living room. Aside from the sofa, there was the chair I'd sat in and a Danish modern coffee table that was great for the look of the room, but definitely not right for sleeping.

"Effie, why don't you take a shower or a bath? Donna and I can work out the sleeping arrangements."

"I can sleep on the floor," Effie said.

"Nobody's sleeping on the floor," Nasty and I said at the same time.

"Come with me," I said and led Effie to the bathroom. I pulled clean fluffy pink towels from the closet. "I can get your pajamas from your apartment while you shower. Officer Nast will be here, so you'll be safe. It's going to be okay, Effie. Really. Officer Nast was right. You did the right thing."

Effie told me where I'd find her keys and where I'd find the T-shirt and boxers she usually slept in. I closed the bathroom door behind me and met Nasty in the living room.

"I'm going to tell Effie to take my bed. She's had the hardest night of any of us and I think that's the best place for her to sleep. That leaves you, me, and the sofa."

Nasty looked at the sofa. "It's a long sofa."

"Nine feet."

"End to end?"

"Sounds like a plan. I'm going to get her some PJs from her apartment. Make yourself comfortable. There's wine in the fridge, but not much else, food-wise."

"I didn't expect it to be a bed and breakfast," she said.

Apparently there was still an edge to her after all.

My trip to Effie's apartment was quick. Everything was where she said it would be, which was surprising considering how much of a mess the place was. She paid her rent on time so it wasn't my place to judge her for throwing her clothes on the floor and letting the dishes pile up in the sink. At least they were sitting in a basin of formerly sudsy water. The intent to hand-wash them had been there.

I collected her T-shirt and boxers and turned to leave. An empty pizza box sat open on top of two plastic milk crates that had been pushed together and acted as a coffee table. Next to the pizza box was a teddy bear with a red, heart-shaped sachet stitched onto its paw. I carried the bear with her PJs and locked up behind me.

When I got back, Effie was in the living room with Rocky, wearing the terrycloth robe that I left on the back of the bathroom door.

"He looked lonely," I said, handing her the bear.

"Present from my boyfriend," she said. She hugged him to her chest. "I haven't named him yet." She brushed a couple of crumbs from the seat of the stuffed animal and waved him in front of Rocky.

I told her Donna and I had worked out the sleeping arrangements and led her to the bedroom. She carried the bear with her and Rocky followed. He jumped up like he did every night. I suspected by the morning I'd find him wedged somewhere between Nasty and me on the sofa, assuming he wasn't threatened by her fire-engine red toenails.

When I got back to the living room, Nasty had spread the sheet over the sofa. "Where do you find a sofa like this?"

"Same place I find most of my stuff." I ran my hand over the turquoise and lime green chenille fabric. It had the classic lines of mid-century: low back, low hairpin legs. I'd found it at an apartment building in the area. An older gentleman had been found dead inside his apartment days after his dog had passed away. With no next-of-kin, it had fallen to the apartment complex to empty his unit and arrange for the donation to charity. As it happened, I'd walked by while three men were scratching their heads over how to fit a nine-foot-long sofa into a seven-foot-long truck.

"Can I make a donation and take it?" I'd asked.

"Fifty bucks and it's yours," one of the men said. I pulled three twenties out of my wallet and told him to keep the change. I professionally cleaned the cushions, replaced the stuffing with high-density foam from the local fabric store, and had the chrome frame redipped. It turned out so well I'd kept it for myself.

Nasty tucked the corners of the sheet into the space behind the cushions. I grabbed the top sheet and flapped it open with a *snap!* The yellow cotton fluttered down to the sofa. I tucked the corners of my side between the cushions as well. Silently, we dealt out pillows, pillowcases, and extra sheets. After far too much time spent in the coveralls I'd worn at the Tylers's house, I unbuttoned them and stepped out, leaving them in a ball on the floor.

"Do you need to borrow pajamas?" I asked.

"I'm sleeping in my clothes."

"Suit yourself." I went to the bathroom, splashed cool water on my face to lower my temperature, and looked through my stack of clean pajamas for something suitable for tonight's sleeping arrangements.

Flimsy cotton nightgown—no. Chinese silk pajamas—no. Peignoir set—no.

I ended up in a pair of loose fitting blue cotton drawstring-waist pants and a matching pullover trimmed in white eyelet embroidery. Good enough.

The lights were out when I went back to the sofa. I went to the kitchen and set the timer on the coffee maker, and then returned to the sofa and slid between the sheets, lying on my side with my knees bent. I didn't know if Nasty was doing the same. Once I was settled, she spoke.

"I respect you for calling me," Nasty said. "I don't think I would have had the integrity to do the same thing."

"I know you care about him. So do I."

"He's not who you think he is, Madison. He has a dark side you've probably never seen."

"Don't we all?"

"Not like his."

As I thought about how to answer her, I wondered if she was testing me to see if I'd blindly defend Tex. The reality was, I didn't know him that well, and he didn't know me well, but somehow, we'd made a connection.

Lt. Tex Allen had first appeared in my life shortly after I'd found a body under the wheels of my car where it had been parked outside of the pool. That body had led to a murder investigation that had led to more bodies—all dressed in the style and likeness of Doris Day. Since I modeled my image and business after her and her movies, I had quickly moved from the person of interest category to the potential victim category. Tex had taken it upon himself to be my protector. His presence had been laced with an inappropriate amount of flirtation that would have made me, in my vintage clothes, old car, and Doris Day-inspired life, feel like a specimen in a Petri dish, if it hadn't triggered an unexpected latent passion that had been ignored far too long.

Two steamy kisses had been the only physical interaction between us. Other than that, we'd never so much as gone on a date. But somehow, through a routine where Tex occasionally brought me groceries or I occasionally dropped off an interesting item I'd come across during my days scouting for objects d'art, I'd gotten comfortable with him, and he, it seemed, with me.

That's why what Nasty said gave me the chills.

Even breathing from her side of the sofa replaced the silence and answered my unasked question about the purpose behind our conversation. We were done talking. I tucked my hands under the side of my head, closed my eyes, and hoped for sleep.

The sun, the scent of coffee, and the presence of Rocky wedged between me and the back of the sofa conspired to wake me. Nasty rolled over on her end and Rocky lifted his head and opened his eyes halfway. I ruffled his fur. The wall clock said it was five thirty. Just about the time I usually got up to go to the pool.

The pool.

It was the last place I had seen Tex. If he wanted to talk to me, would he try to find me at Crestwood a second time?

I got up and went to the kitchen to get two cups of coffee. When I came back and sat down on my end of the sofa, Nasty kicked her feet, and then rolled onto her back and stretched them out.

"What time is it?" she murmured

"Five thirty."

"You think this is normal?"

"*Nothing* about the past twelve hours has been normal." I held a cup of coffee toward her.

"Copy that," she said. She took the mug and inhaled the scent before drinking.

I went into the bedroom to check on Effie. She was lying on her side, facing away from me. I walked around the bed. She was staring at the wall. "Good morning."

"Hi, Madison," she said. "Thanks for letting me sleep in your bed."

"How are you feeling today?"

"Better. It kind of feels like a bad dream, like it didn't happen, you know?" She rolled onto her back and focused on the ceiling.

"Effie, I think you should go to the police station with Officer Nast and make a formal statement while last night is still fresh in your mind."

"But I told her what happened. Doesn't that count?"

"I'm afraid not," Nasty said from behind us. "I'm not on the force anymore. Consider last night a dry run."

SIX

"Since when are you off the force?" I asked. Tex hadn't mentioned anything about Nasty leaving the police department, although even if there was juicy gossip behind the story, I doubted we would have spent any time talking about her. Somewhere along the way of developing a loose friendship, Tex and I had reached an unspoken agreement not to talk about our respective pasts.

"It's been about a month. I'm working security now. That doesn't change anything I said last night. Effie, I'd be happy to take you to the police department to make that statement if you don't want to go by yourself."

"Yes, okay, that would be nice. Madison, do you think Rocky could come with us, you know, to keep me company?" Effie said.

"Sure, Effie," I said. "He'll like that. I'll be back at the apartment tonight to pick him up."

It was over an hour before the two of them left. Still early enough to squeeze in a couple of laps at the pool. Best case scenario? Tex would show up and I could tell him what had happened to Effie. Worse case? I'd get a workout. I packed my swimsuit, a lime green double breasted blazer and matching pants, a fresh pair of coveralls, and the hardhat, and headed out.

Arriving at the pool late meant sharing space with other swimmers. There were no empty lanes, and two of the six already had more than one occupant. I pulled on my cap and goggles and sat on the deck, dangling my ankles into the lane while the other swimmer, a man in a purple swim cap, approached and flip turned next to my feet.

"Madison, you're late today," said Grace, who appeared to be at the tail end of her water aerobics routine in the slow lane. Her foam noodle was behind her head and her arms were draped over it. Strains of the Beach Boys poured from a small CD player that sat on the ground by the locker rooms. She bounced up and down in time to the beat of "Help Me, Rhonda."

"I had company last night that turned into company this morning," I said.

"It's about time," she said.

"Grace!" I said. "It wasn't that kind of company." I splashed water at her and she laughed.

"I think Mary Elizabeth gets more action at the retirement home than you do. That's not right."

"I bet Mary Elizabeth would beg to differ," I said, winking at Grace's friend who was approaching from behind her.

"I don't think Mary Elizabeth has to beg for anything," Grace said.

"Gracie!" Mary Elizabeth said. "For shame."

I left them to their good natured laughter and their cool-down to the sounds of "Little Surfer Girl" and jumped in.

It felt good to submerge under the water. Familiar. I pulled my goggles down and waited until the purple swim-capped man flip turned at the end of the lane before I pushed off. I wasn't sure which of us was faster, but putting a length of the pool between us seemed like the polite thing to do. Though my muscles were sluggish and not yet warmed up, I easily finished lap one and turned into lap two. Two strokes into the second lap I realized the other swimmer had stopped in the middle of the lane and was treading water in front of me. I lifted my head.

"What are you doing?" he demanded.

"Swimming laps. Like you."

"You don't just get into a lane with another swimmer without telling them," he said angrily.

"But I—"

"That's rude. You wait and then you ask," he said, pushing water toward me. Either his anger or his workout turned his face red.

"I'm sorry. I dangled my feet into the water and let you turn. I thought you would have seen me."

"That's not how it's done." He glared at me.

I was so shocked by his unexpected hostility that I offered a second apology while he pushed off of the bottom and swam away from me, and then got angry with myself for apologizing.

I looked up at Bobby the lifeguard to see if he'd caught the interaction. He shrugged, like it was no big deal. I treaded water until the other guy was at the end of the lane and I started swimming again.

I wasn't used to being yelled at one and a half laps into my workout, and the incident left me annoyed and tense. I'd been swimming at Crestwood since I moved to Dallas. The low impact workout was perfect for my then-freshly injured knee joint, and the natural solitude had fit my antisocial mood. What had started as a way to cope with unresolved emotions had become a part of my day that I cherished. It included several regulars who had their own reasons for swimming each morning. Purple cap was a newbie, probably a regular from the nearby Gaston Swim Club. They might have rules at their location, but at ours, we operated on a protocol of politeness.

I powered through the first several laps of my workout, again losing track of my lap count. Adrenaline from the encounter had kept me moving and, in an attempt to calm down my mind, I let it wander.

Even though I'd left my world behind in Pennsylvania, and started over when I was not quite forty-five, it turned out I liked surrounding myself with the familiar. I'd created a new life in the Lakewood suburb of Dallas, Texas, one that was entrenched in routine. Swim in the morning. Scout dumpsters or estate sales midday. Spend time at my studio in the afternoon. Volunteer at the local movie house that shows classic pictures in the evening. Go home, go to sleep.

Lather, rinse, repeat.

At the time, I'd moved to Dallas from Pennsylvania with little more than the belongings that could fit in my car. My purchase of the apartment building on Gaston Avenue had been transacted over the Internet, and the rental of my Mad for Mod studio space had happened shortly after I'd gotten settled. I'd had big plans for establishing a new life, and I wasn't going to let the realities of hard work, heartbreak, and zero clients derail me.

The sound of the bubbles surfacing through the water replaced my own churning thoughts about what was really missing in my life.

I was searching for something to hold on to, something to ground me. When I'd moved to Dallas, a city I barely knew, I did so with the hopes of severing ties with my past and starting over. But after a killer almost took my life and the story of the Pillow Stalker became part of the news, my former lover tracked me down. He offered a reconciliation that had ended badly. These days, I was starting to expect the very chaos I'd left behind when I fled Pennsylvania.

Is that why I had found myself oddly attracted to Tex when he'd shown up in my life? Was it a case of being drawn to an opposite of myself, or did he represent the newfound thrill of chaos, heat, and passion that I'd denied myself after my last big breakup? Would I ever be happy with the routine I had once craved?

Even though my arms were tired and I wanted to stop and catch my breath, I flip turned next to purple cap, who was resting by the end of the lane. My feet kicked up a splash of water. I hit a groove and picked up the pace. My thoughts picked up as well.

When Hudson, my handyman, had been in trouble, I believed in him. And when I was in trouble, he had done the unthinkable and gone to Tex behind my back and asked the lieutenant to look out for me. Kinda like what I'd done by calling Nasty to help out Tex.

My, what a wicked web we weave.

I glided to the end of the lap and pulled my goggles up. The lane next to me had emptied out and Purple Cap had moved into it.

"Sorry about that back there," he said. "I've been a little wound up lately and I'm afraid I took it out on you. Hope there's no hard feelings."

I defaulted to my cordial Doris Day voice. "I've always found the pool to be a good place to work off tension," I said, hiding any trace of anger.

"Here's hoping. I'm running out of things to build in the garage. I'm Jake, by the way."

"Madison," I replied. I bent my knees underneath me and let the water cover me up to my shoulders. "And I agree. When the pool isn't available, construction works too."

He raised his eyebrows. "You do construction?"

"It's part of my job." I pulled my cap off and dunked my head underwater. When I popped back up, I slicked my hair back with one hand and tucked my cap and goggles under the side of my bathing suit. "Nice talking to you," I said. I climbed out of the water and went into the locker room.

I got ready quickly. My naturally blond hair picked up sun-bleached highlights from time spent in the chlorine, and a lifelong attachment to sunscreen kept me looking far younger than my forty-eight years.

Being pale in my twenties had made me less than popular around my peers, but it all evened out now that they were pricing Botox treatments and microdermabrasion processes and I used whatever moisturizer was on sale at Rite-Aid.

I dressed in the lime green, double-breasted pantsuit and slipped my feet into patent leather flats with white daisies on the front. I left the locker room and dawdled by the bleachers. Still no signs of Tex. I hoisted my bag on my shoulder and went out to my car. A man stood on the steps out front typing something into his phone.

"Madison—it's Madison, right?" he said. "Wait up."

I turned around. "Do I know you?"

"Jake. We just met in there?" He pulled a purple swim cap from his bag. "We shared a lane?"

"Oh, right."

"You said something about construction being part of your job. What did you mean by that?"

"I own a mid-century modern interior decorating business. Sometimes before I can get started on the decorating I have to do a bit of construction or demolition."

"You're kidding."

"Afraid not," I said. By now we were next to my car. My yellow hardhat, dirty coveralls, and canvas sneakers sat in the back seat. It was pretty good evidence that I wasn't making this up.

He reached into the back seat and picked up a piece of wood painted with four streaks of the paints Mitchell expected me to endorse. He'd given it to me as a nudge. The streaks hadn't been dry when I set the wood in the back seat, and a drip of turquoise had edged close to red. Tahitian Turquoise? Caribbean Coral?

I needed a vacation.

"Interesting palette," he said. I didn't offer an explanation. He turned the wood over. A white sticker with the Paintin' Place logo, address, and phone number was affixed to the bottom edge. I took the board from his hand and set it back in the car.

"You ever hire out freelancers?" he asked.

"On occasion."

"Here." He pulled a business card out of his wallet and held it out. "I'm new to town and it's hard to find job leads. If you need an extra set of hands, I come cheap."

His card said Jake Morris with a phone number and email below. No address, website, or endorsement quotes.

"Thank you, Jake. I'll keep you in mind." I opened the car door and set the card in the cup holder.

"You're not going to lose that, are you? You want some extras?" he asked, reaching inside his wallet for more cards.

"I'm not going to lose it," I said. "Nice meeting you." I put the car in reverse and left before he could say another word.

*   *   *

I stopped off at my local mechanic and found him filling out some paperwork behind the counter. He greeted me with a big smile. "Madison, my favorite customer."

"The only reason I'm your favorite customer is because I drive an old car that constantly needs work."

"True, true, but it doesn't hurt that you look like the girl I took to the prom in 1959. What's the trouble today?"

"Easy. Broken tail light."

We walked around the back of the car and he tapped the plastic. "Could be a short. Want me to check it now?"

"Yes, please."

I helped myself to a cup of coffee from behind the counter while he checked the bulb. A few minutes later, he came back. "Good as new," he said.

"What do I owe you?"

"Five dollars for the bulb."

"What about the labor?"

"If I charged you for that, I wouldn't be able to sleep at night."

I peeled a ten dollar bill out of my wallet. "Buy your wife something pretty," I said. He shook his head at me and I left.

I drove to the Tyler house. Yesterday, I hadn't known if I'd be coming back, but today I knew the work would be the distraction I needed.

Cleo met me at the front door. Today she wore a fitted red sweater that highlighted her probably-not-real bust line and narrow waist. Short white shorts showed off long, tan legs that ended in gold, high-heeled sandals. It was going on nine o'clock and even in my pantsuit I was painfully underdressed.

"Hi, darlin', I wasn't sure if we'd be seeing you today."

"A busy decorating job is probably the best place for me to be. Have you had a chance to look at the bathroom?"

"I had Molly clean the room up after you left. It's gorgeous!"

I cringed. Cleaning up a job site was my job, not her

housekeeper's. "I'm going to finish up in there first, and then I'll come find you to talk about the removal of the glass wall."

"You sure you want to tackle that yourself?"

I was pretty sure I *didn't* want to tackle it myself. I remembered what the man at the pool said about taking out frustrations around the house. "I think it'll make for good therapy."

"Honey, I've been in analysis for twenty years and it hasn't done a darn thing. If tearing down that glass wall helps you, maybe I'll have to get into the decorating business myself."

Cleo walked with me to the bathroom. I cracked the door and peeked inside, and then, delighted with the way the fixtures had turned out, I opened the door wide and stepped into the room.

It wasn't often that you found a mid-century house with a pink bathroom in mint condition. The former owners had done the poor man's version of renovating the room, and their frugality had served to protect the fixtures under the latex paint. It had easily come off with the paint remover, and now matched the ceramic tile that trimmed the walls and the small pattern of tile in the floor. A trip to my storage locker would net me an era-appropriate light fixture for over the sink. The cabinet under the sink would have to be replaced. A custom construction job would be best.

I pulled a notebook from my wicker tote and made a quick list: Light fixture, cabinet, throw rugs, curtains, towels. "It's perfect, don't you think?"

"It's pink, that's for sure."

I turned to face Cleo, again wondering about her and her husband's motivation in hiring me. "Are you sure this is what you had in mind?"

"Darlin', you're the one with the vision. Dan and I agreed on this. Whatever you say goes."

"Is Dan here?"

"No, you don't have to worry about any more of his outbursts. Today it's just us girls. Too bad we can't have any fun." She pouted as if she wished the Chippendale dancers had shown up instead of me.

Inside, I relaxed. Dan's anger over his brother's death and his hostility toward Tex had made for a tense working environment. I was happy to be able to work without fear of a second confrontation.

"Cleo, about what Dan said yesterday, about the mentality of a cop..."

"Don't think twice about what Dan said. He's never accepted how his brother changed after joining the force. George was a mild-mannered guy who dated the same woman for four years. Six months after he graduated from the police academy, he changed."

"With all due respect, that's one person. That's not everybody. Tex isn't like that. He takes his job very seriously."

"Sounds like maybe you know this Tex better than most."

I looked down at my notes, flipped the notebook shut, and clipped my pen to the spiral binding at the top. "He took a bullet for me a few months ago," I said quietly.

"I suppose if a police officer took a bullet for me, I'd defend him too," she said. She raised her glass to her lips and took a long drink. "I'll be outside by the pool if you need me," Cleo said.

I left the bathroom and sat by the wall of glass blocks in the living room. Cleo and Dan had hired me for the works, and that included removal of the carpet, removal of the glass block partition, paint, new lighting, new furniture.

Self-described as having no talent or interest in decorating, they had written me a check for half of the job estimate I gave them, and it had been a hefty estimate. I'd deposited their check, set timetables, and planned out which tasks I could do myself and which I couldn't. As much as I wanted to test out the theory of demolition as therapy, I recognized that I needed backup. I dug my phone out of my bag and called Hudson.

"Madison," he said in his deep voice. It was like dark chocolate coated in espresso and dipped in cigar smoke. "Hope you don't mind that I have you on speaker. I'm in the car."

"Of course," I said. "I didn't expect you to answer."

"Have you been trying to reach me? Shoot. I went backpacking and didn't bother with my phone. Suspended my service for a while. Is everything okay?"

"Sure, I wanted to talk to you about a job."

"Should have known. The consummate businesswoman."

I listened for something in his voice, a hint that he'd missed me, or that he'd been hoping I'd called for another reason, but the background noise his cell picked up made it impossible to hear anything but the sound of the wind.

Hudson wasn't the first handyman who had answered my ad, but once we started working together, he became the last one I needed. If we'd met under different circumstances, who knows what might have become. But I was jaded about things like happily ever after, and the possibility of trading our comfortable connection for a romance that came with no guarantees wasn't worth the risk. I relied more and more on his talents and let my other contacts lapse. But even he had moved on. It had been a year since I'd learned the truth about Hudson's past, and in that year I'd had to deal with my own demons when they came knocking on my door. When Hudson had resolution, I hadn't. And now that I had resolution, Hudson wasn't around. I missed him more than I thought I would.

"Are you back in Dallas?" I asked.

"Not yet. I don't know when I'll be back, to tell the truth. I still have a couple of states to cross. If it's urgent, why not call one of the contacts I gave you when I left?"

"I can do that." Our conversation dropped to silence for a few seconds.

"Sure is good to hear your voice," he said. "I'll see you soon."

"Bye, Hudson."

I didn't realize that Cleo had reentered the room while I was on the phone. I closed the sketch pad and notebook and put my phone away. "I was making arrangements with my handyman."

"I was hoping you'd call him. Is he the one who was suspected of that murder?"

"He was innocent," I said in Hudson's defense. "How do you know about that?"

"It was all over the news. Makes a great story, you know? Why do you think we hired you?"

SEVEN

"You hired me because of my history? Because of my involvement in a homicide investigation?" I asked. Even saying it out loud didn't make it sound more rational.

"That's how Dan and I found out about you and your business. Truth is, we'd like to talk to you about buying the rights to your story. Could make a great movie," she finished in a sing-song voice.

"Cleo, I don't know how I feel about this. What happened last year isn't my story. It involved a lot of other people too."

"But you were at the center of it. If you sell to us, we'll build the whole thing around you."

The rundown house and the carte blanche mid-century decorating job were starting to make a bit more sense. Cleo and Dan were movie producers with money to burn, and I was the novelty act du jour. I didn't need to subject Hudson to an environment like this, where his past would be the deciding factor in getting the job.

"My regular contractor is out of town. I'll be hiring someone else to work with me."

"Boo-hoo," she said, pushing her glossed lips out in a pout. "I was so hoping to meet him face to face. But speaking of being out of town, I've decided to throw a pool party while Dan is gone. How does Saturday night sound? I know you won't be done with the renovations, but is there anything you can do in the interim, you know, to make it seem more special than, well, than it is right now?"

I flipped through the pages of my sketch pad until I reached the one with the list of renovations. It was going to be a long time until their house was ready for entertaining.

"What part of the house do you want to be available to guests?"

She stared at me as if she didn't understand the question.

"Cleo, once I tackle this wall of glass blocks, it's going to be a mess in here. Right now you have an empty room. I can stage it with furniture and knickknacks from my storage locker, but that's going to cost you—"

"Like a rental? Don't worry, I'll pay whatever you want. What's the going rate?"

"I was going to say it would cost you in time. It's going to take time to clean up this room, bring furniture in, have your party, and take the furniture out."

"We've got all the time in the world."

Cleo's lackadaisical approach to the completion of her deadlines had been bothering me. Add in her confession that I was hired because she and her husband were interested in the development rights to my story, and I was growing less and less enthusiastic about her and Dan's business. They'd paid me generously to start the work on their house, and under just about any circumstances it would have been difficult to turn down the opportunity to work on a Cliff May house so in need of repair. But still, I was starting to feel like the entertainment.

"Before I agree to anything, I have to check my calendar and see if I have any other commitments."

"I know this is in addition to what we hired you to do. Make sure you track the expenses and hours, and if you need another installment, just let me know. Now, why don't you come up with a game plan and let me see some new sketches?" She turned to the wall behind her and waved her hands in small circles. "I'd love something Japanese." I was reminded of *Broadway Danny Rose* when Mia Farrow talks about doing a room in bamboo.

"Sure, I'll see what I can come up with," I said. I scribbled *Japanese? Check storage locker* on my sketch pad and flipped it shut.

"Oh, and you're invited, of course," she said. "Wear your swimsuit and bring a date. Eight o'clock?"

"Cleo, are you sure it's a good idea to throw a party while Dan is away? In light of what's been happening around Lakewood?"

"Madison, you are delicious, you know that? You're all a kerfluffle over there, trying to look out for me. It's cute." She handed me a pre-printed invitation, which let me know in no uncertain terms that "not doable" had not been an option. I headed out to see what I could come up with on the fly.

It was going on lunchtime and I hadn't eaten all day. I didn't want to spend a lot of time or money, so it would probably be fast food. As I grew closer to my studio, I passed the parking lot to the shopping center where Kate Morrow's body had been taken. There were half as many cars in the lot as usual. Tex's Jeep sat in a spot in the back. A scruffy version of the man I knew appeared to be asleep in the driver's seat.

I drove past the Jeep to the Hunan Palace located in the corner of the strip mall. It was next to Paintin' Place, and long ago I'd come to appreciate their buffet. I bought two combo meals, left my car parked in front of their shop, and walked to the Jeep. The closer I got, the surer I was that it was Tex inside. He didn't look good.

A faint stubble dusted his normally freshly shaven face. His dirty blond hair fell forward over one eye. His head rested against the headrest, eyes closed, and his chest rose and fell with even breathing.

I wondered how exhausted he must have been to fall asleep in his car in the middle of the Casa Linda parking lot in broad daylight. I had a feeling I knew what he was doing there in the first place.

I rapped on the front windshield, startling him. He stared at me for a few awkward moments, his icy blue eyes cloudy and unfocused from sleep. A stack of flyers sat on the passenger seat.

From where I stood, I recognized images of the missing women. I was struck by the futility of handing out flyers in a parking lot in an attempt to find a lead.

"Night," he said. He looked at my outfit and shook his head. "When are you going to start wearing dresses again?"

"When this job is over. Are you hungry?" I asked, changing the subject. I held up the bag of takeout.

"Hunan Palace?" he asked. I nodded. "Hop in."

I circled the car. Tex moved the flyers from the seat to a webbed pocket inside his door and I climbed in. In the past year I'd learned how to get into and out of a Jeep in a dress; it was one of many new skills I'd picked since befriending the lieutenant. Today I was thankful for the pantsuit.

The car smelled like Christmas. I looked at the rearview mirror, the floor mats, and the pockets in the door, eventually spotting a green tree-shaped air freshener sticking out from under the seat.

I handed Tex a small container of white rice, took one for myself, and left additional containers of orange chicken and pork shu mai open between us. Nasty's words flashed through my mind. *He's not the man you think he is.* At least fifty different questions fluttered through my brain while I ate, none of them appropriate for the moment. All of the shu mai and most of the chicken was gone before I spoke.

"Do you want to talk about this thing that's going on with you?" I asked.

"Not much to tell. Not yet, anyway."

"I saw the news."

"That's only half of the story."

"If I thought it was the whole story, I wouldn't have gotten into your car."

"Night, I would never hurt you."

"I know." It was obvious that Tex didn't want to talk about the abductions. I tried out silence for a while, but when that proved awkward, I went with good old-fashioned get-to-know-you small talk. "Do you have any family around here?" I asked.

"What?"

"Family. You know, a mom. A dad. The people who raised you. Do they live in Dallas?"

He stared at me like I'd grown a second head. He finished chewing and leaned back against his seat, staring ahead at the windshield. I looked away and bit down on a messy piece of chicken.

"My dad split when I was six. My mother passed away when I was in high school."

"Brothers? Sisters?"

"Both."

"So there are more of you out there?" I said, trying to get a smile.

"My sister lives in Austin."

"And your brother?"

"Killed in action."

My initial assumption that he might like some company seemed far from accurate, and the shortness of his replies told me that he wanted me to leave.

"What about you? What's your story?" he asked.

"You know my story. I worked at Pierot's in Philadelphia. Fell in love. Got lied to and left."

"That guy was a part of your life, but the way I've been figuring, there's a lot of life that you're not talking about."

"What else do you want to know? I came to Dallas to start over. And then one day after I was done swimming, I found a dead body under the wheels of my car. You were there. You know the rest."

I sat, silent, waiting for Tex to badger me into talking. I waited for three minutes, if the clock on the dashboard was to be trusted. As it turns out, three minutes is a relatively long amount of time.

"My parents died in a car crash when I was twenty-one," I said. "I remember because it was the night before my midterms. They were the only family I had. When they were gone, it was just me."

"What about your extended family? Aunts? Uncles? Cousins?"

"My parents were both only children. When they died, I was on my own."

I stared at the empty containers scattered inside his car. Not only had I not gotten Tex to open up, but I'd succeeded in exposing my own old wounds. This wasn't going well.

"I should be getting home," I said. I picked up the empties and opened the car door.

He reached a hand out to stop me before I was out. "I'm here because I can't sit around at home wondering what's going on. Kate Morrow was abducted from this store."

"You're planning to make the parking lot your new residence?"

"Not just here. One of the other women was abducted from the bowling alley on Turtle Creek Boulevard. Another from the Mexican restaurant on Greenville, and another from the Cineplex."

"So you've become a one-man surveillance operation."

"There has to be something we're missing. Officially, I'm on leave. Unofficially, I can sit in a parking lot and look for something unusual to happen."

"Has anything unusual happened yet?"

"Aside from you showing up with the Chinese food? Not really."

I smiled. "Are you going to be here tomorrow?" I asked.

"I don't know where I'll be tomorrow." He hesitated. "But maybe I'll be back here tonight."

"Okay, well, maybe I'll bring you dinner."

We held each other's stare for a few seconds but neither of us moved. When I opened the door a second time, Tex didn't stop me from leaving. Halfway to my car, the Jeep started. Tex pulled up next to me and rolled down the window.

"The Chinese takeout was a nice touch," he said. "Next time bring eggrolls." He smiled and drove away.

I stopped at Mad for Mod for the references of other contractors that Hudson had left for me and drove home. Effie and her boyfriend Chad sat on the front steps. Rocky lay on the sidewalk, legs spread out behind him, paws in front, face on the ground. He looked pooped.

"Sorry I'm so late. Something came up."

"Madison, you remember Chad, right?"

I looked at the guy and smiled. "Yes, nice to see you again."

He nodded his head once.

"I have to talk to Madison," Effie said to him. "Alone."

"I'll wait by the car," Chad said without looking at her. He pulled himself up with a hand on the loose metal banister and walked to the car parked by the curb.

I took Chad's place on the steps. Rocky stood, turned around, and laid his head across my lap. "How did things go today?" I asked.

"Officer Nast was great. She took me to the police department and told them she wouldn't let them talk to me without her. When we were done she gave me her phone numbers and email and told me I could call her anytime I wanted to."

"Did she tell you she wasn't a police officer anymore?"

"Yes, but she's a security officer now so I'm still going to call her Officer Nast."

"I'm glad things worked out."

Effie reached out and rubbed the top of Rocky's head. Her lips were pressed together, making their normally rosy shade turn white.

"Effie, what's on your mind?"

"Chad thinks it's a good idea if I move in with him. You're not here every night, and even though I know you put in all those security devices, I don't want to stay here alone."

"I understand," I said, because I really did. Even if I said I would stay in the building, we'd have separate schedules. Coming and going to the mostly empty complex would still have a solitary feel.

"I'm going to get my stuff over the weekend. I paid my rent

through the end of the month, but once I'm out, I won't come back. I know I should have given you sixty days. I'm sorry."

"Don't even worry about that. You can stay here as long as you want. If you decide to get your own place, let me know and I'll write you a referral. You've been a very good tenant."

"Madison, there's something else." She looked down at her feet. They were pointed toward each other, and the rubber of her worn-out sneakers was peeled away in two places. She reached down and pulled off a piece, tossed it to the side, and looked up at me. "I know you said Lt. Allen couldn't have been the person who approached me last night, but I'm still scared of him. I know he comes here to see you and I don't want to see him."

"I thought when you saw him on the news, you knew it couldn't have been him."

"Yes, but I can't help it. I'm still scared of him. That's why I think it's a good idea that I go with Chad."

I looked at her boyfriend, leaning against his Prius, using his thumbs to type something on the screen of his phone. He was a tall, skinny guy in a faded Kiss T-shirt and ratty jeans, but to her, he was her protector.

"You can come visit Rocky whenever you like," I said.

"Maybe he can come visit me?" she asked.

"Sure. When you're ready, you give me the address and we'll come by." I stood and helped her up after me. We hugged. She got into Chad's car and he pulled away.

And then there was one.

I drove back to the studio to check out my Asian-themed inventory. Before I moved to Dallas, Mad for Mod had been a vacant storefront on Greenville Avenue. The storage locker behind the shop had been in disrepair, with the doors falling off their hinges and the roof leaking in five places. In addition to the locker, the property came with a Dumpster, four parking spaces, and an unfortunate red zone in the front that had led to more than one parking ticket.

Half of the interior of the studio was staged with furniture to demonstrate the styles of room I'd design if a client hired me: Nelson bubble lamps, Saarinen tulip chairs and tables, low sofas with classic right angles, and the occasional bachelor bar, all filled the space. I'd recently rotated the inventory from the storage locker and set up Tiki windows, with collections of mugs, hula girls, Polynesian lamps and ashtrays. I even found a couple of old blowfish lights in the trash when La Calle Doce renovated, and put them to good use, suspending them from the ceiling and using battery-operated dollar store flicker lights to illuminate them.

The other half of my studio was my office. Less than half, actually. A narrow hallway led to the back portion of the store, and my office sat on the left-hand side. One wall was covered floor to ceiling in cork squares where I pinned inspiration pictures and stills from Doris Day movies for potential rooms. Cleo and Dan Tyler had taken a particular liking to the cork wall.

Two weeks ago I'd pinned the four paint chips from Paintin' Place to the top of the cork wall. At the time I'd thought surrounding myself with the swatches would keep me from forgetting them. Maybe I should go with famous architects. Paul McCobb yellow. Yellow like corn. On the cob. Corn on the McCobb Yellow.

I was losing my mind.

I sat behind my desk. It was a patchwork of surface, drawers, and mismatched legs from different pieces of furniture that were otherwise unsalvageable. Two Barcelona chairs sat opposite the desk. A molded fiberglass desk chair sat behind it. Cabinets next to the desk held swatch books and blank sketch pads, an electric coffee pot, and an industrial-sized box of vanilla wafers, my current favorite afternoon pick-me-up snack.

Rocky curled up on his fluffy dog bed and chewed on his rope bone. I located a list of contractors from the file and left messages with the first four on the list. The afternoon sun was high in the sky, bringing with it the perfect amount of sun to illuminate the storage locker. I put the paper aside and planned to try again later.

I filled bowls with food and water for Rocky and left him in the office while I went out back to root through my inventory. I amassed a pile of bamboo, paper lanterns, and stacks of pillows with vintage Oriental needlepoint patterns. The bright sun had brought an uncomfortable level of heat and humidity with it, but I was too lost in the project to quit.

"Excuse me," said a voice from the doorway.

I looked over my shoulder. A strange man in a dark uniform blocked the exit. I was wrangling a long red tufted cushion between a table and a bookcase when I turned to face him.

"Can I help you?" I called.

"Dunno. Are you Madison Night?"

"I am."

That's when I saw the knife in his hand.

EIGHT

The sunlight backlit the man's figure. He stepped into the locker. I stepped back. He lifted his knife. It was curved like a hook. I raised the cushion in front of me. He came closer. A lamp tipped over and glass shattered on impact. I tried to scream but my throat was dry and no sound came out.

"Madison Night, right? The decorator?" he said. "Hudson told me to get in touch with you. Says you was looking for a contractor? I tried to call but nobody's answering your phone."

"What did you say your name was?" I called. He hadn't, but I didn't care.

"People call me Lyndy. Are you sure you're okay back there? You look trapped."

"Mr. Lyndy, can you wait out front for me?" I said from behind the cushion.

"Sure."

I waited until the storage locker was silent and shifted the cushion onto the top of a boomerang coffee table. I didn't have much in the way of weapons, but I wasn't going out unarmed against a man with a hook-shaped knife. I picked up an aluminum trash can lid and a fireplace poker and made my way out front, feeling more Monty Python than Doris Day.

The man leaned against the back door of Mad for Mod. He was older than I'd originally assumed. Dark, tanned, deeply creased skin glowed against his white hair. He was shorter than I was, exacerbated by the curve of his spine.

"I hope I didn't scare you back there. I've been banging on the front door for about twenty minutes afore I came around the back.

Saw the door open and saw your legs sticking up, got a little scared myself."

Rocky's barking sounded from inside the shop. The knocking must have riled him up. "Mr. Lyndy, you said you know Hudson?"

"Ain't no Mister, just Lyndy. Yeah, I know Hudson. Taught him a thing or two about construction. Boy's a fast learner."

I knew Hudson had been raised by his grandmother, but I'd never stopped to think about how he'd gotten into construction and woodworking. I'd always figured he'd picked it up on his own.

"What's that?" I asked, pointing to the knife in his hand.

"That's my carpet knife." He held it up. "Truth is, I'm on foot. Don't live far from here and I didn't want to bring my whole tool box if you wasn't around. Hudson called me yesterday and said you were looking for someone to help you on a project. I thought I'd show up ready for a job. I don't do many jobs these days, but if Hudson wants a favor, I'll do it."

I was still wary of the knife and wondered exactly how far he'd walked while holding onto it. It seemed I had even more evidence to support my argument that most Dallas residents didn't pay attention to the threats right in front of them.

"I can see it makes you uncomfortable. I lost my old one. This one's new. I had it in my pants, but after a while I kept feeling the tip poking into my thigh. I didn't even realize I was holding it when you saw me. Sure am sorry about that." He set the carpet knife on the ground by the toe of his boot, and then eased it forward, away from him and toward me. It was an odd gesture. I'd seen people do it in old movies, when bad guys are told to stand down. In the movies, the bad guys usually have another weapon strapped to their ankle.

"Do you have any referrals?"

"I told you, Hudson," he said.

"No, I mean client referrals."

"Most of the time I do the work and get paid cash. I don't ask people to write up referrals. But I've worked on most of these buildings out here. Been laying carpet since the sixties. I did the

Granada Theater at the end of the street, and the Szechwan Pavilion on Buckner before they renovated."

"Is there a way I can reach you? Do you have a business card?"

"You can write down my phone number."

The longer I stood outside talking to Lyndy, the less wary I became. He seemed like a nice old man who was willing to do a job, but I wasn't the same trusting soul I'd once been. I was going to need more than first impressions to put him on my payroll.

"When did you talk to Hudson?" I asked.

"This morning. Boy knows I get up early. He's in one of them square states now but he said he's on his way back. I got the feeling he wanted me to help you out until he got here so he could pick up where I left off."

"Let me get your number, and if things pan out, I'll be in touch." Instead of going inside, I went to my car and pulled a pen and business card from the center console. Lyndy rattled off seven numbers, I prompted him for the area code, and he looked at me like I was crazy.

"Two-one-four," he said. "I've been around longer than them new area codes."

I thanked him for his time and watched him walk to the edge of the parking lot. When he turned around, I noticed sadness in his red-rimmed eyes. "Miss Night, Hudson said you were a good lady. I've been down on my luck and I could use the work, even if it does only last until he gets here. I understand you gotta call him and make sure I'm not lying about anything I told ya. I'd want my own girls to do the same thing if they were still alive." He raised his hand to me in a cross between a tip of the hat and a wave. I waved back and watched him disappear into the streets behind Greenville Avenue.

I went back through the file of contractors that Hudson had left me. The last name on the list, one that I hadn't gotten to because of the early time, was Emil Lyndy. The phone number matched the one the old man had given me. For the first time since he'd shown up by the storage locker, I felt myself relax a tiny bit.

Maybe he was just a man with a tragedy in his past who was looking for a job.

I locked up the storage locker and spent the rest of the day designing the Japanese-inspired temporary interior for Cleo Tyler's party. I tried to recall any pertinent scenes in the Doris Day movies I knew so well, but came up empty. Not a tragedy, I figured, since the room would be temporary and torn down when the time came to finish the rest of the Tyler house.

I made a shopping list: paint for the walls, brushes and ink to create a minimal design on it, string lights for the paper lanterns, and bamboo. I downloaded a photo of the Tyler living room as it currently was, diluted the colors enough that only a hint of walls, floor, and ceiling lines were present, and printed five copies. I placed a sheet of tracing paper over the photo, and with a sharp black marker, sketched on the placement of a long, low bench that could serve as a dining area, rectangular cushions like the red one I'd been wrestling in the storage locker, plants, and a portable sake bar. Once I replaced their light fixtures with suspended paper lanterns, it would take on a cartoony Asian flair, less aesthetically pure but higher in entertainment value—something I suspected Cleo would respond to.

I closed down the computer, locked the front door, and left out the back sometime after seven. The temperature didn't change much between the time the sun was up and when it dropped, and the air held the beginning of what would soon become months of summer humidity. I envied Cleo's ability to jump into the pool when she wanted to cool down. Maybe I'd take her up on her offer to attend the party. I closed the storage locker and drove to Thelma Johnson's house.

I'd inherited the two-story stucco house from the son of a woman who had been murdered a year ago. It was located in the M streets, so named because all of the streets had names that started with that letter. The inheritance had required me to clear the back taxes on the property, and at the time, the idea of a secret hideaway had been appealing. I cleared up the bills and moved in. Turns out it was just in time. When my past came knocking on the door of my apartment, I'd needed a place to go. A place where nobody knew to look for me. And for the most part, this house had continued to be just that. A place where I could get away when I wanted to not be found.

Staying at Thelma Johnson's house had started out as a once or twice a week thing, and had turned into my more regular residence. Now that Effie was moving out of my apartment building, I found that I didn't want to stay there all by myself. The initial luster of buying the property and building my own small community through rentals had been tarnished by recent events. The community I'd built had vanished into thin air. I was forty-eight years old and had established that I didn't want or need anybody in my life except for my dog. At least that's what I wanted the world to think. Personally, I was starting to feel like a fraud for pretending to be so independent when more and more I craved companionship.

I carried Rocky from the car past the hedge, and then set him down. He took off across the yard, making a dash for the row of trees that lined the property. He lifted his leg by a purple Japanese maple that had been there for decades, and then raced in circles around the sidewalk. I guess when you spend your day cooped up inside a small office, you need a place to let off some steam.

I studied the vegetables in the garden while he played. A white butterfly caught his attention and he trotted along behind its irregular path. I picked the almost ripe tomatoes from the vine and called to Rocky.

"Time to go inside." He looked at me, then back at where the butterfly had been. It wasn't there. He dropped his head and trotted to the door like a sad but obedient dog. When I unlocked the door, a litter of takeout menus fell to the floor. I scooped them up and noticed a note scribbled on the one from Hunan Palace. *Same place. Midnight.* I opened the menu and found several items circled. Eggroll was underlined twice.

Tex was one of the few people who knew I sometimes resided

at Thelma Johnson's. His own history with the house ran a little deeper than mine. He'd dated the original owner's daughter. Being discovered in my secret hideaway was like having a stranger discover the Batcave. Surprisingly, Tex had been considerate when it came to respecting my privacy.

I turned on the television. News reports had dwindled from full scale stories with press conferences to one sentence updates reporting on the lack of leads. And if the police didn't have any leads, I wondered if that explained Tex's surveillance mission.

Tonight, the female reporter who had lost control of the interview with Chief Washington stood in front of the Casa Linda shopping center. "Earlier this evening, a store employee said he saw a police officer force this woman into the back seat of his car. At this time, the police are operating under the assumption that she is the latest victim of the Lakewood Abductor. If you have seen her, if you have any information about her whereabouts, please call this number." The photo of the recent abductee filled the center of the screen.

It was Cleo Tyler.

NINE

My chest tightened. I'd been at that shopping center hours earlier. So had Tex. And now, Cleo had been abducted. I clicked to the other local news channels, searching for more information. The reports were all the same. Cleo Tyler had gotten into the car with a police officer outside Paintin' Place and nobody had seen her since.

I called Dan Tyler. After four rings, the call went to voicemail. "Dan, this is Madison Night. I heard about Cleo. I'm so sorry. I was with her at the house this morning. Please let me know if there's anything I can do." I left my number and hung up.

Next, I called the police station and asked to speak to whoever was in charge of the abductions. I was connected to a Sgt. Osmond.

"Sergeant, this is Madison Night. I'm calling about Cleo Tyler's abduction."

"You and everybody else around town. She hasn't been missing for twenty-four hours. That news reporter jumped the gun, and I don't have anything to report."

"I'm not calling with questions. I'm an interior decorator and Cleo Tyler is one of my clients. I met with her earlier today at her house."

His tone became more lively. "What time was that?"

"It was around lunchtime."

"Before you left, did she say anything about her agenda for the rest of the day? Did she mention where she was going or anybody she planned to meet?"

"Not really. I got the impression that Cleo didn't leave the house much. She lounged around the pool."

"Did you talk to her since then?"

"No. They're saying on the news that she was abducted from the Casa Linda parking lot. That's where I went after I left her house."

"How long would you say you were there?" he asked.

"Forty-five minutes, somewhere around there. I had Chinese food takeout and ate in the car. I was at my apartment building by one thirty." For now I kept Tex's name out of it. "Sergeant, when did the cashier see her?"

"Half past four. He was collecting the shopping carts in the parking lot. She was at the end of the lot by the paint store. He said she got out of her car and into a black sedan with red and blue lights mounted on the bumper. He didn't think anything until he heard barking from inside her car."

"Daisy."

"What?"

"Her Chihuahua. He was tiny. He fit in her handbag. She never left him in the car."

"The cashier looked inside her car and saw the dog. On the floor he saw a gold shoe. That's when he called us. Can you tell me anything else?"

"Where's Daisy now?" I asked. "You didn't leave her in there, did you?"

"One of the officers took her for the night."

"Do you have any leads on what happened to Cleo?"

"Only what I told you. The cashier doesn't even know if the car turned left or right."

I gave Sgt. Osmond my contact information and hung up. My hands were shaking. I called Dan again, and again the call went to voicemail. Cleo had said he was out of town, and I didn't have his cell. I should have asked the sergeant if they'd been able to reach him but I doubted he'd tell me if I called back.

The passage of time ticked by slowly. Tex was expecting me to show up in the parking lot with dinner at midnight, but would he be there? Did he know about Cleo's abduction? Would it be safe for him to camp out in that parking lot now?

At eleven forty-five, I left. I picked up the order I'd called into Hunan Palace and circled the lot twice before locating Tex's Jeep across the street, parked outside of an all-you-can-eat buffet-style restaurant. I left the first lot and parked in the second and then got into his Jeep. He tore into the Hunan Palace bag before I had the door closed.

"Did you bring the eggroll?"

"What's with you and the eggroll?"

He pulled out the wax paper bag and extracted one of the deep fried rolls of cabbage and pork wrapped in phyllo dough. He finished it before I had a chance to hand him the duck sauce packet.

"Started back when I first became a cop. Stakeouts. Surveillance. We got Chinese food. Now, whenever I'm stuck in a car for any period of time, I crave eggrolls."

"How long have you been stuck in this car?" I asked, noticing that the stubble on his chin seemed to have grown since earlier in the day.

"Not long enough. Something's going on around here and I'm supposed to stay out of it."

"This has to do with your case?"

"It's not my case."

"You know what I mean."

He stopped eating for a second. "Night, what do you know about what's going on?"

"Only what they've been saying on the news—that you're connected to the abductions."

He pulled a pair of chopsticks out of a paper wrapper and tossed the paper behind his seat. "The guy who's doing this planted my badge in the woods near Kate Morrow's body and then called in a tip to the police. If those two hikers hadn't found the body, the cops would have."

"Jeez," I said. I knew the police had something big that connected Tex to the crimes, but I hadn't expected it to be his badge.

He shot me a sideways glance. "'Jeez?' I've been saying a lot stronger stuff than 'jeez.'"

"How'd somebody get your badge?"

"It's a fake. You know you can order these things on the internet? I can tell the difference—anybody in the department can—but to the general public, this looks better than what they see on cop shows on TV. The chief has my real badge. He strongly suggested that I take a voluntary leave of absence while they work the case. I don't blame him. He had to do something. But it's not me out there doing this. Somebody's pulling women over, showing them my badge, and taking them who knows where. Kate was the first victim to turn up and somebody leaked that my badge was found near her body. And as long as people think it's me, nobody's going to find out who it really is."

"I don't want to sound flip, but if they really thought it was you, wouldn't you be in jail?"

"Something happened yesterday. I heard Nasty came in with a potential vic who made a statement. Seems it was close enough to what's been happening that they couldn't hold me."

"Effie."

"What's an Effie?"

"Not a what, a who. Remember Effie? The college girl in my building who sometimes watches Rocky?" He nodded and bit down on a barbecued rib. "Someone attacked her. She said it was you."

"What made her think it was me?"

"He had a nametag pinned to his uniform that said 'Lt. Tex Allen.'"

"I don't wear a uniform, and if I did, it would say Lt. Allen. It wouldn't say 'Tex.'"

"I know. That's why you're out."

"What does Nasty have to do with any of this?"

"Effie wouldn't talk to the police. She doesn't trust them. I asked if she'd trust Nasty and she said yes."

"*You* called Nasty?"

"I don't think you want to criticize that particular judgment call."

For the next few minutes we ate. Tex kept his eyes trained on the entrance of the store. When the barbecued ribs and foil wrapped chicken were gone, we leaned back against the seats and relaxed as best we could. I didn't know what Tex was hoping to discover by keeping up surveillance on the shopping center, but for the time being, I didn't have any better ideas. I felt him closing off, dropping into his own world. As long as I was there, I needed to offer him a lifeline.

"Here's what I know," I started. "The guy impersonating you approached Effie on foot outside the Landing. He said she had a tail light out. Weird thing is, I was pulled over three days ago for a broken tail light. Remember, I called you?"

"Did you get a ticket?"

"I got a warning and fixed it this morning. Do you think that's how he's choosing his victims? Not how he's choosing them, but how he's able to follow them."

"It's one theory. Guy watches a place, sees who comes and goes. He sees a pretty girl get out of a car with out-of-state plates, he waits until she's inside and breaks one of her tail lights. Easy enough to follow her when she drives away. Either approaches her on foot or follows and pulls her over."

"The cops are finding cars abandoned in parking lots."

"I bet some of the women get out of the car because they want to see for themselves."

"That's what Effie said. He asked if she wanted to see for herself."

"How'd she get away?"

"She threw the car in reverse and knocked him down. She didn't stop to see if he was okay."

"That was smart." He ripped the package off of a wet-nap and wiped the barbecue sauce from his fingers and mouth. "So he's getting bolder and approaching women on foot. That would seem less threatening. I'll make sure the chief knows about this."

"He already should. Effie made a statement and told him. But the thing is, Tex, she thought it was you because of the name tag. She never even looked at his face. She's still afraid of you even though she knows you couldn't have been the person who approached her."

He jammed his chopsticks into the carton of rice and threw it at the dashboard. Tiny white grains flew out and stuck in clumps to the steering wheel.

"Lieutenant, everybody knows it wasn't you. You were standing next to the chief of police when she was approached. Whoever's trying to frame you is doing a really bad job."

"People who watch the news know, but people from out of town might not know anything about it. If it wasn't me, it would be another officer. He's using what we stand for to get women to trust him and he's abducting them."

I set down the rib that I was eating, my appetite suddenly gone. "What's the real reason you're camping out around Dallas?"

He jutted his chin toward the parking lot across the street where we'd been earlier in the day.

"I left that parking lot after you left. Went home. Crowd of news people were poking around the neighborhood, asking questions about me. I can't handle that, not now. I went to the gym to work off some steam. There was another news van in the lot when I came back, so I cruised around for a while and then came here."

"When was that?"

"Around five. Why?"

"There was another abduction today. A store employee saw a woman get into an unmarked police car with a man in a uniform."

"Why didn't he do anything?"

"The cashier didn't think anything of it until he heard barking from inside the woman's car. When he looked inside, he saw her Chihuahua and a single gold shoe. Tex," I said, putting my hand on his forearm, "the woman is one of my clients. Cleo Tyler. I was at her house just this morning and now she's gone. She could be dead."

Tex punched his steering wheel and the grains of rice that had stuck fell off. I felt his anger at the lack of control building up. He reached out for the dash and gripped it in both hands, his knuckles turning white.

"The news crew you saw in the parking lot broke the news. I talked to Sgt. Osmond earlier today." My voice came out shaky. "He said the news is making them look like fools because they didn't even know she was missing when they broke the story."

"Cleo Tyler. Married to Dan Tyler?" he said. He kept his voice even.

"Yes. You know her?"

"Him. His brother George was on the force. Died in a drunk driving accident."

"I know. Dan told me."

"We were friends, me and George. Worked a couple of cases together. I was at Jumbo's the night of the accident. George wasn't the only one who died—two teenage girls died too. It didn't look good for the precinct and a lot of officers tried to distance themselves from the scandal. Not many went to his funeral. When I offered my condolences to Dan, he took a swing at me. Called me part of the problem, not part of the solution. Said someday the tables would be turned and I'd know how he felt."

I thought back to Dan's anger when he'd first heard that Tex was a suspect. He hadn't mentioned that he even knew Tex, but clearly he did. And now he goes out of town the same time his wife was abducted.

"People deal with grief in different ways. Even though Dan knew about George's drinking problem, it was easier for him to blame the police force than to blame his only brother. You probably represented everything about the department that he had come to hate."

"He was right. A cop dies in the line of duty, he's a hero. No matter what the job does to you, you have that. But George didn't even get that. All the good work he did, it didn't matter. When he died, he was the bad guy. Dan Tyler was right. You know what the worst thing was about that?" He paused for a second, but I didn't think he really wanted me to say anything. "Within the month everybody was back at Jumbo's. It was like George's death never even happened."

TEN

Tex dropped his hands from the steering wheel and suddenly punched it again. The horn sounded a brief blast that startled a couple of pigeons in the middle of the lot.

I put my hand on his arm. "You can't blame yourself for what's happening now. You can't sit here in this car all day and all night and hope to find this guy. It's not going to happen that way. For starters, you're probably all kinds of cramped from sitting in here. How long has it been since you got up? How do you—never mind."

"Public bathroom outside the gas station. I picked the lock. I got out of the car and stretched right as the sun was coming up. I don't usually get to see the sun rise. Nice time of day. Nobody out here except for me and the crickets."

"Aren't you worried the security camera is going to spot you?"

"See the camera up there?" He pointed to the roof of the store. "Not hooked up to anything. After I went in to talk to the Chief, we requested the tape. The manager said the camera is a dummy. Meant to deter people from stealing shopping carts. Once people are out of their store, they don't care much what anybody does."

"Even with what's been happening here? Aren't they concerned about the safety of their employees?"

"Employees park in a lot in the back. Completely safe. They used to have someone collect the carts every hour but now they stop when the sun goes down and start back up in the morning."

"How do you know all this?"

"Surveillance."

"You can't sit in this Jeep all day staring at the front of a grocery store."

"There's not much else I *can* do. Reporters are camped out at my house, going through my trash, talking to my neighbors. I don't know how long I'm going to get away with sitting here, but it's my only option."

"Have you come up with anything? Any leads?"

"Whoever's doing this knows something about the way the department works. Could be a cop, a former cop, or somebody with a relative on the force."

"Like Dan Tyler," I said. "He went out of town this morning and then Cleo was abducted. They just bought a second house here."

"I'd like to see when they moved here and how it matches up to the abductions."

"I have that at the studio. Who else?"

"If it's not a cop, maybe it's a felon, somebody with a grudge. I've been going over past cases in my head and one sticks out." Tex leaned back. "It was my first case after I went into homicide. I was in the middle of a fifteen-hour shift. We'd been going over evidence for so long that I couldn't see straight. I went for a walk around the neighborhood to clear my mind. To this day I don't know why, but this one house caught my attention. Lawn was overgrown, trash was overflowing, and the front door was wide open. I called it in and went to the door to check it out. The place was filthy. Hadn't been cleaned in weeks. I walked through room by room, looking for whatever it was that set off my radar.

"There was a closet in the middle of the room with a mirror attached to the outside. I heard a scratching sound from inside. I turned the knob and caught the reflection of a guy behind me. He'd been hiding behind the sofa. I turned around and he fired a gun at me. I fired back, four shots. A cat ran out of the closet and startled me. My last shot went cockeyed into the sofa."

"What happened?"

He was quiet for a moment. "There was a woman behind the

sofa with him. We think he was hiding her there. That fourth bullet went through the sofa and killed her."

"What happened to the guy?"

"We arrested him."

"He's off the streets because of you."

"No, he's not. The DA couldn't make a case against him. If he was holding the girl against her will, we'll never know."

"What's his name?"

"Jacob Morris."

"Is he still in Dallas?"

"Last I checked he moved out of state." Tex put his hands up and rubbed his face vigorously. "Sometimes I drive past that house as a reminder of her. Looks like any other house out here. I wonder if the people who own it have any idea what happened inside."

"It's probably better that they don't. Do you have any other theories about who's doing this?"

"Couple of things here and there, but nothing big. I gotta get some sleep so I can focus."

My thoughts whirled around, potential solutions to Tex's situation so tangible I didn't know which way to turn.

"What if I gave you the keys to Thelma Johnson's house?" I asked.

"You're asking me to move in with you? Night, I'm flattered."

"Hardly." Not counting the abandoned apartment building, there was one other place I could go if I needed to get away from it all. One place that would be available for a few days, at least, as long as Hudson took his time crossing those square states Lyndy had said he was driving through.

"I need to pack a few things tonight, and I'll leave the key under the Dracaena plant around back. You can come and go as you wish. But if we do this, it comes with conditions. Number one: you don't ask where I'm staying."

"I figured you'd be staying at your apartment or at the studio. Now I'm curious. Where are you planning on staying?" he asked. He laced his fingers together and rested them behind his head. For the first time since I'd slid into the car, he smiled.

"Do you not understand the meaning of 'conditions'? Because you just violated the first one."

"Go on."

"Number two: twice a day you check in with me."

"For what purpose?"

"So we can exchange information. I'll tell you what I learn from the news, you tell me what you learn from camping out in front of the store."

"No. I'm not involving you in this."

"Lieutenant, in case you haven't noticed, I'm sitting in your car discussing your suspect pool. I already am involved."

"Don't you have a TV at Thelma Johnson's house? Shit, Night, why are we still calling it that?"

"Because of respect."

He was silent for a few beats while he appeared to consider that. "So, is there a schedule to these check-ins?"

"We can figure that out when we talk. Right now, it's about an hour past my bedtime and at this rate I'm not going to make it to the pool tomorrow."

"You really get something from swimming every morning, don't you?"

"Don't knock it till you've tried it." I opened the door and slid out of the seat. "Goodnight, Lieutenant."

"See ya, Night."

As I drove to Thelma Johnson's house, my mind raced with what Tex had told me about Dan Tyler. I understood the anger Tex said Dan had demonstrated at the funeral of his brother. Anybody would be angry. But now that Cleo was missing, was Dan going to turn to the police for help in finding her, or did his distrust of the police department run so deep that he would try to find her on his own?

I called Sgt. Osmond. "Sergeant, has there been any word on Cleo Tyler?"

"Not yet. Still can't reach the husband, either."

"Cleo told me he went out of town for a few days. I don't know when he's due back. Are you any closer to finding the other missing women?"

"Ma'am, we're doing what we can. Nobody wants to find those women more than we do, but these phones are ringing off the hook and every phone call that doesn't give us information takes us away from looking for them."

I thanked him for his time and hung up.

Tensions were running high—at the police station, at the local businesses, and among the community. The apartment building, Thelma Johnson's house, and Mad for Mod—none of them felt safe. I packed a turquoise and white vintage Samsonite suitcase like I was packing for a weekend getaway, put Rocky on his leash, and rooted around in the junk drawer in the kitchen until I found two house keys on a small silver ring. The keys belonged to Hudson.

He'd given me the keys before he left town. In case of emergency, he had said. At the time, I'd just inherited the house from Thelma Johnson's son. I didn't know how to tell Hudson that the house where I'd been living had previously been owned by the family of the woman he'd been suspected of killing, so I took the keys he offered and tucked them away in a drawer, where they'd stayed until tonight.

The personal drama that had followed Hudson for twenty years had reached a resolution thanks in large part to me. I suspected that he, now freed from his past, was interested in more than a working relationship with me, but my own walls were still up, not ready to let anyone else in. Had I asked him to stay in Lakewood, he might have, but that wouldn't have been fair.

As hard as it had been to watch him pack up his truck and leave, it would have been selfish to ask him to stay on my account. Offering me his keys told me he still wanted me in his life; taking them showed I wanted to be there. No matter what, I was happy for that connection.

There had been days when I drove past his house with the keys in my pocket. Days when I had slowed down, and even one when I pulled into his driveway. But there was a difference between spending time in his house while he was away and spending time with him. Every time I'd been there, I'd turned around and driven home. Except for the one time I let Rocky relieve himself on the post of Hudson's mailbox.

I didn't know how long it would take Tex to determine that he wanted to shower and sleep in a real bed, and I didn't want to be around when he showed up. As much chemistry as the two of us had together, we were both still very independent people with very different lives, in some ways worlds apart. It would be easier if this temporary setup respected that.

I drove to Hudson's house. Rocky hung his head out the window and let the passing wind hit his small furry face. There were no cars on the road save for those parked by the local bars, and we arrived quickly. I pulled up to a stretch of curb in front of the house next to his, collected my suitcase and Rocky, and went in through the front door.

Rocky sniffed every inch of the hallway while I felt around for a light switch. I walked into the corner of a long, low coffee table and cursed as it bruised my shin. Before I could stop it, a vase with long cat-o-nine tails tipped over and landed on the floor. I dropped to my hands and knees and felt over the carpet for the scattered sticks. A light came on, blinding me.

"Who's there?" said a dark chocolate coated in espresso and dipped in cigar smoke voice.

Very slowly I peeked out from behind the coffee table.

On a good day, Hudson was a gentle, artistic soul wrapped in a fitted black T-shirt and faded jeans. Today he was half naked in drawstring waist pajama bottoms. His longish black hair had been shorn into a Mohawk, the top long, the sides starting to grow in.

"Madison? Is that you?" he asked, squinting at me. "What are you doing here?"

"Picking up the cat-o-nine tails."

"Leave them."

Slowly, I stood. "Surprise," I said.

"I can't imagine a much better surprise than finding you in my house." His voice was low and gravelly from having been woken up. He stepped closer and I reached up and brushed his longish hair away from his amber eyes.

And then a door opened in the hallway and I heard a soft female voice. "Hudson?" she called. "Can you bring me a glass of water before we go to bed?"

ELEVEN

My hand froze in place and instantly I felt clumsy. I lowered my arm and stepped back. "I should leave," I said. I looked around for Rocky but he wasn't there. "I'm leaving. Right now. As soon as I find Rocky."

"Wait here," he said. He walked down the hall toward the door that separated the house from the garage. I heard a door shut, then open, then another door shut.

I bent at the waist and called out to Rocky. "Hey—Rocky— where are you?" I whispered. I turned my head to the left and right, looking for traces of his fluffy tail. Not paying attention to where I was walking led me to bump my head on the wall of the dining room. "Ow," I said to myself.

I straightened up and found myself face-to-face with Mortiboy, Hudson's black cat. He was lounging across the back of the orange sofa. He stretched one paw out toward me and did whatever it was cats did to make their claws pop out. When he laid his paw on the fabric, his claws got stuck and he twitched his shoulder a few times to try to free himself.

"Hold on, Mortiboy. No need to get all riled up, I'm on my way out." I lifted his paw and extricated his claws. Once he was freed, he looked up at me and meowed. A ball of white and caramel fluff jumped onto the sofa and swatted Mortiboy's long black tail. He hissed in Rocky's face and then jumped down and ran into the dark hallway. Rocky followed.

"Rocky!" I whispered. "Get back here." I tiptoed around the table and into the hallway.

A door opened and Hudson came out. He'd added a pajama

top, and in one arm, he held Rocky. His other hand held that of a young blond girl who hugged a stuffed bunny to her turquoise pajamas.

"Madison Night, meet my niece, Heather. Heather, this is my friend, Madison."

"Is he your dog?" Heather asked.

"Yes. His name is Rocky."

"Can he sleep in my room?"

"We were about to leave."

"Why did you come over if you were going to leave?" she asked. Hudson's eyebrows raised as if he wanted to hear the answer too.

"I didn't know Hudson had company."

The girl looked up at Hudson and curled her bunny under her arm. "Uncle Hudson, can the puppy sleep over?"

"If it's okay with Madison," Hudson said.

"Please?" the little girl said to me.

I looked from her face to Hudson's. "My sister and Heather kept me company on the drive back to Texas. They're staying for a few days."

"If you let your dog sleep in the room with me, I promise I'll be extra quiet," Heather said. "Mom won't even know he's there."

Hudson let go of the girl's hand and rested his palm on her shoulder. "Let's get that glass of water for your mom before Madison and I work this out."

"Okay," Heather said.

"I'll be right back. Stay put," he said to me. They went to the kitchen where the faucet ran for a few seconds, and then down the hall with Heather leading the way. They stopped by a door on the right and Heather opened the door. Hudson set Rocky down and he went inside. Hudson pulled the door shut behind him but didn't close it all the way.

"Now we need to find a place for you to sleep," he said.

"I'll take the sofa."

"You could take my bed." I must have looked shocked, because he quickly added, "And I'll take the sofa."

"I should probably be out here in case Rocky acts up."

"Rocky. Sure."

I finished cleaning up the spilled cat-o-nine tails and righted the vase on the coffee table. When I went to the kitchen, I found Hudson putting a bottle of wine back into the refrigerator. Two glasses on the counter were half full of a crisp white, and already beads of condensation were running down the outside of each glass.

"You look like you could use this," he said. He handed me one of the glasses, clinked rims with me, and we both took a sip.

"Come with me," he said. He opened the sliding glass doors at the back of his house and hooked his index finger around mine, gently pulling me outside. We sat down next to each other on the white rope hammock.

"I read about what happened with your ex-boyfriend," he said. "Too bad it had to end that way."

"It's over. Life goes on."

We both sipped at our wine. I silently auditioned several different ways to explain why I'd showed up at his house but none of them sounded quite right.

"You didn't seem all that surprised to find me in your living room," I finally said.

"I gave you a standing invitation. Just think, if I'd stopped off in El Paso like I originally planned, I might have never known you were here."

"Lyndy said—"

"Lyndy called you?" He smiled. "I wasn't sure if he would."

"He came by the studio this morning."

"He's a good guy. He learned carpentry and construction from his father and he taught me. He had two daughters, but they died a few years ago."

"How come you never told me about him?" I asked.

"There's a lot I haven't told you about."

I wondered for a split second about how much I knew about the people in my life and how much they knew about me. Nasty's

WITH VICS YOU GET EGGROLL   87

warning about Tex floated through my thoughts again. *He's not the man you think he is.* Wasn't that the truth about everyone? That we projected our feelings, intuition, and what we wanted someone to be onto them, only to discover in time that they weren't who we thought they were.

"Something brought you to my doorstep, Madison," Hudson said gently. "Do you want to talk about it?"

I drank more than a sip of wine and tipped my head back, appreciating the taste of the sweet cold liquid before I swallowed. How to start?

"Someone has been abducting women around Dallas. So far one woman has been found dead. You might have heard about it on the news." Hudson nodded once. "Remember Lt. Allen?" I rushed ahead, not wanting to draw attention to the other man in my life. "Whoever's been doing this has been impersonating him. Using his badge to get women to trust him. He's on voluntary leave, but the press has been camping out by his house. He needed a place to stay."

"You gave him yours," Hudson guessed correctly.

"Because I thought I could stay here."

"You still can."

"It's a little more complicated now."

"Not to me, it's not."

"Lt. Allen came after you for the murder of Thelma Johnson's daughter," I reminded him. "I don't expect you to make any sacrifices on his behalf."

"Tex was doing his job. We're good now."

I turned and looked at his face. He ran his index finger down my cheek.

"Hudson, Lt. Allen and I might be more than friends."

"If you and Lt. Allen were more than friends, you wouldn't have come here to spend the night."

"But Lt. Allen and I have been spending time together. He's trying to find who's committing these crimes. Now that the news broke about his badge, he can't come and go as he pleases. He needs eyes and ears to keep him informed."

"For a woman who can't open herself up long enough to start a relationship, you sure are trusting."

"With Lt. Allen, it's different. I know he isn't the man abducting those women. Just like I knew you weren't guilty of murder. As long as people are focused on him as a suspect, nobody's out there looking for the real villain. Only one of the women has been found, and even though she'd been missing for a month, she'd only been dead for a few hours. That means the abductor is keeping them somewhere. Hudson, I know two of the women who were approached. One is a client, one lives in my building. They're not strangers to me. Neither is Lt. Allen. Too much of my life is rooted in coming and going as I please. These abductions are changing all of that—not just for me, but for everybody."

Hudson readjusted himself on the hammock, his hand resting against my leg. Heat from his hand seared through the fabric of my pants.

"I think I understand why you're letting Tex stay at your house, but why'd you come to my place instead of your apartment?" he asked.

I looked down at my hands. "The last of my tenants moved out. The building is empty except for me. Here, well, here I would have felt like you were with me, even if you weren't."

Hudson and I had developed a trusting rapport, an easy dependability that hinged around tables and chairs in need of repair. Once my decorating business was on solid footing, I'd repeatedly asked if he wanted to become partners—my way of establishing a more permanent connection. He always declined, and I always felt like he'd given me a present by saying no.

"The building's empty?"

"Yep."

He dropped his eyes to my hands and nodded slowly, his lips pursed. I failed at stifling a yawn. "We can talk more tomorrow. You need to get some sleep." I followed him back inside. "If you need anything, my room is the last one on the left. The bathroom is the first door on the left."

I waited until his bedroom door closed behind him and carried my bag to the bathroom. I changed into a cotton nightie and splashed cool water on my face. Sleep. Right.

The next morning I woke up disoriented. The living room was flooded with light, showing off the wooden Witco wall hanging above the sofa, the chrome globe lamp that rested on a two-tiered end table, and the brass magazine stand that sat next to the reclining chair. In it were back issues of *Atomic Ranch* magazine and the *Better Homes and Gardens Handyman Guide* from 1957 that I'd given him for Christmas last year.

I knotted a pink cotton robe over my nightgown. According to the starburst clock in the hallway, it was after nine. Under normal conditions, I would have been up for the past three and a half hours. Then again, nothing about the past few days had been normal.

I listened for sounds that would prove I hadn't dreamt the whole encounter with Hudson and his niece last night. The house was silent. I went straight to the bathroom, did what I needed to do, and went to the kitchen. A pot of coffee sat on the counter, anchoring a handwritten note. *Madison—I took Heather and Nettie to the World Aquarium. Help yourself to anything you want. I'll be back around four. Had an idea for you. —H.*

I poured a cup of coffee and sat in the breakfast nook. Out back, Mortiboy wandered the perimeter of the yard. Rocky ran up to him, then ran away. The wooden fence provided an enclosed area for both of them to explore. I knew Mortiboy had been on the road with Hudson for the past few months. He must have been happy to be back in his environment if he was tolerating Rocky's attack-sniff-retreat routine.

I finished my coffee, took a quick shower and changed into a geranium red dress. After applying my daily slathering of sunscreen, I secured my hair into a high ponytail, slipped black ballerina flats on my feet, and collected Rocky. Mortiboy seemed unconcerned that we were leaving. I added a note to Hudson that I'd see him later.

It was too late to bother with the pool. Not only would the lanes be overflowing with lap swimmers who had slept in, but the sun was already hot, and there was only so much my sunscreen could do. I wasn't about to risk skin cancer for a late workout. I'd be back in the pool tomorrow.

Rocky and I headed to Mad for Mod. I unclipped his leash and he went straight to my office. By the time I caught up with him, he was on his dog bed fighting with his rope bone. Snarls and growls came from the floor while I checked my messages.

There was one from Joanie Higa, who ran Joanie Loves Tchotchkes, a local thrift store. She claimed to have acquired a collection of vintage melon, yellow, and aqua Spaghetti String glasses and a matching pitcher with my name on them. The second message was from Richard Goode, the head volunteer who ran programming at the Mummy Theater. He wanted my opinion on the tackiness level of planning a night of kidnapping movies. The fact that he was asking the question told me he already knew the answer.

The third message was from Sgt. Osmond. I called him back first.

"Sergeant, this is Madison Night. Do you have any leads on Cleo Tyler?"

"Ms. Night, that's not why I called. It's starting to look like you might have been the last person to talk to Mrs. Tyler, so can you tell me anything else about yesterday morning? Did you ask her to go to the paint store?"

"No, in fact, I don't know why she was there. We've discussed swatches that I took to her, but it's my job to order the paint and supplies, not hers."

"Do you do all the work yourself?"

"I do as much as I can, and what I can't do, I freelance out. I have a network of contractors that I like to work with. Hudson James is on the top of that list."

At the mention of Hudson's name, Rocky looked up from his rope bone and yipped. I reached down and tugged the toy out from under his paw and tossed it into the hallway. He charged and retrieved it like a pro.

"Is Mr. James working with you on this job?" Sgt. Osmond asked.

"He will be. He was out of town when I first took the job, so I called around to the other contractors he recommended."

"Do you have a list of these other contractors?"

"Yes. Why?"

"It seems that after you left her, she drove to the paint store, where she was abducted. We don't know if she was followed from home or picked out at random in the parking lot. We're following up on everything she did, everybody she might have interacted with. It's thin, but we're looking at it all."

I glanced at the list of contractors. I'd left messages for most of the men. Emil Lyndy's name was at the bottom. "Sergeant, I can email this to you if you'd like. There's only one on the list who I actually spoke to, and he showed up here before I called him. His name is Emil Lyndy."

"Know where I can find him?"

"I only have a phone number." I rattled off Lyndy's digits. Sgt. Osmond thanked me and hung up.

Ever since taking the job with Cleo and Dan Tyler, my studio hours had been limited. Considering what they were paying me, I could have closed my doors to new business and still been financially secure. But the decorating business was a game of feast or famine, and being closed to new business wouldn't work out well for Mad for Mod in the long term.

I tried to reach Dan Tyler again. This time he answered.

"Hello, Dan? This is Madison Night. Have you heard from Cleo?"

"The police tracked me down this morning. I'm heading back

now."

"I just spoke to the police too. They're following up on everything they can. They're going to find her." I spoke with more confidence than I felt.

"You don't get it, do you? Those cop friends of yours don't care what happens to her or to any of those women. They want to protect their image and look good. It's up to me. By the time they'll treat her like a missing person, she could be dead."

"What are you going to do?"

"I'm going to mobilize a team to help me find my wife and I'm going to tell that woman on the news what I know about how the Lakewood Police Department operates when it comes to protecting their own."

"Dan, they're trying to help."

He cursed. "Mind your own business, Madison. And consider your services terminated."

TWELVE

I repeated Dan's name a few times before accepting that he'd hung up on me. I set the top half of my donut phone back on the receiver, completing the circle, and sat back, staring at the notes on my desk.

Cleo had said that Dan would be out of town for a few days. Now Cleo was missing and Dan was circumventing the police to try to find her. Did his anger toward the police run so deep that he would destroy the reputation of the department to get back at them for what happened to his brother? Or was there something else behind his actions?

Like, did he know more about the abductions than he was letting on?

Try as I might, I couldn't relax, not completely. Watching the news had become a compulsion—waiting to hear if the police had any leads or, worse, if another woman was missing. I tried not to let it get to me, but everywhere I turned, I was reminded of my isolation. My client had been abducted. My last tenant had been approached by the abductor. My former clients were out of town, and I'd just been fired.

As a single woman in Dallas, I should have been afraid to leave the house alone. Instead I found myself confronting latent feelings about two men. Was it the fear of the abductions that forced me to acknowledge what Hudson and Tex meant to me? Or a greater fear of sitting passively by, letting life happen around me? I was a woman with very few personal connections and that had been fine. Until now. But regardless of which way I went, I couldn't turn my back on one person in order to have a life with the other. That went against my nature.

What did I really know about the abductions? Not much, but that could change in an instant.

I pulled up the internet news of the abductions and wrote each of the vics' names on an index card: Linda Gull, Susan Carroll, Kate Morrow, and Cleo Tyler. I wrote the date each woman was reported as missing on the bottom, and then pinned them to the wall on top of the still-unnamed paint swatches. When I was finished, I had a timeline that spanned five weeks.

If something connected these four women, I didn't know what it was. They varied in ages, races, and economic backgrounds. Cleo and her husband had moved here recently, and Kate, an only child, had been in town visiting her mother. Linda had been passing through on her way to Shreveport to meet up with friends, and Susan had been headed to the airport after a reunion weekend where she and her siblings celebrated their parent's fiftieth wedding anniversary. The police had confirmed that they were all from out of town. So was there a pattern to the abductions, or was the pattern completely random?

I sat up straighter and remembered Effie. There was no report of her attempted abduction in any of the papers. I wrote "Effie Jones" on an index card and thumbtacked it to the board to the left of the article about Cleo. But Effie didn't fit. She had Texas plates on her car, and she wasn't from out of town. Plus, as far as I knew, she was the only person who could give a statement about the attacker.

The attack on Effie had come when Tex was at the press conference. That bit of odd timing had moved suspicion from him, even though her would-be attacker had worn Tex's name pinned to his shirt. It was a pretty sloppy mistake if someone was trying to set him up.

I leaned back in my chair and considered what that might mean. Did the same person approach Effie as the other women, or was someone taking advantage of the situation? Was her so-called attack a copycat crime?

"What do you think, Rocky? Does anything stand out to you?" I asked. Rocky, tired of his bone, lifted his head and looked at me. I pointed at the pictures on the wall. He cocked his head sideways and then laid it back down on top of his paws.

"If you think of anything, let me know. Lt. Allen is counting on us."

I stared at the wall again. The abductor clearly knew a thing or two about how the Lakewood Police Department conducted their business. How else would he know how to get Tex's badge, or know what would pass as a believable uniform, or what to say to get someone to pull over and trust him? But these things were also the flaws in his plan. Why impersonate Tex, a homicide detective, who didn't wear a uniform? Who didn't pull people over and hand out traffic violations? Or drive an unmarked police car?

That made me think it was a personal attack against Tex. Using his identity mattered more than the accuracy of the impersonation. That's why he targeted women from out of town. They wouldn't know who Tex was. The Lakewood Abductor could operate under relative anonymity while the entire police department was looking for him.

I didn't like the thought, but the more I tried to reason it through, the more it felt like I was onto something. I needed to bounce my thoughts off of someone. I considered my options and, regretfully, ended up with one person. For the second time in a matter of days, I called Nasty.

"Donna, this is Madison." I was met by silence. "Thank you for your help with Effie. She was really shaken up, and I don't think she would have made a statement if you hadn't gone with her."

"What do you want?" she asked.

I pushed aside my petty anger at her rudeness. "I've been going over what I know about this case. I know you're not on the force anymore, and I know we're not exactly friends, but I thought we could put aside our differences to help Lt. Allen."

"No."

"What?"

"No. I told you. That life—being a cop and being with Tex—is in my past. I've moved on."

"This isn't about me, it's about a man we both know, a man we both care about."

"You're enabling him, you know that? You're allowing him to manipulate you into helping him. You're putting yourself in danger for no good reason. As long as you're asking yourself questions, try to answer this one: what is it you get from this situation?"

"Donna, four women have been abducted. One is dead, and three are still missing. Lt. Allen needs our help."

"No, he needs to help himself. Get any ideas of you and me working like partners out of your head. We're not Cagney and Lacey."

And for the second time that day, someone hung up on me.

Shortly after noon, Rocky and I left the studio and drove to the Casa Linda shopping center. I circled the lot twice, looking for Tex's Jeep. It wasn't there. Just as I was about to leave, I noticed a long, flat pizza box jutting out of the trash. *Go to Keller's* was written on the side.

Keller's Hamburgers was a drive-in burger joint a few miles away. Going to Keller's was like going back in time. Dressed as I was in a secondhand dress from the early sixties, it seemed fitting. Tex's Jeep was parked at the end of a row of cars and trucks. A few bikers on motorcycles idled around the front of the restaurant by picnic tables. My Alfa Romeo fit in perfectly. I parked next to Tex, and Rocky and I moved from my car to his.

He looked at Rocky and then at me. "I ordered you a vanilla shake and a burger. Okay?" he said.

"Sure. No fries?"

He turned to the speaker. "Add an extra burger, no bun, and an order of fries."

"I was kidding."

He ruffled Rocky's fur while we waited for the food. Rocky walked from my lap to Tex's, turned around, and came back to me. He jumped down to the floor and curled up on top of my feet. When the food was delivered, Tex distributed the burgers and shakes and set the fries between us. He unwrapped the second burger and tore off a piece for Rocky. I covered my lap with napkins and bit into mine. I hadn't realized how hungry I was until I stopped three bites in and caught Tex staring at me.

"Did you want me to wait?" I asked.

"Nope." He unwrapped his burger and caught up to me. We finished our burgers and picked at the fries between sips of our shakes.

"You didn't go swimming this morning," he said.

"How do you know?"

"I was there."

"I forgot. You like to pop up from time to time."

"No, I was there. In the pool. Six o'clock."

"You went to Crestwood to swim? Lt. Allen, you surprise me."

"You were right. Being in the water provides a certain outlet for tension. It's no shooting range, but it's something."

"Is that where you normally go to let off steam?"

He raised an eyebrow. "It's not my number one choice, but it works. Besides, you had a good point about getting out of the car and changing my scenery. So, what, you had another job this morning?"

"Not exactly." I suspected Tex was looking for clues as to where I had slept. The memory of spending the night at Hudson's was still too fragile to talk about. "How'd you sleep?"

"Fine, once I got used to the pink floral comforter."

"Sorry. Would airplanes and fire engines be better for a big strong boy like you?"

"Maybe." He grinned. One last slurp of his shake gave evidence that the white Styrofoam cup was empty. He set it in the cup holder and bit off another fry. "Can I ask you a question?"

"Sure."

"You ever wonder about your life? About all of the decisions that brought you to this place, right now? Do you ever wish you did things differently when your ex showed up?"

Leave it to Tex to ruin a perfectly good vanilla shake and basket of French fries by bringing up my past.

Brad Turlington was the reason I'd left Pennsylvania. While on a romantic getaway at the Poconos, on the top of a black diamond ski slope, in the middle of our torrid love affair, he told me he was married. I'd skied away. Skidded on the ice. Lost control and fell. Tore a couple of ligaments in my knee.

As if that wasn't bad enough, two years later, he showed up in Dallas. The marriage, the whole confession, had been a lie. He claimed to be ready to come clean about the skeletons in his closet, and when I realized how much trouble he was in, I let him back into my life.

"I should have slammed the door in his face. The whole thing was a manipulation. I spent two years building a life on my own in Dallas. Sure, he hurt me. But if I had one do-over, I wouldn't have given him the chance to hurt me again."

"Relationships hurt. That's reality."

"You've been hurt by love? Mr. Love them and leave them? Who was she?"

He sat back against the seat. "Night, there's no 'one who got away', if that's what you're driving at. I just never met the right girl."

"Either you stopped looking when you were a fourteen-year-old Boy Scout, or you might want to rephrase that sentence and use the word 'woman' this time."

"You think I'm sexist, don't you?"

"I think you can do with a couple reminders of equality here and there."

He moved his hands from behind his head to his thighs. "I think that's my favorite thing about you. You don't care that I'm a cop. You're willing to call a spade a spade."

He turned his head away from me and looked at a passing

black Escalade.

"Lieutenant, I don't think you're a spade."

"Oh, yeah? Then what am I?"

I considered the question. "I don't know what you are."

"Is that why you gave me a place to stay and are checking in on me twice a day? You're trying to figure me out?"

"I don't know about that either."

He leaned close and I smelled the sweetness of the shake on his breath. "You're here because you don't understand what this is," he said, moving his hand back and forth between us. "Just like me." He sat back and looked out the window. "I realized last night when I was trying to sleep on your pink sheets that I don't need to understand it."

I fought the urge to tell him where I'd slept last night. I didn't know why I'd wanted to keep it a secret when I thought Hudson was out of town, but now, getting into the details would be plain old messy. Tex didn't need that kind of drama, not when he was trying to find a killer. And I didn't need that kind of drama, not when I was finally sorting out my life.

"Dan Tyler fired me this morning," I said. "I called him to see if there was any news on Cleo and he said I should consider myself terminated."

"Does he know you know me?"

"Yes."

"I'm sorry, Night."

"Don't be. I'm not going to lie about who I associate with. But speaking of associations..." I bit my lower lip and wondered if maybe I should consider lying when it came to Nasty. "I was looking at the articles about each of the known abducted women and I don't think the person who approached Effie is the same guy who took the other women. There are too many inconsistencies. Her guy was on foot, but the others had a car. He had a name tag with your name on it. The other guy had a badge. All of the others were from out of state but her car has Texas plates. I think someone took advantage of the situation to scare her, but that's all."

"A copycat."

"Maybe. Effie's story doesn't match what we know about the others. She was at the Landing. And she wasn't abducted. She drove away."

"The police are following up on her statement."

"But if her situation was meant to be a distraction, then whatever they're following up on isn't going to lead them to the right guy. Any time that's spent searching for him is time not spent searching for the guy who took the others. Do you see what I'm saying?"

"It's one theory."

"Do you have a better one?"

He tore off another piece of hamburger and held it out to Rocky, who moved from my feet to the driver's side with Tex. "I wish I could figure out the connection. Whatever it is that ties me to these women, or ties these women together. That might give us a clue to where they are."

"What do you have so far?"

"At first we thought he was impersonating a cop to get women to pull over. Make us look bad while he commits his crimes. I don't think it was ever about making a mockery of the Lakewood Police Department, but I think it's about me."

"What makes you say that?"

He reached under his seat and pulled out a small black wallet. When he flipped it over, I saw his badge. "I thought that was found on the body of Kate Morrow. How do you have it now?"

"It's another one. I found it in the parking lot by the paint store."

"That's where Cleo Tyler was abducted."

"I know. Seems whoever is behind this is dropping clues to keep me under suspicion."

THIRTEEN

I thought back to when I'd been pulled over earlier in the week and had asked Officer Iverson to show me his badge. "So the warnings on the news aren't going to protect anybody. If someone gets pulled over and asks to see a badge, they're going to trust that it's real."

He nodded. "Ever since Kate Morrow's mother accused me of abducting her daughter on the news, my name's been connected to the crime. Doesn't look like that's going to change."

"Why aren't the police staking out the Casa Linda parking lot?"

"Patrol cops circle through on their route, but the abductions haven't all happened there. The force is already spread thin because of this. If the chief puts a car there around the clock, that's a car that can't be somewhere else. He's managing the best he can with limited resources. If someone's following what the reporters have been saying, they'd know the police suspect an impersonator."

"Unless that someone was from out of town."

Like Cleo Tyler. But Cleo knew about Tex. Her husband had an obvious dislike of the police, and now I knew his affiliation with Tex wasn't random. So how had an impersonator gotten her to go with him? She should have known the man who approached her wasn't the man we watched on TV. Or did she trust me so much that she ignored any warning bells that had gone off when she saw his name on the badge? Had my reassurances that Tex was innocent led her to fall for a trap?

I ate two more French fries and moved the empty red and white checkered carton to the trash bag with the Styrofoam shake cups. "What are you going to do now?" I asked.

"I don't know. I'm trying to find the connection to me. I've been over every old case, every guy I put in jail, every ex-girlfriend."

"You must be tired."

I caught him off guard and he chuckled, and then grew serious. "Criminals always return to the scene of the crime. He took Kate and Cleo from the Casa Linda parking lot. I'm going back to keep watch."

"You don't think someone's going to report your car as being suspicious?"

"I'm not conducting an investigation. I'm sitting lookout. I told you, there aren't enough cops in the department to plant somebody there around the clock. If I see something, I call it in. That's all I can do."

"Lieutenant, you can't keep up surveillance on the parking lot for twenty-four hours of the day. It's not healthy."

"Twenty-three hours, if you count the pool this morning."

"I'm serious. Take the night off. Stay at Thelma's."

"It doesn't work that way, Night. Until this guy gets caught, I'm on watch. Besides, I've got you to check in on me twice a day, right? So, tonight? Midnight? Are you in or are you out?"

"I'll see what I can do."

Tex and I went separate directions. I drove Rocky back to the studio and unpinned the images of the abducted women from my cork wall. I tried brainstorming paint color names (Turquoise Target, Dead-On Red, Hopeless Taupe, and Yell for Yellow) before recognizing I was in a dark mood. I moved on to the important task of doodling the blank page of my notebook with sketches of boomerangs and wing dings until I remembered what the mall employee had said. He saw Cleo get into a car in front of the paint store. Not the grocery store.

I called Paintin' Place. "Mitchell, it's Madison."

"Did you finally come up with names for those swatches?"

"I'm working on it, but that's not why I called. I heard a woman was abducted from the parking lot in front of your store yesterday."

"Yeah, and now I got reporters hanging around like I'm giving away free coffee."

"Did you see anything?"

"She came into my store and took a bunch of paint swatches, but she didn't buy anything. After she left, I went back to restocking the drop cloths. Some new contractor was in that morning and wiped me out."

"So you didn't see her talking to a police officer?"

"No."

"How did you find out what happened?"

"That lady reporter who broke the news came in. She asked me a bunch of questions like the ones you're asking. Once her story hit the air, the reporters multiplied. Only thing I keep hoping is that one of them will decide they want to paint their house."

"Thanks, Mitchell," I said.

"Listen, Madison, I don't want to pressure you, but are you any closer to coming up with paint names?"

"Soon, I promise."

"You're putting a lot of thought into it."

"It's not every day I get the chance to endorse a line of mid-century paint colors. It's a big responsibility in my world."

"Well, if you don't come up with names soon, I'm going to have to pull the plug on the whole idea. This is peak home renovation season."

"I'm on it."

When I hung up, I looked back down at the page hoping maybe there was something there that was better than I thought. Sadly, I'd been right the first time. I wrote "Cleo Tyler" in a blank space on the side of the page, and then sat back. Why would Cleo have been getting swatches from the paint store? She and Dan were paying me a fair amount to decorate. Why do it herself instead of tasking me out for that very project? She was a woman who had a maid clean up after her dog. Something—or someone—had drawn her there.

At quarter to four, Rocky and I headed to Hudson's. Mortiboy and Hudson were in the backyard. Rocky raced to Mortiboy, who hissed in his face. He looked at me with guilty Shih Tzu eyes, and then back at Mortiboy, who stared at him with a feline expression that said, "don't even think about charging me again."

Hudson reclined in the rope hammock that we'd sat in last night. He kept one foot on the ground, moving the hammock side to side. Mortiboy and Rocky were on the deck. It seemed they'd reached an agreement to coexist.

"So it really wasn't a dream," Hudson said.

"Funny, I thought the same thing when I woke up. Where's Nettie?"

"She took Heather out to a matinee."

"I hope you didn't pass up something good on my account," I said playfully.

"Disney princesses aren't my thing." His expression changed. "I asked around today and found out Lt. Allen's troubles are worse than I thought. You're not turning into a thrill seeker, are you?"

"I think I've had my fifteen minutes of danger already," I said, trying to keep my voice light. "You don't have to worry about me."

"Come here," he said. He shifted to the side of the hammock and it rocked back and forth.

I crossed his backyard. He held a hand out and I took it. I didn't put up a fight when he gently pulled me closer. I sat, facing him, with my legs dangling from the side. He ran his thumb back and forth over the palm of my hand.

"When you came here last night, you didn't know I would be here. Now that I'm back, are you going to leave?"

"I don't think so," I said.

"Good."

I felt the cozy warmth I'd been missing since Hudson had left town. The tension, fear, and anxiety that surrounded me since the abductions started now dropped away, like I'd entered a soundproof booth that shut out the world. In the yard, a Monarch butterfly hovered by a row of bamboo plants. Mortiboy stood up and swatted at the butterfly, and then chased it a few feet. Rocky followed close behind. Mortiboy turned and swatted Rocky in the nose. Rocky whimpered, looked at me, and back at the black cat.

"Pretty soon they won't remember what life was like without each other."

"I don't think I'd go that far," I said.

"We're very accepting around here. You might be surprised."

I stared up at the blue sky and closed my eyes for a second. The early humidity stuck on my face like an invisible washcloth. I'd come to accept the hot, humid days in Dallas, but I didn't think I'd learn to like them.

"Your note this morning said something about an idea for me," I said.

"Yes. You said your apartment building is vacant, right? Good time to do some major renovations. If I remember correctly, those carpets are looking pretty shabby."

"It's like you can read my mind. I was just thinking about that yesterday."

"If I could read your mind, I like to think we wouldn't be talking about renovating your apartment building. Besides, I don't know if I would have gotten the idea if you hadn't mentioned Lyndy."

"You never called in backup on a job before. Why now?"

"You're talking about tearing carpets out of an entire building and refinishing the hardwood floors underneath? I'm flattered that you think I can handle that myself, but unless you want the place to be under construction until Christmas, I'm going to need some help. Lyndy's a pro. Carpets are his specialty."

"Do you want to head over there later, do a walk-through and give me a quote?"

"Don't need to. I went over today and did a walk-through."

"And?"

"I'm pretty sure you can afford me. But Lyndy's not going to come cheap." He smiled.

Something was happening between Hudson and me, and as much as I wanted to give in and see where it went, I was still scared. After about a minute or so, I stood up and let go of his hand. "Aside from your living room and your guest bathroom, I've never really seen the interior of your house. Any interest in giving me a tour?" I asked.

"Why don't you go inside and check it out on your own? Help yourself to anything you find. I'll be in shortly."

I left Hudson out back and wandered into his house. I knew I would have done this very thing the previous night if he hadn't been here, but knowing he was right outside, allowing me the same chance to get to know him through his residence, made me feel like he had invited me into his private world instead of me showing up and crashing it.

Tempted as I was to beeline for his bedroom and take a peek, I didn't. I walked down the hallway, pausing to study the paintings on the walls and the books in the bookcase. I was already familiar with his living room, a study in wood paneling with an orange tweed sofa and matching round cushions. I kicked my shoes off and walked barefoot over the plush shag carpet. In front of me was the boomerang table that I'd knocked the vase of cat-o-nine tails from the previous night.

The kitchen was homey. Avocado green appliances from the seventies shared space with a microwave, blender, and popcorn popper. The room was wallpapered in a green, gold, orange, and cream print of vegetables. A wooden pull-down room separator was in the up position above a counter with two bar stools nestled underneath it.

Past the kitchen was a breakfast nook with a small round table and four chairs. The style of the table was like that of my custom desk at Mad for Mod: a patchwork of materials that previously had come from different abandoned pieces. Four mismatched legs had been recut and attached to a rough cross-section of wood that had been coated in polyurethane to protect it. Above the table hung a chandelier of glass fruits and vegetables.

It seemed the whole place was a time capsule house, maintaining the groovy vibe of the late sixties/early seventies. Within the first five minutes I felt completely at home. Down the hallway, I opened the door to the room where Heather and Nettie had slept. Yellow shag carpeting met pale green walls with oversized flowers hand-painted on as if growing from the white baseboards. Yellow blankets trimmed in satin covered each bed.

As comfortable as I felt in Hudson's house, I couldn't help thinking about how uncomfortable Tex must be in mine. Before inheriting Thelma Johnson's house, I had moved most of the furniture out, and had only recently layered in a twin bed, a sofa, a TV, and a portion of my wardrobe. He had accepted my generosity and found himself sleeping under pink sheets. I giggled at the thought, then immediately grew serious when I considered the alternative. I fished my phone out of my handbag and called him.

"Where do you live?" I asked after he answered.

"Why?"

"You said you're avoiding your house because of the press. I can go, get you a few things, you know, to make your stay at Thelma Johnson's house more comfortable. Change of clothes, teddy bear, whatever you need."

"I don't think that's such a good idea," he said.

"Why not? It's the middle of the day. Surely women have reasons for going to your apartment in the middle of the day that don't raise your neighbor's suspicions. Or do you need me to dress like a maid?"

"I'd like to see that."

"Forget I suggested it."

"Too late. The image is already there." He was silent for a second. "There are a few things I could use, but you'll need my keys to get in."

"Are you at the shopping center?"

"I'm close enough. Meet me there in twenty minutes."

"Deal."

I went out back and watched Hudson toss a branch across the yard. Rocky raced after it. When Hudson saw me, he turned away from Rocky, who was trotting back with the branch between his teeth. I held my hand out to stop Hudson from approaching.

"I have to go do something and I don't know how long it's going to be before I get back. I can't tell you much more than that. Can you watch Rocky?"

"Madison, I've been away for four months. It's nice to be back. It's nice to have you here, but even if you weren't here, I'd be too tired to do much more than watch the animals. You do what you gotta do. Take the spare set of keys from the pegboard in the kitchen and I'll see you when you're done."

I made it to the Casa Linda parking lot faster than expected. Tex's Jeep sat along the far end of the lot, next to the abandoned field. Under the bright Texas sun, the car shone like it had just been washed. From across the lot, I saw a man in a dark uniform leaning into the driver's side window. He straightened and pulled a black duffel bag out of the window. A rush of heat climbed my throat, leaving me lightheaded.

The man tossed the bag into a black sedan next to the Jeep, jumped inside, and took off. I grew nearer and made out the silhouette of a person inside the Jeep, but by the time I pulled into the space next it, I knew the person wasn't Tex.

The person wasn't even a man.

Sitting behind the steering wheel, looking battered and bruised was Cleo Tyler.

FOURTEEN

I was out of my car before it stopped moving. I jumped into the Jeep and worked the gag from her lips down to her neck. One of her eyes was shaded with a deep purple bruise. The other was swollen shut. The seatbelt had been secured over her arms handcuffed together. Dark welts were visible on her wrists.

"Is that yours?" I asked, pointing to a cell phone sitting on the floor. She nodded. I picked it up and called 911. "I'm at the Casa Linda parking lot in a black Jeep along the back row of cars. One of the abducted women is with me. She's still alive but she needs help."

"Water," Cleo choked out. She cut her eyes to the cupholder, where a plastic bottle of water lay. I set the phone down, uncapped the water, and held it up to Cleo's mouth while she drank. An overflow of liquid spilled down the side of her mouth onto the tight red sweater she'd been wearing yesterday when I was at her house.

Cleo picked up her handcuffed hands and reached for mine. She fed her fingers through them and clutched me like a toddler learning to walk. "Is he gone?" she whispered.

I hadn't stopped to think that the man who did this might still be close. I pulled the door shut next to me and locked it, but still felt exposed. Who had put her here? Was he still around? The only cars in the lot were in a line waiting to exit. I was too far away to see the plates, make, or model.

"Do you remember anything? How you got here?" I asked. She shook her head. "Do you know who brought you?" Again, a head shake.

I looked at the interior of the car, hoping to find some clues as to where Tex had gone. There was nothing. No trash under the seats, no napkins by the dashboard. It smelled like Armorall, that plastic scent infused with lemons that was particular to cars newly detailed.

She closed her eyes and leaned back against the headrest. I untied a strip of Caution tape that had been wound around her ankles. Sirens sounded close by. When I sat up, a fleet of cop cars headed toward us, their blue and red lights diluted by the waning sunlight. Officer Iverson was the first one out of his car. He raced to the driver's side of the Jeep and yanked the car open. He looked surprised to see me inside with Cleo.

"What's going on here?" he asked.

"I found her in the car. She was gagged. Her hands are cuffed."

He fished a set of handcuff keys out of his pocket and unlocked the metal restraints. The door next to me opened and two medical technicians faced me. "Are you hurt?" one asked me.

"No."

"Wait over there," he commanded.

I climbed out of the Jeep and watched Iverson. He had the look of someone who was very tired, who'd been jolted awake. Bags under his eyes told of sleepless nights, but the ease with which he managed the scene gave the impression that he had an autopilot setting. He stepped back and gave the medical technicians access to Cleo. Her sweater had been torn in two places and her white shorts were streaked with grass stains. Her feet were bare but clean.

I turned around and scanned the parking lot, my hand shielding my eyes from the sun. A handful of cars were scattered about, most parked close to the entrance of the stores in the strip mall. An employee in a red vest rounded up carts that had been left in the far corners of the lot. He looked over at us with curiosity, as did a small group of people standing in front of the entrance. More employees clustered outside of the rest of the shops, pointing our direction. A Jeep, surrounded by four police cars and an ambulance. I expected the news van to arrive any second.

From where I stood, I could smell the Chinese food. The scent had clung to everything I'd worn since becoming Tex's eggroll supplier.

Officer Iverson approached me. "Ms. Night, how did you know Mrs. Tyler was in the Jeep?"

"I didn't. I thought this was Lt. Allen's Jeep. I didn't see her until I was out of my own car."

Iverson studied me. "How do you know Mrs. Tyler?"

"I'm doing some decorating work for her." I didn't mention that her husband had fired me earlier that day.

"Did you know she was missing?"

"I heard about it on the news last night." I wrapped my arms around myself and scanned the parking lot. Had the person who did this left in the row of cars I'd seen driving away? Or was he sitting in the parking lot now, watching us, taking note of how the police were conducting the investigation? Instinctively, I stepped closer to the professionals who were processing the scene. They were busy with their individual tasks and the last thing they wanted was for me to be there, but I was too unnerved to care that I was in their way. Standing even a foot away felt too separated from safety.

Before I could continue, a small gold BMW sped into the parking lot and pulled up next to us. Dan Tyler jumped out of the car. Iverson tried to stop him.

"Sir, you have to stay back."

Dan pushed him out of the way. "She's my wife. She needs me," he said. He pushed his way through the others until he reached Cleo. "Baby, I thought I wasn't going to see you again."

Tears streamed down Cleo's face. Her hands had been freed from the handcuffs, and she held one arm around him. The other was in a sling. I didn't know what kind of internal injuries she'd sustained.

Officer Iverson watched Cleo and Dan for a few moments, and then turned to me. "You said something about Lt. Allen. Was he here?"

I stood back and stared at Tex's Jeep. Something wasn't right and I didn't know what it was. I couldn't lie to the officer and he knew it. I knew the pressure to find the Lakewood Abductor—whether he turned out to be a police officer or not—was making every cop on the force follow every procedure they had with zero leniency.

I took a deep breath of air scented by fried rice from Hunan Palace, and then exhaled. "It's a setup," I said suddenly. "We're supposed to think this is Lt. Allen's Jeep but it's not."

"I know you're friends with Allen, but you're not helping him by lying."

"I'm not lying. It's not his Jeep. Do some legwork. Run the plates, check the registration. It's not Lt. Allen's Jeep."

"I already know it's not Lt. Allen's Jeep. I'm more interested in knowing how *you* knew it wasn't Lt. Allen's Jeep. It's the same make, model, year, and color. Anybody remotely familiar with Lt. Allen's Jeep would have made the assumption it was his. Why didn't you?"

I had been hoping to catch the officer by surprise, have him run the plates and tell me something I didn't know. But he already knew what it had taken me twenty minutes to figure out.

"Ms. Night, Lt. Allen is one of us, but if he's involved in something illegal, I'm not going to protect him. If he's caught in somebody's web, then the truth will come out. Mrs. Tyler is going to be okay, but there are women out there who might not be so lucky."

"When I saw the Jeep, I thought it was his. But Lt. Allen and I had Chinese food in his car. The smell gets into everything. This car is too clean, too new. Other than that, I don't have any information for you. I saw a man in a dark uniform move away from the window. He got into a black car and drove away. He must have done this."

"Did you get any identifying information? License? Description?"

"I was too far away to recognize him, and when I got closer and saw Cleo, I had to help her. She was gagged and looked hurt. I think the sedan pulled out of the parking lot, but I can't be sure."

For a few uncomfortable seconds, we stood facing each other, no words said. The technicians moved Cleo into the back of their ambulance and Dan climbed in with her. Iverson joined three officers who stood by the side of the Jeep talking amongst themselves.

"Officer, if you don't need me for anything else, I'm going to be going," I said.

"Be careful, Ms. Night," he said. "There's a maniac out there."

I left with the sound of his words ringing in my ears.

Unless coincidence was on the side of the bad guy, whoever was pulling the strings seemed to be calling all of the shots. I didn't like it. But for everything we didn't know, it seemed that one thing Tex had hit upon might be true. The abductor hadn't chosen Tex at random. The Jeep that was just like Tex's Jeep, the fake badge, and the identity leaked at the first press conference said one thing. This whole setup was personal.

FIFTEEN

Last night I'd called Nasty in an effort to find someone to help me reason through the information. Her response had thrown me for a loop, but it didn't stop me from wanting to figure this out. Again I remembered Effie's attack, and again it felt off. Different. There was something about her story that didn't fit with what we knew.

I drove to Mad for Mod, where I kept the resident applications for the apartment building. While being a landlord only overlapped with being an interior decorator insomuch as a 1957 building occasionally needed repairs and the occasional paint job, keeping my tenant records at the studio had solved two problems: storage and confidentiality. Well before my tenants knew I was the owner of the building, I implemented a system to keep correspondence addressed to The Night Company and files locked in a cabinet behind my desk.

Once inside my studio, I went straight for the cabinet and pulled Effie's application. As suspected, her emergency contact was her boyfriend, Chad Keith. His address was listed as Luxury Uptown Lofts. I checked directions on MapQuest and left.

The Luxury Uptown Lofts were on Lemmon Avenue on the other side of Highway 75. If it had been earlier in the day, it would have taken less time to get there, but on a Friday afternoon with people cutting out of work early, rush hour interfered. I parked by a curb and walked half a block to the entrance. A directory of apartments hung by the lobby. I scanned the listing until I found Chad's name. There seemed no other way to gain access to the apartments than to ring the buzzer.

"Hello?" Effie answered.

"Effie, hi, it's Madison Night."

"Madison! It's great to hear your voice. What are you up to? Did I forget to sign something?"

"Actually, I'm in the area, and I thought I'd see how you were doing."

"Where are you?"

Despite the obvious, considering I'd buzzed her from the lobby, I answered. "I'm downstairs."

"Oh, duh, of course. I'll buzz you up. We're on the second floor."

The gate let out a sound not unlike a bug zapper and I yanked it open. "I'll be right up."

The lobby of the building was a study in shiny Italian marble. Brushed chrome fixtures mirrored the elevator wells. There were no hallmarks of any particular design era other than the sort of minimalism that said "young and affluent." I wondered what the rent was at a place like this, and why so many college grads preferred to sink their money into a unit here instead of one with character. It certainly would be a change of pace to Effie, who had spent her college years in a mid-century box with fifty-plus-year-old carpeting.

When the elevator doors opened on the second floor, Effie was waiting for me. Disappointment in her face quickly said she'd been hoping that a visit from me meant a visit from Rocky. She recovered and gave me a hug.

"I wasn't sure the building allowed pets," I said. "Rocky's with a friend today. Next time I come to visit I'll bring him, I promise."

"Sure, that was good thinking. I don't think Chad would have a problem with him, but I should ask."

I followed her to the apartment at the end of the hall. She turned around before opening the door. "You're probably not going to like the way he decorates."

"It's okay, Effie. People have different tastes."

She was right. Chad Keith had not only embraced the

minimalistic concepts portrayed in the architecture of the new building, but he'd shown off his own personal interests with a state of the art gaming console and sound system. The living room was white with a black sofa, black coffee table, and black entertainment center. Sleek chrome speaker stands flanked the massive television, and additional speakers were hardwired into the walls. Interrupting the stark interior were two signs of Effie: a pizza box on the coffee table, and a pair of bear paw slippers tucked underneath it. She took a seat on the sofa. I sat in the black and chrome chair.

"I hope you don't mind the impromptu visit," I said.

"No, I'm happy you're here. Chad's out doing something and he asked me to stay here until he got back. I didn't think he'd be gone so long. I can't figure out how to work his remotes, so I'm pretty bored. How'd you know where he lived?"

"I checked the emergency contact information on your lease."

"You really are a good detective. I was telling Chad about everything that's happened to you and he's impressed. He said he never would have expected a woman who looks like June Cleaver to be able to take care of herself."

"Chad watches *Leave it to Beaver* reruns?"

"I watch it at night. It's on Antenna TV." She looked embarrassed. "I think he meant it as a compliment, even though it doesn't sound like one."

I waved my hand to show it didn't bother me. "I guess you two have been together a long time."

"We've been on-again and off-again for most of college." She shrugged and picked at a tear in her workout pants. "We used to hang out in high school. Not like dating, but my friends and his friends were a group. You know how high school is."

Considering Effie was more than half my age, I was flattered by her comparison.

"Did you bring that referral letter? That's why you're here, right?"

"Actually, I came to talk to you about what happened the other night."

"Oh."

I leaned forward and put my hand on her thigh. "Your statement made a difference. I'm proud of you for going to the police department and talking to them."

"Okay, so I talked to the police. Why can't it be done now? Why does everybody want me to keep talking about it?" she said. She crossed her arms and turned away from me. "First Chad, then you. I just want to forget it ever happened."

"Effie, what happened to you was a very scary thing. Chad probably wants you to talk about it so it doesn't end up haunting you."

"What about you? Why do you want to talk to me about it?"

"I'm afraid my motivation is a little more self-serving. Another woman was taken a few nights ago. She's a client. The police found her abandoned in a Jeep in the Casa Linda parking lot. " I looked down at my hands for a second, and back at Effie's face. Her shoulder was still turned away from me, but her head was facing me. "You know Lt. Allen is my friend. Your statement helped him, but it also raised a lot of questions. I was hoping you'd be willing to go over it with me again. There might be something you can tell me that nobody else knows."

She raised her hand to her mouth and chewed on a fingernail. After a few seconds, she lay her hands in her lap.

"I don't know how I can help, but I'll tell you what I told the police."

"Thank you."

She leaned back against the cushions and stared up at the wall in front of her. Before she started, she turned to me again. "You heard most of this already, but I have to start at the beginning. Okay?"

"Okay."

She straightened in the chair and focused on the wall again. I got the feeling she was taking a trip back in time to before the attack had happened. "My friends and I went to the Landing for happy hour. Angie's older sister Barbie just moved here, so a bunch of us stayed for dinner so we could celebrate her new job. I had a beer during happy hour, but I switched to Pepsi when the food came."

I nodded and she continued. "We ordered a bunch of appetizers for the table instead of getting individual meals, and we picked off all of the plates. French fries, potato skins, chicken fingers, and onion rings. We had two baskets of onion rings. Barbie wouldn't eat them because she was planning on going to her boyfriend's house after we left."

"Did anybody talk to you inside?"

"Barbie started dancing in front of the jukebox even though there's not really a dance floor, and then she realized her necklace had come off. She freaked out. The bartender gave her a shot of vodka on the house to calm her down, and then somebody said they found her necklace in the bathroom. I left after that."

"You didn't stay with the rest of the group?"

"It's no fun being the sober one in a crowd of party girls. I left around nine."

"What happened when you left?"

"I've been over this so many times, you know? My car was in a space by the back of the lot. There are tons of lights all over the place, so I wasn't scared. A couple of people were by the back door smoking, but they went back inside when I left. I backed out of the space and was about to drive off when the officer came over to me."

"What can you tell me about him?"

"He had on a uniform and a name tag that said Lt. Tex Allen. He had a hat on too, a cowboy hat with a sheriff badge in the middle of it. It was pretty big and cast a shadow over his face."

"Lt. Allen is a police lieutenant, not a sheriff. He wouldn't wear a hat like the one you're describing."

"I should have known that, shouldn't I?"

"Not necessarily," I said, reassuring her.

"It was dark and I was scared. He popped up out of nowhere. If he wasn't dressed like a cop, I wouldn't have even rolled down my window."

"Do you remember what he said to you?"

"He told me I had a tail light out and he asked me if I wanted to get out and see. That's when I saw the knife in his hand. Madison, I've never seen anything like it before. It was curved, with a point on the end. I got scared. I threw the car in reverse and then took off."

"You told me you thought you knocked him over?"

"I don't know what happened to him. I kept looking over my shoulder to see if he was following me, but nobody was there." Her eyes were wide and filled with tears. She tipped her head back and then side to side, letting the tears run into her hairline. "Excuse me," she said. She stood up and went into a room in the hall. Seconds later I heard her blow her nose.

Her account today wasn't that different from what she'd told me when it had happened. A few details had surfaced in the passing days, but it was hard to trust the accuracy of them. The mind could create memories, and if Effie had been pushed hard enough to remember specifics, she might have populated the actual recollections with bits and pieces of things she'd seen throughout the day without even knowing she was doing it.

But one detail stuck out: the knife. I could close my eyes and picture it as if it had been in front of me. Because it had. Her description perfectly matched the strange curved knife that Lyndy had been carrying the day he showed up at Mad for Mod.

SIXTEEN

I didn't know what to make about that one particular detail, but I knew it was important. I also knew that Emil Lyndy was Hudson's friend and, in some ways, responsible for teaching him what he knew about carpentry. Could the small man be somehow responsible for the attacks? I didn't want to think so, but when he showed up in my storage unit wielding his knife, he'd certainly scared me.

When Effie came out of the powder room, I met her halfway. "I'm sorry to have upset you," I said. I smoothed her long hair back and looked at her red face. "How about Rocky comes to visit tomorrow? We'll only talk about what you want to talk about."

"Okay," she said. She sniffled again and I sensed that the tears were only very barely under control. I hugged her tightly and promised to be back the next day.

It was close to eight by the time I returned to Hudson's house. I could have made it there earlier, but I got turned around outside of the Luxury Uptown Lofts and ended up taking three left turns before I was headed the right direction. I left three voicemails and two text messages for Tex, who was still missing in action. I even went out of my way and drove through the neighborhoods near the Casa Linda shopping center. I didn't think I would actually find him, but I was giving him a chance to find me. He didn't.

Hudson had left the garage open. An arrow had been cut from neon orange paper and attached to a sign that said "Park here and come out back." I pulled the car inside and closed the garage door.

Hudson was in the yard behind his house. Two thick steaks sat on a plate to the left of his grill next to a couple of misshapen blobs wrapped in tinfoil. Rocky sat at the base of a tree, looking up. I followed his stare and found Mortiboy sitting on a low branch.

"Perfect timing," he said. "I was about to toss a couple of steaks and potatoes on the grill. Mortiboy and Rock thought they were getting something fancy tonight."

"They still might," I said. I scooped up Rocky and gave him a kiss, set him back down and held a hand up for Mortiboy to sniff. "I'm not all that hungry."

Hudson set the tongs down. He gently turned me around, placed his hands on my shoulders, and massaged my muscles.

"Do you want to talk about it?" he asked

"Not yet." I reached over my shoulders and put my hands on top of Hudson's. "What I would like is a cool shower. Do you mind?"

"Use mine. Mortiboy's litter box is in the one in the hallway. I'll throw the potatoes on the grill." He gave me a couple seconds more of massage, and then pulled his hands away. "Once the potato clock starts ticking, you've got forty-five minutes."

Hudson's bedroom was the only room in the house I hadn't explored when he gave me the opportunity. I slowed down as I approached it, as if opening that door and going inside was significant.

Where the rest of his house maintained the early seventies style his grandmother had favored before passing away, his bedroom was less decade-specific. His bed was made but the covers were folded back. White pillowcases. White sheets. A plaid comforter in shades of navy blue, forest green, and yellow rested by the foot of the bed. Two small tables sat on either side of the headboard. One held the lamp I'd given him for Christmas two years ago, a white ceramic Chinese man with a Fu Manchu mustache. When I'd found the lamp, it had been little more than a paperweight. Hudson was the person I turned to for object d'art restoration, but in this case I sought out the help of an employee of Lowe's, who sold me a lamp kit and gave me the confidence that I could fix it myself. It had taken the better part of a Saturday afternoon, but when I gifted it, the light bulb over the Chinese man glowed like he had a great idea.

On the other nightstand was a worn Agatha Christie paperback. There was no television set in Hudson's bedroom, only a small cart with an old turntable on top and a collection of dog-eared albums underneath. I crossed the room and lifted the top of the record player to see what he'd been listening to. An old Julie London album was on the turntable. The jacket was on top of a Clash album. I pressed the power button on the record player and placed the needle on the record.

As the sounds of bluesy horns and throaty vocals filled the room, I walked around the bed, my fingertips trailing over the cotton of the comforter. Along the wall in front of the bed was a tall maple armoire, and on the armoire were Hudson's keys, an ashtray of loose change, a pair of sunglasses, and a couple of guitar picks. A hook over the back of the door held a necktie hanger filled with skinny ties. I'd never seen Hudson in a necktie. I'd never seen him in anything other than a T-shirt and jeans until the night I'd found him in his pajamas. But the evidence in front of me told of a life of his that I wasn't a part of. The twinge of jealousy I felt surprised me.

I'd spent long enough wandering around Hudson's room to feel like I was borderline violating his privacy. I went into his bathroom, stripped off my clothes, and turned on the water. I climbed in and pulled the shower curtain closed. A large round spigot directly above me poured water onto my head like I was standing in a downpour.

I scrubbed at my skin with the green bar of soap from the caddy then rinsed under the cool water. The sensation reminded me of my childhood summer vacation at the Jersey shore. Outdoor showers had been installed in the yard of the cottage where my family rented a room. After walking back from an afternoon spent at the beach, my parents and I took turns rinsing off the sand and sunscreen before going inside and changing out of our bathing suits and into real clothes. That felt like a lifetime ago, those days when I had a family, when I had people who took care of me. When I asked advice and sought approval. Ever since the month they passed away unexpectedly, I understood that I was the only person who could make decisions for me. I had dropped out of college and taken a job working for a mid-century modern interior decorator in Philadelphia and had been taking care of myself ever since.

I'd spent my days at the showroom and my nights studying Doris Day movies. Sharing a birthday with the actress had provided a natural connection that my parents had encouraged by buying me one of her movies every April third. In those early days of being alone, in the dark with no company but Doris and one of her leading men, I felt like my parents were there with me. I had wrapped myself in the vintage styles I saw in the movies and created a world of my own, where nobody could tell me I didn't fit in.

Twenty-seven years had passed since their death, and my private world had become a tower of emotional isolation. The only person I had let in had violated my trust in such a way that I closed and locked the tower doors and threw out the keys. I was content to live my life with Rocky as my companion. I was good at decorating, and the job allowed me to maintain a connection with the world through my clients while not risking my heart.

But somehow, when I least expected it, my tower had been demolished. I found myself longing to become a part of something bigger than the world I'd created. The chaos that had surrounded me in the past year had awakened emotions that I'd long denied, but had also awakened the fear of loving someone who might not be there when I woke up the next day. Chronologically, I was forty-eight, but emotionally I was back in touch with my twenty-one year old self with an unmistakable fear of abandonment.

Forever twenty-one wasn't necessarily a good thing.

I heard a knock on the door. "Madison?" Hudson's voice

asked. "You okay in there?"

I dunked my head under the water and tried to answer. "Yes," I said. I hadn't realized I'd been crying until I choked on my reply.

The door opened and Hudson's tanned arm reached into the shower and turned off the water. I held the shower curtain up in front of my body and looked at his face. He tore the curtain down from the silver hooks that held it in place, snapping the plastic from the holes one at a time. I wrapped the curtain around my torso and he wrapped his arms around the plastic. I fell against his shoulder and melted into him.

He put his knuckle under my chin and tipped my head up so I was looking at him. "It's going to be okay," he said.

"You don't even know why I'm upset."

"It doesn't matter. Whatever it is, it's going to be okay."

He brushed a kiss against my lips, and then a second one. His lips were soft and tender, like a ripe tomato. They lingered for only a moment. I caught his breath in my own.

The third kiss was more intimate than the first two. Our bodies pressed together. I became very aware that I was wet and naked under a plastic shower curtain.

When we pulled apart, he rested his forehead against mine. "I've wanted to do that for a long time," he said in a gravelly voice barely above a whisper. "Why don't you get dressed and meet me outside?" I wondered for a second if my emotions were as transparent as the shower curtain. "If I don't get back to that grill, our steaks are going to taste like shoe leather."

I waited until he closed the bathroom door behind him to look at myself in the mirror. My blond hair was in clumps around the sides of my face. My eyes were bloodshot. The cool water had kept my face from turning a blotchy patchwork of red like I'd feared, but my reflection was far from my A-game.

I dried off and changed into a yellow sleeveless sundress with a drop waist and a full skirt. Yellow and white brick-a-brack in the form of a chain of daisies decorated the collar and the faux placket down the front. I slipped into green ballerina flats, combed my hair away from my face, and added a touch of mascara to my fair lashes. I was taking too long and I knew it. What I didn't know was what I was avoiding. Telling Hudson about finding Cleo Tyler? Or giving in to the attraction I'd fought for so long?

Rocky sniffed me out and scratched the outside of the bathroom door. I let him in, closed the toilet, and sat on the lid. Rocky jumped onto my lap and licked the side of my face. I hugged him and then he wriggled out of my arms and ran away.

I dusted some translucent powder across my nose, packed everything up in my overnight kit, and looked out the window. Hudson stood by the grill with the tongs in his hand. He had a straw hat on his head and his black hair curled against his collar from under the back of it. Rocky had returned outside and now jumped around Hudson's ankles. Mortiboy was on the hammock where Hudson had been earlier. It could have been a photo shoot for the Sears catalog. A smile replaced the sadness. Whatever had brought me to this particular moment was worth it.

I carried my personal items out of the bathroom to my suitcase in the spare room. I heard Hudson's voice and figured he was talking to Mortiboy the way I talked to Rocky. I headed to the back of the house and put my hand on the latch to unlock the sliding door.

And then I saw who Hudson was talking to. Tex!

SEVENTEEN

I purposely hadn't told Tex where I'd stayed last night. It was supposed to be my secret. So why was he here? And what did this visit mean?

I dialed back the initial instinct to whip the door open and ask them what the hell they were planning and instead pressed myself against the side of the refrigerator and listened to their conversation through the open window.

"Madison's been great, but this whole thing has gotten bigger than I thought. I can't put her in danger. If you see her, do whatever you have to do to keep her from getting involved," Tex said.

"Allen, I wonder if you know what you just asked me to do," Hudson said.

"I know I couldn't take it if she was hurt because of something that had to do with me. The best way to trap this guy is to make myself vulnerable. Draw him out. I can't do that if I think Madison is at risk."

I peeked outside. Tex crossed his arms and stood with his feet shoulder width apart. It was his intimidating cop stance. It didn't seem to have any effect on Hudson.

Hudson flipped the steaks, but didn't say anything. I wondered if he'd told Tex that I was in the house. It didn't sound like it. But Tex wasn't stupid. Once he figured I wasn't at my studio or my apartment or Thelma Johnson's house, it would have only been a matter of time before he came looking for me here.

"You do what you have to do, man," Hudson said. "And if I see

Madison, I'll do what I can. But I'm not you. I'm not going to tell her what she can and can't do. She's got a brain and she's going to do what she thinks she should." He picked the potatoes up and set them on the plates, and then tented tinfoil on top of each of them. "That's what we both love about her."

Love. The word hit me like a taser to the heart. Hudson looked up at Tex and the two of them stood there staring at each other for what felt like an hour but was probably two seconds. I shouldn't be listening, but I couldn't step away.

Tex pulled his sunglasses off of his face and tucked them into the pocket of his T-shirt. He held his hand out to Hudson. "Thanks," he said. Hudson shook his hand and nodded. Tex's eyes cut to the two plates, the two potatoes, and the two steaks. He scanned the backyard, as if expecting to find me hiding behind a bush. "I'll let myself out," he finally said.

He turned toward the house. In two steps he'd be close enough to see me. I dropped to my hands and knees and crawled through the living room to the hallway, and then stayed low and ran to the spare bedroom with Rocky by my side. I pushed the door shut behind me and shushed Rocky.

The back door opened. The back door shut.

The front door opened. The front door shut.

A loud roar of an engine started. I stood on the twin bed and peeked out the window. A large white camper pulled away from the curb and drove off. I memorized the plate number before it was out of my line of vision.

It wasn't until after the truck was out of sight that I wondered exactly why I'd been so worried about Tex finding me at Hudson's house. I let Rocky out from the spare room and wasted a little time plugging my phone into a charger in the kitchen, and then followed the scent of the steaks to the backyard.

"Hey," Hudson said. "I was starting to worry about you."

"I would have been out sooner but I saw..." My voice trailed off. I studied the expression on his face and I realized with very clear certainty that he was not going to tell me about Tex's visit.

"Saw what?"

"Your collection of Agatha Christies. I didn't know you were a mystery fan."

He smiled. "It was my granddad's collection first. They came with the house. That's my favorite thing to read at night. I like that Poirot."

"How's dinner coming?"

"Just about done. Can you hand me the plates?"

I held the white china plates out while Hudson used the tongs to transfer the steaks and potatoes to each of them. When he finished, I carried them to the wooden picnic table on the small concrete rectangle of patio that separated his back door from his yard. He followed close behind me, with a bottle of wine in one hand and two glasses in the other.

"Red okay?"

"Sure."

He filled the glasses and handed me one. For the next few seconds, conversation ceased while we each dressed our potato and cut into our steaks. Juices ran out and mingled with the melted butter, pooling on the lower corner of the plate and indicating that the table was not 100% level.

For everything I'd ever wanted to say to Hudson, I found myself surprisingly tongue-tied. I knew why. With Tex, I could say anything. We were so different that the barbs we shared were anticipated. From the minute we'd met, neither one of us expected to get along. That had been the surprise. But I wanted to confide in Hudson. I wanted him to know how scared I was.

I set down the knife and fork. "I've been working on a house on Sweetwater. A couple from Hollywood—Dan and Cleo Tyler—decided they wanted a mid-century ranch and bought one sight unseen. It's a Cliff May in serious disrepair."

Hudson whistled. "Restoring a rundown Cliff May. Nice."

"The bones of it are intact: east-west windows at the top of the wall by the ceiling joints, open floor plan, partitions, but the last owner did a number on the interior with a bad eighties remodel.

The Tyler's heard about us on the news. That's why they hired me."
I didn't mention their plan to buy the rights to the Pillow Stalking
case because now, with Cleo's abduction and subsequent release, it
no longer seemed relevant.

Hudson drank his wine. "Sounds like a big project."

"I've been spending three days a week at their house—
Tuesday, Wednesday, and Thursday. The husband fired me this
morning."

Hudson looked surprised. "Why?"

"I was at their house the day the police announced the
evidence that Lt. Allen was involved in the abductions." I studied
Hudson's face for an indication that he knew this, or that he was
going to acknowledge that Tex had just been at his house. When he
didn't respond, I continued. "Dan's brother was a cop. He died in a
drunk driving accident. He was the drunk driver. Two teenage girls
died in the same accident. Dan is anti-cop, and he's especially anti-
Tex. I don't know why."

"Cleo and Dan Tyler. Why do I know their names?"

"Cleo Tyler was abducted two days ago."

"And?"

"She was found today. Still alive."

"That's good news. Where was she?"

This was no time to beat around the bush. "Hudson, I found
her. I'd made plans to meet Lt. Allen in the Casa Linda parking lot,
and that's where she was. I went out there to find him but I found
her instead."

I told him about her being inside the Jeep that matched the
make and model of Tex's car. I told him about how I'd figured out
that it wasn't Tex's car, and how the police officer seemed to
already know that. "I figured a few things out today and I need to
talk to Tex. I don't know where to find him. He's trying to figure
this out alone."

"Maybe he *needs* to figure it out alone. Sometimes that's the
best way to find answers."

"Is that why you left? Because you needed to be alone to figure things out?"

He reached his hand across the table and set it on top of mine. "I left because I couldn't stay. I had closure. You didn't. And I had to let you make your own decisions."

"You might not always like my decisions." I raised my hand and entwined my fingers with his, stroking his palm with my thumb. "My circle is fairly small, Hudson. When I moved to Dallas, I thought I knew all the people I was going to know in my life. And then, when I hired you to help with Mad for Mod, I knew I wanted to spend more time with you." I swatted at a mosquito that was buzzing around my head. "Do you know how many times I thought about us—you and me—together? But I was scared of what would go wrong so I blocked those thoughts. What we have now is pretty special. I don't want to jeopardize it. I don't want to risk not having you in my life."

"Madison, I'm not going anywhere."

"Hudson, Lt. Allen is in my life too. Turns out I don't like isolation as much as I thought. I need to do what I can to protect my circle."

"Who am I to you?" he asked.

"Is this a quiz?"

He ran his fingertips down the length of my nose. "Your life is so rooted in Doris Day. She had a lot of leading men. Is that what I am to you? One of a cast of leading men?"

"I can't explain who you are to me," I said softly. "I can't explain any of these emotions."

He dropped his hand and curled his calloused fingers around mine. "Madison, I walked away from you once. I'm not doing it again."

"Even if it means I might tell you something you don't want to hear?"

Hudson's hand stilled, but he didn't pull away. "You're trying to tell me something now, aren't you?"

I looked away from his amber eyes, wishing the mosquito would return to provide a distraction. Even Rocky and Mortiboy were being particularly well behaved, providing me no escape from what I had to say.

"Do you remember Effie, the college girl who lived in my apartment building?"

"She watches Rock sometimes, right?"

I nodded. "A few nights ago, she was approached by a guy dressed like a police officer outside of the Landing. She thought it was Lt. Allen."

"How do you know it wasn't?"

"It was the same day someone found his badge in the woods near where they found Kate Morrow's body. Tex was with the police chief on a live TV interview. There's absolutely 100% no way it could have been him."

Hudson nodded. "That's not what you want to tell me, is it?"

I shook my head. "I went to see Effie today. She's staying with her boyfriend. She's the only person who had an encounter with this person and walked away unscathed. I thought maybe she could tell me something new, something everybody's overlooked."

"Did she?"

"The guy approached her on foot. He was in uniform, and he said she had a broken tail light and asked her to get out of the car. She saw the knife the guy was carrying and took off instead. It was the same one your friend Lyndy had."

He pulled his hands away from mine and his face went rigid. "Lyndy's not a killer," he said.

"Hudson, I don't have the same history with Lyndy that you do. I saw his knife. I gave his name to the police."

"You think he had something to do with these women getting abducted?"

"I don't know. The police wanted a list of every contractor that I spoke to, and of everybody on that list, he's the only one who came to me instead of me reaching out to him. He popped up at my studio the day after my client was abducted."

Hudson stood up quickly. The picnic bench he'd been sitting on flipped backward. He stormed into the house, the screen door banging against the frame after he disappeared. Seconds later he returned.

He held up a blade like the one Lyndy had set by my feet. "It's a carpet and linoleum knife. Cuts on the pull," he said, miming the motion of hatchetting the knife into flooring and pulling toward him. "I told you Lyndy's trade is carpet installation. He's one of the best." He set the knife on the table between us in the same manner that Lyndy had set it down on the ground. He tapped the wooden handle with his index finger. "This knife cost me less than four bucks at the hardware store. I've had it for twenty years. I'm surprised you don't have one considering you're a decorator. There's probably a carpet knife in every garage in Dallas."

For every part of a renovation job that I did myself, carpet tear out and installation was one job that I left to the professionals. It was a physical limitation, not a professional one, that kept me from adding it to my resume: my bad knee.

When I moved to Dallas from Philadelphia, I'd brought two things: a van filled with my meager possessions, and a torn ACL. I bought the apartment building, started my business, and adopted Rocky all after moving. The knee injury was a constant reminder of the days before I shut out the world and made a life for myself. Because I didn't like to ask for help, I'd learned to do most things for myself, but kneeling on the floor while installing or tearing out carpets was one act that I'd never be able to do.

I picked up the knife and traced my fingertip along the side of the blade. Hudson's faith in Lyndy was as unshakable as my faith in Tex. I couldn't fault him for his loyalty. I focused on the tip of the knife. I'd been so sure that the knife meant something that I wasn't willing to admit that it didn't.

"Madison," Hudson said softly, "it would be one thing if you found Lyndy's knife at the scene of the crime, but you didn't."

"How would I know Lyndy's knife?"

"His daughters gave it to him for Father's Day, two weeks before they died. It has his initials scored on the handle."

I looked at Hudson. "How did Lyndy's daughters die?"

"Car accident," said Lyndy, appearing at the side of Hudson's house. "Five years ago my daughters were killed in a head-on collision with a drunk police officer."

EIGHTEEN

My hands shook with nerves. Lyndy's daughters had died in the accident with George Tyler. That had to be the connection.

Before I could say anything, Hudson jumped up from the bench. "Lyndy, you know Madison, right?"

I remained seated and looked back and forth between the two men. Lyndy looked angry at having walked in on a conversation about him. His eyes were narrowed and he watched me with what felt like distrust. Hudson approached him and put a hand on the small man's shoulder. "I'll toss another steak on the grill for you."

"Don't bother," Lyndy said. "Don't know if I'm staying." He stayed his distance.

Lyndy was obviously more than a fellow contractor to Hudson. I could see that from where I sat. I walked over to him. "Lyndy, I'm sorry."

He waved his hand in front of him. "I could tell you didn't trust me the other day when I came to your store. Said I wasn't going to hurt you but it was in your eyes."

"You caught me off guard."

Lyndy looked away. "Don't matter," he said. "I'm used to it."

In the course of owning Mad for Mod, I'd taught myself a few tricks of the trade, but I'd also learned to hire those who could do what I could not. That's what had brought Hudson into my life. But before Hudson, the contractors that I'd worked with had had the same rough-around-the-edges qualities that Lyndy did. Some of the most skilled carpenters were people you might not think of taking home to mother. Even Hudson had turned out to have a sizeable skeleton hanging in his closet, and if I'd known about his past when I met him, I might not entertain the thoughts that were becoming more and more present. But that was his past. He'd chosen to build a quiet life for himself where nobody could judge him for his demons. Maybe he'd learned that from Lyndy.

"Lyndy, stick around, would you? I'll get you a beer," Hudson said.

"Beer's good."

Hudson caught my eye and I forced a smile. He went inside and Lyndy and I were left standing awkwardly by the side of the house.

"Did you walk here?" I asked.

"I walk most everywhere."

"Then you must be tired. Let's sit down."

I led the way to the picnic table where Hudson and I had been eating. We sat across from each other. Lyndy folded his hands in front of him and stared at his dirty thumbs.

"How long have you lived in Dallas?" I asked.

"Whole life. That's over seventy years if you want to know. Grew up in Oak Cliff and moved around lots. Been a carpet layer since as long as I can remember. Worked on lots of the fancy buildings around here. Dallas Grand Hotel downtown, the Manor House, even that fancy department store. Easy to get work back then."

"I bet this was a nice area to raise a family."

"Was back when I had a family."

Lyndy fell silent and I didn't prompt him to keep talking. Hudson returned with a bottle of beer and handed it off to Lyndy. He drank half of the contents before setting the bottle on the table.

"It's a hard thing to lose a child. Changes your whole life. My oldest was sixteen years old. She'd just gotten her license. First person in our family who was going to graduate from high school, can you believe that? She even talked about going to college. Now she's gone. Both of them are."

My skin prickled. I looked up at Hudson, who shook his head

almost imperceptibly. Lyndy lifted the bottle of beer and finished it off. "You got another one of these for me?" he asked Hudson.

"You know I won't let you sit around here and drink your dinner."

Lyndy stood from the table. "Just as well. Time for me to be gettin' home." He glanced at me, and then walked back the way he'd come.

Hudson waited until he was out of sight. "I know you two got off on the wrong foot. I thought it would be a good idea for Lyndy to come over while you were here, so the two of you could get to know each other."

"It's him," I said. "Tex was at the bar the night it happened. George's brother is Dan Tyler, the client who fired me. The husband of the woman who was found today." My voice spilled out of me, words that made little sense independently of each other but, strung together, created the connection I'd been looking for. "Lyndy's daughters were killed by George Tyler in that accident. Lyndy's still angry about what happened that night and is out to exact revenge for lives lost. I have to tell Lt. Allen about this." I turned away and went to the kitchen to grab my phone.

Hudson caught up with me. "Lyndy isn't doing this," he said.

"You don't know that. You don't know what it must have done to him to lose his daughters like that."

"That accusation could destroy him."

"But if there's a chance he's involved—Hudson, you have to see that I need to get this information to the police."

"Go ahead, call them," he said.

I put my phone in my handbag and reached for Rocky's leash.

"You're going to meet with Tex, aren't you?" I didn't answer. "He said he doesn't want you involved."

"And you said I have a brain of my own and you can't stop me from doing what I want," I said. I watched the shock of having his words cited back to him cross his face, as the realization that I'd heard the whole conversation sunk in. "Being involved with you doesn't mean I'm going to turn my back on him."

Hudson took Rocky's leash from me. "Madison, be careful."
I left out the front door.

Half an hour later, armed with takeout bags from the Hunan
Palace, I knocked on the door of the white camper parked in front
of Jumbo's Topless Club. When I hadn't spotted Tex in the Casa
Linda lot, I widened my circle. Jumbo's boasted stiff drinks,
tattooed women, and eighties rock. If Tex didn't answer the door to
the camper, I wasn't going inside to find him. Even I had my limits.

I heard movement inside seconds before the door opened.
Something fell. Someone cursed. Another few sounds of items
banging around, and then the door opened. Tex stood in front of
me in a white undershirt and faded blue jeans that hung low on his
hips. His hair was slicked back away from his face, and the facial
hair from a few days ago had morphed from stubble to beard. He
looked like he still hadn't showered.

I held up the bags. "Hungry, Lieutenant?"

He stepped back and let me in.

I climbed up and moved a broom and plunger that had fallen from
a cabinet. I felt his eyes on me while I unpacked the cartons of
Chinese takeout and set them out on the counter. I didn't look at
him and I didn't say anything. When I was done, I tore the paper off
of a pair of chopsticks and turned around.

"You look like crap," I said. "Doesn't this thing have a
shower?"

He flashed me a smile. "What's the point of showering when I
have to put the same dirty clothes back on?"

"You seem to have contacts with the outside world that bring
you eggroll and beer. Surely you can get new clothes."

"Priorities."

"If you've been wearing the same underwear since last
Wednesday, I don't want to know."

"I'll show you mine if you show me yours," he said. I threw a
balled up napkin at him.

I picked up a carton of orange chicken and dug around with my chopsticks. "I think I'm their number one customer. The owner gave me an order of snow peas for free."

"They're getting ready to close," he said. "Chinese food doesn't keep overnight."

"What do they do with the leftovers?" I asked, before realization dawned on me. "They know I'm getting this food for you, don't they?"

He finished his mouthful and swallowed. "About ten years ago the restaurants around here kept getting robbed. My partner and I made a habit of patronizing the restaurants every night. Thought if we made it known that there were police around, the perps would leave them alone."

"Did it work?"

"We never caught the guys, but the robberies stopped. Sometimes that's the best we can do."

"And you've been hooked on Hunan Palace ever since."

"They make a good eggroll." He bit into his second since I'd arrived.

Having already eaten most of the steak and potatoes with Hudson, I wasn't as hungry as Tex appeared to be. I moved past him and sat on a small padded bunker. Tex sat on the one opposite me and leaned back against the wall.

"How'd you know where to find me?" he asked.

"I watched you drive away from Hudson's house earlier today."

He didn't react. "White campers aren't that uncommon."

"I got the license plate."

He grinned. "Night, I do like the way your mind works." He finished off the second eggroll and set his container of rice down next to him. "You shouldn't have come looking for me."

"I thought that's what you wanted."

"I don't know what I want." He rubbed his eyes with the thumb and index finger of his left hand. "No, that's not true. I want to find the women who are still missing. I want more than two hours of sleep. And I want you to stop calling me 'lieutenant.'"

"What should I call you?"

He grinned a lazy half smile that gave away the fact that his whole mind wasn't occupied with thoughts of the case. "It's a shame my mind is fuzzy from lack of sleep. I'm going to wake up in the middle of the night with a very good response to that question." He bent one leg and put the heel of his boot on the edge of the bench. "Okay, so you're here. Considering you were at Hudson's when I showed up, I'm going to go out on a limb and say he knows you're here. Did he try to stop you?"

I wanted to return Tex's playful smile, but I couldn't. Not when I thought about the knife and the girls and the car accident.

"I think I found the connection you've been looking for," I said.

Instantly the playfulness was gone and he was all business. He put both feet on the ground and leaned forward, forearms on his thighs. "Yeah?"

"First, you know about Cleo Tyler, right? That she was found today?"

A shadow crossed his face. "Iverson told me."

"Why didn't the abductor kill her? He killed Kate Morrow. If he's escalating his violence, he wouldn't go backward."

"I don't think he ever intended to kill Mrs. Tyler. I think she was a message."

"Why weren't you there? In the parking lot. I found her because I was there to meet you."

"Something came up on the scanner that I needed to check out."

I waited for Tex to tell me what it was. He didn't. He finished his beer while I moved my rice around inside the carton. I'd lost my appetite. I set the carton down.

"Remember how we talked about George Tyler? Cleo's husband's brother?"

"Sure. Why?"

"Two girls were killed in that car accident. Their father is a man who sometimes works with Hudson. His name is Lyndy."

"Emil Lyndy? Carpet layer?"

"You know him?"

Tex bent down and picked up a stack of manila folders. He flipped through the contents of the second one until he was about halfway through. "Sure. He's been picked up on a couple of drunk and disorderlies. Sleeps it off in a drunk tank and gets out the next day. Doesn't own a car so he doesn't drive. You say his daughters were the ones killed in the accident?"

"Yes."

"What else can you tell me about him?"

"He came to Mad for Mod looking for work, and he had a carpet knife with him. It had a long curved blade and a wooden handle. It's the same kind of knife the guy who approached Effie had. Hudson has one too. It's not expensive—you can get them in just about any hardware store."

"Did this guy threaten you?" Tex said. His jaw clenched.

"He scared me at first, but only because I was in the storage locker and I didn't know he was there. But listen to me. You have three people who died because of that car accident. Dan Tyler lost his brother and Lyndy lost his girls. You were here the night it happened, but so were a lot of other cops, right? So why are you being targeted?" My words tripped over themselves.

"I've been trying to figure that out." Tex set the folder on the floor and looked at me. His stare was laser sharp. "That case I told you about, Jacob Morris. Iverson checked into him and found out he left Arizona a few months ago. Hasn't turned up yet."

I looked away. Nausea claimed my stomach and I wished I hadn't eaten anything.

"When you went to the pool to swim, was there a guy there in a purple cap?" I asked.

"Yes. Why?"

"This might be nothing, but his name is Jake Morris. He told me he's new in town. He's a contractor. He showed up two days after Kate Morrow's body was found at Lockwood Park."

NINETEEN

Tex's eyes bore into mine. "Describe him."

"He was wet and he wore a purple swim cap and goggles. He came over to talk to me when I was trying to leave, but truth was, I was annoyed so I didn't pay him much attention. I have his card in my car if you want it, but you're not going to get much. It only has his name and his phone number."

"I want you to stay away from him."

"Do you really think he was holding a woman against her will?" I asked.

"The district attorney said he didn't have a case."

"That's not what I asked. Do you believe he was guilty?"

"Yes." Tex made a phone call. He turned his back to me, but I could still hear him. "Jake Morris. Could be Jacob Morris. Keep an eye out." He hung up and turned back.

"Do you think it could be him?"

"Hard to say. He's worth looking into."

"But you're not convinced."

"It doesn't feel right. Why would he come back here and commit the same crime we accused him of? And why impersonate me? It's almost too obvious."

"Have you heard anything about Cleo?"

"I think Mrs. Tyler was a distraction. She hadn't even been classified as a missing person when you found her. If the press hadn't picked up on her disappearance, she wouldn't even be a part of this."

"Distraction from what?"

He looked down at his hands. "There was another abduction yesterday. College graduate. She'd been out partying on Wednesday night. Went to her boyfriend's to spend the night, but she never made it home the next day."

"Do you have a name?"

"Barbie Ferrer."

The blood drained from my head. "She was at the Landing with Effie the night Effie was approached."

"When was that?"

"Wednesday."

"We got the report yesterday afternoon. Still no leads. She could still be alive out there with the others. We need to find them."

"Lieutenant, if this guy is going to such lengths to single you out, then maybe he's holding the women somewhere that has a connection to you too."

We were interrupted by three rapid knocks on the camper door. I went rigid. Tex sat forward and held his hand up to silence me. After a pause, a second series of knocks that sounded more like dull thuds followed. Tex relaxed. "It's Iverson. Wait here." He moved to the back door and cracked it. I heard another male voice. "Nah, not tonight. Thanks, man," Tex said, and closed the door. When he came back inside, he was holding a six pack of Lone Star beer.

"And here I thought you needed me to look after you. Let me guess, the dancers perform in the parking lot when the bar closes?"

"Only on Thursdays." He smiled.

This time I threw half an eggroll at him. He caught it and popped it into his mouth, and then screwed the top off of a longneck and took a long pull. I tried to stifle the sensation that I was hanging out with Burt Reynolds. He set the beer down and moved the empty containers to the fridge.

"Okay, Night, you told me why you're here. Now you want to tell me why you're not there?"

"Where?"

"Hudson's."

"I'm not there because I'm here."

"You know what I mean. You overheard a conversation between me and Hudson. You learned things that probably you would have found out in due time. I appreciate that you want to help me more than you can imagine, but there's something else going on with you. Want to talk about it?"

"With you?"

He looked to the left and then to the right. "You see anybody else around?" He paused. "C'mon, humor me. I've been trapped in a camper with nobody to talk to and the thoughts in my head aren't the stuff of Doris Day movies. Give me a lifeline."

I popped the plastic that contained my fortune cookie and pulled out the slip of paper from inside. IF YOU SPEAK HONESTLY, EVERYONE WILL LISTEN. I crumpled the paper up and set the cookie on my lap.

"I don't know if I have the energy to do it all again," I said. "The thing with Brad...I don't know. You date from time to time. Don't you get tired of the game?"

"What's worse? Connecting with somebody, even if it's only for a couple of hours, or not taking the chance? Or taking yourself off the market because you think the biggest romance of your life is behind you and nothing else can compare?"

"Is that what you think I'm doing?"

"I wish I could figure out what you think." He leaned back and stared at me. "Strike that. I think the sexiest thing about you is that I don't have a clue what you're thinking."

"That is funny. Because I think I've been pretty consistent when it comes to me telling you what I think of your playboy ways."

"True. Problem is, you keep showing up in my life and I can't stop thinking about the way you kiss."

Heat climbed my face. "I was confused."

"You were vulnerable."

"Weak."

"Open to possibilities."

"Stupid."

"You're saying you had to be stupid to kiss me?"

"No, I wasn't stupid. Desperate?"

"For me to kiss you?"

I raised my gaze and looked directly into Tex's clear blue eyes. "I was desperate to know I could still feel something."

We sat that way, facing each other, in silence. For the first time in days, my mind was clear. I didn't want to think about what it all meant, or whether I'd made a mistake by coming here. I knew the answers. Tex meant something to me, and even though I couldn't define what it was, I couldn't walk away.

"Night, I appreciate everything you're trying to do for me, but I'll take it from here. I don't want you involved."

"I already am involved. I have access to Cleo and Dan from my client files, Effie from her tenant application, and Lyndy if I hire him. Tell me what you want to know about them and I'll find it out."

"No."

"What do you mean, 'no'?"

"I mean, I'm not putting you any further in the middle of this. Night, somebody is out there abducting women and he's killed at least one of them. You shouldn't be here helping me. You should be scared to death like the other woman in town. Under normal circumstances, I would hunt this perp down and make sure he can't do this again. But I can't do my job because some Ted Bundy wannabe made it personal. Do you understand what I'm saying?"

"You're letting him get to you."

He gritted his teeth and balled up his fists. "Night, this is going to get worse before it gets better. There are things I have to do in order to figure this out, and I can't do them if I'm worried about you following me around and putting yourself in danger."

"You weren't worried about me when I brought you eggrolls," I said. "So, what are you going to do? Live in a camper parked outside of a topless club? Drop out of society and become a vigilante? Shut out the very lifeline you just asked for?"

"I don't need you to be my conscience. Somebody's got to stop this guy." He stormed past me. He grabbed a set of keys from the counter and left out the back door. I followed him. He tried to slam the door but I caught it with my palm. He crossed the parking lot and went into Jumbo's.

Screw this. I went back in the camper and checked my handbag for my own keys. They weren't there. That's when I remembered I had set them on the counter next to the Chinese takeout. Where they no longer sat.

This was not happening.

I exited the camper a second time and looked at the bouncer. He stared at me, standing in the middle of the parking lot in my yellow and white floral dress and green ballerina flats. He crossed his arms over his chest. I closed the camper door and approached him.

Sometimes a woman has to do what a woman has to do.

TWENTY

If a fortune teller had predicted that I'd walk into a topless bar after midnight, I would have had her license revoked. Yet here I was, inside the poorly lit red and gold interior of Jumbo's. I looked away from the stage where a woman in a cowgirl outfit danced to "Mustang Sally," and I scanned the crowd for Tex. I found him at the bar, his back to the stage, sitting next to Officer Iverson. Two empty shot glasses sat in front of Tex.

As I passed a table of rowdy young men, I felt something brush against my hip. I looked down and saw one of the men holding a wad of one dollar bills. "Hey, Sandra Dee! Cool. I didn't know it was amateur night. You up next? These singles got your name written all over them."

I shook my head and kept walking.

By the time I reached Tex and Officer Iverson, they were aware of my presence. Iverson looked amused. Tex looked angry. I caught my reflection. My expression matched Tex's.

"Go home, Night," Tex said.

"I can't. You took my keys. If you don't hand them back in the next five seconds, I'll be forced to drive that camper home instead of my car. I have no problems doing that, but in all fairness, I should tell you, the clutch on the Alfa Romeo sticks."

Tex stood from the bar stool and patted down his front jeans pockets, and then the back ones, and then the pocket on his T-shirt. His angry expression turned to confusion. He turned around and looked at the bar, the stool, and the worn wooden floor boards.

"This isn't a joke, Lieutenant," I said.

"I don't have them," he said. He turned to Iverson. "You see a set of keys?"

"Nope," Iverson said. He picked up his drink, a clear glass tumbler filled with ice and liquid, and poured it down his throat. "Good luck, man," he said. "Hotel California" came over the sound system. Iverson patted Tex on the back and moved to a seat closer to the stage.

The bartender, a slim man in a black T-shirt and jeans, leaned against a wall filled with bottles of booze and dried a glass with a white terrycloth towel. His attention was on the stage.

"Night, I don't know what to say. You have a spare set, don't you?"

"Not with me."

"So I'll give you a ride home."

"Between the two beers in the camper and the empty shot glasses in front of you, I'd say you're not driving anywhere."

"So, what, you're going to hang out with me and watch the stage show? You really are an enigma."

"They must have fallen out of the camper when you left. Come help me look."

Even with pain throbbing in my knee joint, I made it to the exit before Tex. As I passed the bouncer, I cut my eyes to him for a second. He stifled a smile.

"It's not what you think," I said.

"It never is," he replied.

We scanned the lot between the doors to Jumbo's and the back of the camper. My keys weren't there. Tex asked the bouncer if he'd seen them, and the bouncer shook his head. Tex rejoined me.

"Tell you what. I'll have your car towed to a safe lot overnight and you can pick it up in the morning."

"And in the meantime I just accept the fact that my keys are gone?"

"Night, they didn't spontaneously combust. They're probably in the back of the camper."

Tex pulled the back doors open and climbed in. I watched him from the lot. He squatted to the floor and looked around the table and the bench. "You got a nail file?"

"Not on me."

"What kind of a woman are you?"

"The kind who is rapidly losing patience with you."

He looked down at me. "Your keys are wedged between the bench and the table. The way I see it, you've got two options. Give me a ride to Thelma Johnson's and take the camper—"

"Or?"

"Spend the night here with me and we figure it out in the morning."

I grabbed the camper keys from him. "Buckle up, Lieutenant. I've never driven a camper, but I'm pretty sure it's going to be a bumpy ride." I went around to the driver's side and climbed up into the cab. I was thankful that it was the middle of the night and the roads would be close to empty.

The engine turned over easily, but the camper jumped when I put it into reverse. It took a second to find the emergency brake, and then we were off. I checked every mirror three times and eased the behemoth out of the space, cut the wheel to the right, and left the parking lot.

The drive to Thelma Johnson's house was slow and steady and filled with more mirror checking than backstage at a beauty pageant. I was surprised that Tex had asked me to bring him here. I parked the car out front and walked around back to check on him.

He wasn't there.

What had happened to him? Had he climbed out the back while I was stopped at a traffic light? Why? Simply to make me mad?

The man was infuriating.

I threw the camper in reverse and backtracked over the route I'd traveled. I made it most of the way back to Jumbo's without seeing any sign of Tex. When I turned the corner, the five police cars, spiraling red and blue lights, and scattered crowd of uniformed officers in the parking lot out front distracted me from my annoyance.

I threw the camper into park and got out. A young cop put his hand up to stop me from getting closer to the crowd.

"I'm sorry, ma'am, but this is a crime scene. I can't let you get any closer."

"But I was here earlier tonight. What happened?" I looked past him to the crowd and picked out Officer Iverson talking to a uniformed officer I didn't know. Iverson looked out of place in his civilian clothes, a chambray shirt and jeans over cowboy boots. Behind them, several of the dancers from the club huddled together, each wrapped in blankets that covered their near-nudity. Iverson spotted me. He raised his chin and then nodded in a sign of recognition. "Let her through," he said. The young officer stepped back.

"Officer, what happened?" I asked.

Iverson put his hand on my shoulder and turned me away from the others. "You left here with Lt. Allen, right? How long ago was that?"

"Ten—fifteen minutes. Why?"

"Where's he now?"

I studied Iverson's face. I didn't know where Tex was, but all of a sudden I was afraid to acknowledge that.

"Ms. Night, I'm on Allen's side. I think you are too. But unless we can prove he wasn't anywhere near Jumbo's in the past ten minutes, we got ourselves a problem."

"Why?"

"Because somebody dumped the body of another of the abducted women."

TWENTY-ONE

I swayed with a bout of vertigo. When I opened my eyes again, I saw the body on the asphalt. She was face up, her legs bent underneath her at an unnatural angle. Her arms were out on either side of her, as if to say, "Come and get me."

"Who is she?"

Officer Iverson turned around and stared at me. "Her name is Linda Gull."

I chewed on my lower lip, too stunned to answer. Linda Gull was the second woman who'd been reported as missing after Kate Morrow. She'd been abducted while on her way to Shreveport. It wasn't until after she failed to meet her friends that someone noticed the abandoned car left outside of the Mexican restaurant on Greenville and put two and two together.

"How did she die?" I asked.

"You don't want to know," Iverson said.

"I need to know."

"Her throat was slit."

I turned away and bent over, anticipating dry heaves. The ground spun below me. I dropped to my knees and put my hands out in front of me so I was on all fours. Pain shot through my knee cap. I curled into a ball and wrapped my arms around my head, trying to erase what was happening.

Officer Iverson stooped down and put a hand on my shoulder. "You okay?" he asked.

"No," I said. "No, I'm not okay. This can't have happened. It can't." I slowly righted myself. Iverson stood and held out a hand. I took it and he pulled me up until I was standing.

"When is this going to end?" I said.

"When justice is served," he said.

I looked at the empty space where my car had been parked. "Where's my car?"

"The Alfa Romeo?" asked the man who'd been tending bar earlier. "That guy you were with earlier called. Said to have it towed."

Great. Now I was minus one police lieutenant and minus one car. On my worse day in the softball league in high school my batting average was better than this. If it hadn't hinted at the proximity both Tex and I had had to the person who dumped the body, it would have been laughable.

Another man in a dark suit approached me. I recognized him as being in Tex's precinct, but I didn't know his name. "Madison Night?" he asked.

"Yes."

"Sgt. Osmond," he said, holding out his hand. "We spoke on the phone about Cleo Tyler."

"How is she? Do you know anything?"

"She's going to be fine. The hospital is sending her home tomorrow."

She was going to be fine. Except for the nightmares.

"Ms. Night, Officer Iverson says you were here earlier tonight. I'd like to ask you a few questions."

I darted my eyes behind him to Officer Iverson. He stared at me but didn't make a move.

"Sergeant, Officer Iverson said her throat was slit. Remember when we talked about the contractors? Have you tracked down Lyndy? He carries a sharp carpet knife with him, the same kind that was used to threaten a woman on Wednesday night."

He took more notes. "What were you doing here tonight?"

"I was here earlier with Lt. Allen."

"Arrived together?"

"No, but we left together." It took every ounce of emotional strength to let my words hang out there without any additional explanation. We were in the parking lot of a topless joint frequented by police officers. Tex had a reputation as a ladies' man among them. Now was not the time to defend my honor.

"Lt. Allen and I left in the camper," I said, pointing to the big white vehicle. Behind Sgt. Osmond, the two guys who had mistaken me for Sandra Dee snickered between puffs on their cigarettes.

The sergeant looked at them and then back at me. "You don't look like the type to go off in a camper with Lt. Allen," he said.

"I don't know what type you take me for, Sergeant, but I can assure you that I'm able to take care of myself when it comes to Lt. Allen."

"You said you and the lieutenant arrived separately. Where's your car?"

I wasn't the best liar under regular circumstances, and while my number one priority was helping Tex, I didn't think inventing false leads was going to do a whole heck of a lot to help his case. "I thought the lieutenant took my keys by mistake. I went in to get them but he claimed he didn't have them. We found them wedged in the back of the camper, and neither of us was equipped to get them out. I offered to drive him home and then take the camper to my house."

Sgt. Osmond made notes on an iPad.

"Sergeant, Lt. Allen told me there was another abduction, Barbie Ferrer. She's a friend of a friend. Are you any closer to figuring out where these women are being held?"

"We heard about Ms. Ferrer yesterday afternoon. The press was all over the Cleo Tyler disappearance, which we knew nothing about. Made us look like fools," he said. "When your call came in about Mrs. Tyler, I was with the Ferrer family, getting details about her last twenty-four hours."

"She was out with friends on Wednesday night," I said. "She left the Landing and went to her boyfriend's house."

"He's the one who called us. She left his place in the morning but never made it home. Her sister thought she was with him. We don't know when or where she was taken."

I looked away again, but there was no place to look that didn't remind me of what had happened.

"Ms. Night, has your contact information changed?"

I could give him the address of the apartment building, but I knew I wouldn't be there. I could give him Thelma Johnson's address, but there was a decent chance Tex would be there, and I didn't want him to walk into a trap. And then there was Hudson's address, where I'd spent last night. I didn't want to draw Hudson into this mess. And after how I'd left, I didn't even know if I was still welcome there.

"You can reach me at Mad for Mod." I gave him the address to the studio. Sgt. Osmond made a note and clicked a button on the side of his iPad. The screen went dark and he tucked the tablet under his arm.

"Thank you, Ms. Night. You've been very helpful."

Having been given permission to leave the scene, I climbed back into the camper and left the parking lot. I was at a loss as to where to go. If ever there was a night that I wanted companionship, it was tonight, but showing up at Hudson's felt too much like I was using him.

Ultimately, I drove to Thelma Johnson's house. It didn't hurt that Tex had hooked my spare key onto the ring of keys for the camper. I parked by the front curb and moved quickly from the vehicle to the house. The lack of lights told me I was alone.

There was something strange about being inside the house—my house—where Tex had been staying for the past few days. I checked the fridge and found a half-empty case of beer, a carton of eggs, and a block of butter sitting next to my assortment of yogurts and bag of spinach. Saltines, Campbell's soup, and a stack of tuna cans had been added to the existing contents of my pantry.

In the living room, I found a windbreaker draped over the back of a chair and a pair of sneakers pushed underneath it. I turned on the TV; the last channel watched had been CNN. The yellow blanket from my bedroom had been moved to the sofa, along with a pillow in a pink, yellow, and white floral case. Tex might have tried to shake off the Doris Day quality of my residence, but it was hard to escape the daisies.

I climbed the stairs, showered and changed into a clean pair of pajamas, and slipped between the sheets on the bed. The loneliness was stifling. Ten minutes later, I moved downstairs to the sofa and rested my head against the pillowcase that now smelled vaguely of Tex.

After a fitful night of sleep, I dozed off around five. Too bad the sun comes up around five thirty. There was no ignoring the bright rays that flooded the living room. I stretched, stood, did a few toe touches to limber up my joints, and looked out the window. The camper sat by the curb where I'd parked it. A black Jeep was parked behind it. Tex was sitting on the concrete steps out front.

I combed my fingers through my hair, matted and knotted since I'd slept on it wet. I double-checked that the buttons on my PJs were all buttoned and opened the front door. Tex stood up and climbed the stairs. I stepped backward and let him in. He pulled a chair away from the dining room table and dropped into it. I dropped into the one catty-corner his.

"When I realized you weren't in the camper, I went back to Jumbo's," I said.

"If this is about your car, I'll square that when the impound lot opens."

"This isn't about my car, Lieutenant. Another woman is dead—Linda Gull. Her body was dumped in the parking lot outside of Jumbo's after we left."

"Shit."

Tex leaned back, one arm on the table, flipping a pack of matches from Jumbo's between his fingers. The other arm angled down by his side. His knee jiggled, his wrist shook, his fingers twitched. He was wired for sound.

"Do whatever it is you came here to do and then you're coming with me. We're going to the pool," I said.

"I appreciate the gesture, but I don't have time for water aerobics."

I stood up and slammed my palms down onto the table. "You are twitching like a bomb with a lit fuse. You're going to explode if you don't do something soon. I don't care where you spend your nights, and I don't care where you drown your sorrows, but I'm not going to let you destroy yourself because you can't control what's happening to the women who've been abducted. If somebody sees you like you are right now, you're going to go off and that's not going to do you—or anybody—any favors."

He stood up and stormed outside, slamming the doors behind him. I watched out the window as he walked down the sidewalk toward the garage. He stopped halfway and turned toward a gnarled oak tree that sat by the property line. He pulled a gun out of his waistband and shot the tree three times. A branch fell onto the ground. Next door, a window opened and my neighbor pushed her head out.

"Thomas Rexford Allen, are you shooting that poor old oak tree again?"

"Sorry, Mrs. Yoder," he called.

"You better be. You scared the dickens out of my cat Sadie."

"Sorry, Sadie." He sheathed his gun and walked to her property line. I lost sight of him as he rounded the freestanding garage.

Only in Texas. Anyplace else, half the neighborhood would have called 911 at the sound of the shots.

For the first time since I'd met the lieutenant, I was scared of what he was capable of. He was turning his back on the world he knew—the world where he went after the bad guys—because it was protocol, but it was killing him.

I felt for him; I recognized the cage he'd put himself into. For the first time, I saw a glimpse of the darkness that had driven Nasty out of his life. I understood why he wouldn't tell me where he lived, why whenever we got close to talking about something real he defaulted to wisecracks and flirtation. He was separating from the world. But I knew better than most that isolation is never the answer. I also knew I couldn't force him to do anything he didn't want to do.

I went upstairs and rooted around in the closet for a bathing suit. Swimming laps required something more practical than the vintage suits that matched my every day style. Last year one company had a closeout sale on poor selling patterns and I'd cleaned house on what they called their retro floral print, buying the same style in four colors. Today I pulled out the purple and blue one and added a white swim cap and clear goggles. I followed with two faded orange towels.

From a bin that I kept on the lower shelf, I pulled out a pair of mustard yellow men's swim trunks trimmed in light blue that I'd acquired during one of my many estate buy-outs. The tags were still on them. Trafficking in vintage as I did, I found it hard to give up dead stock, even if it was intended for the opposite sex. I changed into a powder blue A-line dress that zipped up the back. An oversized Peter Pan collar and large covered buttons decorated the front. I pulled down a navy blue straw hat that was shaped like a wedding cake and trimmed with tiny wicker bows and set it on my head. When I went downstairs, Tex was waiting for me in the kitchen. He glanced up at my hat, and then shook his head at the style.

"You got a bathing suit around here for me?"

I pulled the yellow trunks out of my bag and held them out. He grabbed them.

"I'll change when we get there. Let's go."

TWENTY-TWO

We walked out together. I was getting tired of driving the camper, but if it was between that and his Jeep, I had a feeling I knew which would win. He surprised me.

"If you can drive the camper, then you can drive the Jeep." He tossed me a set of keys. "That work for you?"

"Sure."

It was going on six a.m., an hour that only morning people cherished. Sunlight filtered through the trees, casting a glow on streets that too soon would be filled with cars and angry drivers. The sound of birds chirping were audible, as they'd remain until horns and radios drowned them out.

We made quick time to Crestwood. Like most of the regulars, I scheduled my workouts between Monday and Friday. The good thing about showing up early on a Saturday was the people who did show up slept in, so at this hour the pool was mostly empty.

Tex went into the men's locker room while I set my bag down on the bleachers. I waved to Bobby the lifeguard.

"Hey, Madison. Brought a friend today?"

"Yep. I guess he got tired of hearing how great the pool was and wanted to find out for himself."

"Where's Rock?"

"He's with a friend. A different friend," I finished.

"I guess I figured you wrong. All these years I thought you were a loner."

I pulled my blond hair back and twirled it around my finger, and then shoved the ponytail up into the rubber cap. The muscles in my body were either sore or tired. I stretched out my arms, shoulders, and neck while I waited for Tex to join me. It was taking him longer than I had expected to change. Was he having second thoughts? I started to suspect he'd left out the locker room window when he appeared.

The extra time he'd used in the locker room had been spent shaving. Gone were the whiskers that had grown in over the past week, and in their place was smooth tanned skin. I'd never seen Tex without a shirt on, let alone in swim trunks. He had a series of scars on his left pec. His fit torso showed off toned abs, a washboard stomach, and a faint trace of blond hairs that traveled south from his navel. When I'd met him, I remember noting a layer of softness that often comes with age. Any sign of softness was gone. I tore my eyes away and focused on the deck of the pool.

He grinned. "Thanks for that, Night. Feels good to be noticed."

I turned around and jumped into the water.

We worked out the logistics of circle swimming and I pushed off the wall and swam through the lane, propelled more by a desire to loosen my stiff muscles than to burn calories. Tex waited until I flipped at the far end before pushing off. We swam in tandem, passing mid-way each lap, for two hundred yards. I stopped at the end of the lane and caught my breath. Tex flip turned next to me and kept going.

"There's enough lanes that nobody has to share today," the guy in the lane next to me said. I pushed my goggles up and looked at him. I hadn't recognized him without his purple cap.

"Jake," I said. "Seems like you're finding your own schedule at the pool."

"Got a lot of free time on my hands these days. I finished working on the basement a couple of days ago. Hard to sit around waiting for the phone to ring. You'll keep me in mind if you have any work, right?" he asked. There was a trace of desperation in his voice.

"I'm between jobs at the moment," I said, "but I still have your card."

Tex glided to the end of the lane. He shook his head so his hair was out of his eyes, and looked first at me, and then at Jake, and then back to me. "You want a kickboard?" he asked.

"Sure."

He hoisted himself out of the pool as if he'd been doing it for years. Jake watched him cross the deck. "Have I seen that guy here before?"

"I don't think so. He's not a regular like me."

Tex came back and jumped into the lane. He pushed a kickboard in front of me. He was trying to be nonchalant, but I saw him take in Jake in a split second, memorizing his face, his physique, his presence. If we hadn't all been coated in chlorine, he probably would have memorized his scent.

Jake picked up his own kickboard from the deck. I didn't want to get caught up in any more conversation than what had already transpired. There was something about him I didn't like, but I couldn't put my finger on it. The desperation of being new in town and trying to drum up business through me? Or was there something else about him and his at first angry, but now overly friendly manner? Was he the man who had shot at Tex all those years ago?

I set the kickboard on the deck, pulled my goggles down, and pushed off. Several laps in, Tex stopped at the end of the lane and positioned himself in the corner by the red and white plastic lane dividers. I'd found my rhythm, though, and didn't stop again until I'd finished a mile. I glided into the wall and joined him.

"Done already?"

"Thought it was more fun to watch you than to keep going. How long have you been coming here?" he asked.

"Three years? Somewhere around there. It's good for my knee. I started when I moved to Dallas."

"You make it look easy."

"So do you." When I'd first suggested that Tex work out his frustrations by hopping into the pool, I hadn't known what to expect in terms of skill level. Crestwood catered to anybody with an interest in doing something good for their bodies. Since the median age was somewhere around seventy, it wouldn't take much for him to be among the younger swimmers like me. He'd surprised me with his ability.

"I used to compete in triathlons in my early days. Hated the swimming part at first, until I found out most other triathaletes hate the swimming part, too. That meant if I could learn to love it, I'd have an edge. I'm out of shape, but the muscle memory is still there."

"You faked yourself into liking what you didn't like. There's a strategy you don't hear every day," I said.

"It worked. I was unbeatable for a while."

"Why'd you stop?"

He bent his knees and bounced low in the water. "Joined the force. Put my energy into the job."

"But you still needed an outlet."

"Different stress called for different outlets. Going to the gun range blows off a lot of steam."

"Did it work today?" I asked. Until now, neither one of us had mentioned Tex's tree shooting incident.

"I let things get the best of me. Sorry about that."

I wasn't an expert, but from the cheap seats, it looked like Tex was headed down a dark and dangerous path. "How about a couple more laps before we call it quits?" I asked, even though I was near exhaustion.

He tipped his head and studied me for a moment. "Sure. You first." I put my goggles back into place and pushed off.

By the time we left, the lanes had been taken over by members of the swim team who wanted to squeeze in an extra workout, and a couple of young children who were getting lessons from Bobby the lifeguard. We each headed to our respective locker room. When I was dressed, I found Tex waiting for me in his Jeep. This time I'd be the passenger.

"Well, Lieutenant? Did the swim help?"

"Night, I don't want you coming back here until this case is solved."

"You can't tell me—"

"Yes, I can. That was him. Jacob Morris."

"What are you going to do about him?"

"I can't do anything. I'm on leave, remember? But I don't want you around him. Get in the Jeep and I'll take you to get your car," he said.

"My car won't do me a heck of a lot of good without my keys."

He dipped two fingers into the cup holder and pulled out a keychain. I snatched them from his hand. "They jiggled lose when you were driving."

"I'm curious. After you found my keys, did you fall out or jump out?" I asked.

"Doesn't matter, does it?" In the broad light of the morning, the lines of exhaustion and determination stood out on his face. He'd aged years in a week. "You took a turn too wide when you hit Greenville. The doors flew open. I hit the curb and rolled." One side of his mouth pulled up in a half smile. "I wouldn't go applying for your bus license any time soon."

"So where'd you go?"

"Someplace safe." I waited for him to elaborate but he didn't. He started the Jeep and drove us away from the pool. "It would have been a bad idea to leave your car at Jumbo's. My cousin Mickey owns a towing company. I called in a favor and he moved it to the police impound lot."

"Police impound!"

"Night, they gotta tow it somewhere. Jumbo's doesn't have an impound lot. The signs out front are deterrents, but if you left your car, it would be there in the morning, and it might have picked up some graphic illustrations on the windows. This way your car was safe, and you can get it without a lot of red tape."

"What are you going to do in the meantime? Lay low at Thelma Johnson's house?"

"I'm not staying there anymore. I already told you. I don't

want you involved."

"But where are you going to go?"

"I got a place. Listen, Night, I need a favor. Get the camper to Nancy and Lee at the Woodshire RV Park. Tell Lee I said thank you."

"Why can't you do it?"

"Night, don't ask questions you don't want answers to."

TWENTY-THREE

Tex dropped me off at the impound lot and told me to ask for Mickey. I hoisted my raffia tote bag onto my shoulder and walked toward the small white wooden booth in the center of the lot. A red-haired man was rearranging keys on a wall of hooks.

"Excuse me. Can you tell me where I can find Mickey?"

"I'm Mickey. What can I do you for?"

"My car was towed here last night. Lt. Allen told me to ask for you."

Mickey tucked his chin and laughed. "So you're Madison?"

"Yes."

"You just cost me twenty bucks."

"How's that?"

"Tex bet me you'd call him 'Lt. Allen' even though he told you to call him Tex. I've met some of the other women he gets involved with, and I thought it would be easy money. Follow me," Mickey said. He headed between two rows of cars and turned left when he reached the back of the lot. "Pretty little car you got there. You ever want to sell it, you let me know, okay?"

"As far as I'm concerned, this car is two months old. I'm planning on keeping it for a long time."

"Roger that," he said. "Did Tex say when he was planning on returning the camper?"

"He told me to get the camper back to Woodshire RV Park. He got it from you? Why would he lie?" I asked, shocked.

"Mighta had something to do with keeping you busy. Sorry,

toots, Tex is family. Can't say I always agree with him, but blood is thicker than water." He laughed again and walked away.

I stopped off at a gas station on my way to Thelma Johnson's house and topped off the tank, then parked in the garage and headed back out in the camper. I wanted little more than to turn it in and be done with Tex's game of musical cars, but that little more that I wanted included Rocky's company. And that meant a trip to Hudson's.

It took most of my concentration to navigate the giant white camper through the streets of Dallas, which was exactly what I'd wanted. Otherwise I'd call myself on the excuse-to-visit-Hudson-in-the-camper plan I'd just created. I was nervous to see him after how I'd left things last night, and I foolishly thought the anonymity of the camper would somehow make my arrival less obvious.

I pulled the camper up behind Hudson's blue-and-primer colored truck. He was in front of his house with his sister and niece. They stood to the side while he loaded one of many suitcases into the back of a minivan. He glanced at the camper for a few seconds, but then turned and hugged his sister. His niece stood next to him, her right hand balled up into a fist that rubbed at her eyes. Her left hand held her stuffed bunny. Rocky sat on the ground in front of her, tail wagging against a patch of grass. It seemed I was watching a good-bye.

Not wanting to spy on their familial moment, I stood up from the driver's seat and moved to the back of the camper. I gave myself a pep talk about getting out of the car, and braced myself for whatever reaction I'd get. Before the pep talk took effect, there was a knock. I fumbled with the locking mechanism and then pushed hard on the doors. They swung open and Hudson jumped out of the way.

He had a red and white bandana folded down into a three inch strip that was tied around his forehead. His black hair jutted up on top. The outline of a star was tattooed on the side of his neck above the collar of his black T-shirt. He held two cups of coffee and a leash. Rocky was on the end of the leash, trying, unsuccessfully, to jump into the back with me.

Hudson held out a cup of coffee and I took it and set it on the counter. He then scooped up Rocky and set him inside. Rocky immediately stood on his hind legs, paws on my knee, yipping for a hug. I dropped to my knees and wrapped my arms around his furry body and held him like the lifeline he was after what I'd seen last night.

After a reunion of puppy kisses, I turned to face Hudson. He watched me with a mixture of happiness and concern. "I want to see my sister off. Will you stick around until after she leaves?"

"Sure."

I unclipped Rocky's leash and set him on the ground. He jumped a few paces forward and then turned back and ran around my ankles to make sure I knew he was there. I waved at Nettie and Heather and walked around the side of the house to the back patio, where I lowered myself into Hudson's hammock. Rocky jumped up and a paw went straight through the open rope weave. He pulled his paw out and walked the length of my thigh, and then flopped on my belly.

Minutes later, Hudson came out the back door. I shifted Rocky and sat up and Hudson joined me. We sat side by side for a few seconds, my feet dangling above the grass, his foot on the ground, gently rocking us back and forth.

"I heard about the victim they found last night. Do you still think it could be Lyndy?"

"Lt. Allen recognized his name. He said he arrested him for drunk and disorderly on more than one occasion."

"Being drunk in public isn't the same thing as impersonating an officer and forcing women to get into your car."

"Hudson, I told the police about him. If he's responsible, they're going to find out."

We rocked back and forth a few times before Hudson spoke. "Nettie and Heather left. It's too dangerous for them to stay here. I'd like to pack you up and take you away too."

"Going away won't make it stop."

"It's not your job to make it stop."

"But if I have information—if I see something or know something that will help the police catch whoever is doing this, then I have to tell them. Somebody is out there terrorizing the women of Lakewood. Last night I saw another one of his victims. Effie's terrified, and who can blame her? Cleo is getting released from the hospital today. I need to check on her. It's going to take longer for these women to recover than the time it'll take for their bruises to heal."

"You're willingly putting yourself in danger and I don't know if I can watch that."

"I'm not used to answering to someone when it comes to the decisions I make. I'm not going to pretend those decisions are rational and well-thought-out, but they're mine. I've had forty-eight years to become the person I am and I think it's too late to expect me to change."

He reached over for my hand and sandwiched it between his. "I don't want you to change. It's you—the person it took forty-eight years to become—who I'm in love with."

I wasn't prepared for that. I thought of how long it had been since I felt loved, and then about the women who'd been loved who were now gone.

"Maybe love isn't enough. My softball coach had an expression: if your head's not in the game, there's no point in playing. I don't know if my head will ever be back in the game." I was quiet a moment. "I don't want to hurt you. And I don't want you to hurt me. And the only way I can see those two things not happening is for us to leave things as they are and not cross that bridge."

"Madison, do you have feelings for me?"

I nodded.

"Then how can you not see what you're suggesting is the one way to guarantee we'll both get hurt?"

"I need time, Hudson, and I don't know how much time I need. I came here to get Rocky. I think it's a good idea if I didn't stay here anymore."

"What about your apartment building?"

"I'm going to sell it."

"Can I ask where you'll be?"

"Remember that house I inherited a couple of months ago? Thelma Johnson's house?"

"Doesn't sound like much of a home if you're still calling it 'Thelma Johnson's house.' Besides, I thought you loaned it to— never mind."

"Lt. Allen isn't staying there anymore."

"You can stay here as long as you want. I have plenty of room, and Rock seems to like it."

"I think Mortiboy and I might have some issues."

"You'd be surprised. Just last night he told me he wanted you to move in."

"That's a pretty bold statement."

"Mortiboy is a pretty bold cat."

He put his hand back on top of mine and we sat there, holding hands, while a playful breeze danced around us. A part of me was pulled toward Hudson in a way I couldn't explain to anybody. He knew me without knowing me—something he'd demonstrated over and over. And the longer I knew him, the more I knew I wanted him in my life, regardless of the capacity. I tabled the attraction and built a connection to him through my business instead. And here he was, offering to take me in and give me an oasis in the middle of a storm.

The part of me that was drawn to everything Hudson stood for was having a hard time ignoring the offer and that scared me. I stood up and let Hudson's fingers drop from my own. "I promised Effie that I'd bring Rocky by today. She's having a hard time adjusting to life at her boyfriend's apartment."

He nodded a few times. "Be careful, Madison. Whoever's making trouble for the lieutenant probably knows you two have a relationship."

I started to deny it, but cut myself off. Hudson saw things the way they were. The only person I'd be denying it to would be myself, and I was getting tired of pretending. I clipped Rocky's leash on and led him out the front door.

"Do you want to tell me about this camper?" Hudson asked.

"It needs to go back to the police impound, but I can't figure out how to do that without ending up stranded."

"How about I follow you there and give you a ride to your car? And if you say one word about inconveniencing me, I'll either charge you mileage or start up a tab that you can repay when you're in the mood."

I blushed.

"That's not what I meant," he said with a smile. "But it's nice to know where your mind went." He winked and pulled his keys out of his jeans.

Rocky hung his head out the window while I drove, and Hudson followed. We reached the impound lot without incident and I turned the camper and keys over to Mickey. He looked behind me at Hudson's truck. "You didn't trade the Alfa Romeo for that, did ya?" he asked.

"Not yet," I said. "But the day is still young."

Hudson dropped me at Thelma Johnson's house. He stuck around until I pulled out, and then drove the opposite direction and waved goodbye. I waved back and took off for Chad's apartment complex.

The early morning swim had only touched the surface of letting my mind wander, and I'd needed all of my concentration to keep the camper between the yellow lines, so I took the scenic route now. Monticello doglegged by Greenville but I stayed on it, eventually turning right on Abrams, which turned into Gaston and took me past my apartment building. The middle of the day on a Saturday, normally the front door would be propped open, people would be coming and going. The scent of food cooking would permeate the air, and the sounds of music would let me know where the party was at. Today the building was desolate and depressing. I fought the urge to run inside and shout to the walls that I was sorry about the neglect.

I ended up weaving through a series of diagonal streets until I crossed the highway and ended up at Chad's Loft. A valet attendant stood out front. I was not the type to valet park my car at an apartment building, so I drove around the block twice, finally squeezing the Alfa Romeo into a narrow spot by a cemetery. Rocky and I walked toward the overgrown foliage on the corner first, where he lifted a leg and watered a small shrub, and then turned around and headed toward the apartment building.

In the lobby, a group of young men stood by one of the tall marble pillars. They were in various versions of the same outfit: backward baseball hat, short sleeved T-shirt over long sleeved T-shirt, cargo shorts, and sneakers. Every one of them had their heads down, staring at their phones. I half wondered if they were texting each other.

I buzzed Chad's apartment and Effie answered. "Hi Effie, it's Madison. I brought you a visitor like I promised."

"Come on up!" she said. The doors buzzed. I hung up and stepped through, and then set Rocky down on the clean marble floor. We walked to the elevator, where Rocky sniffed the brushed metal trim. When the doors opened, he ran inside and resumed sniffing. I was glad we'd made the detour to the corner shrub, because I wasn't prepared to mop the marble floor in the event of an unplanned pee break.

When the doors opened and Rocky saw Effie in the hallway, he charged. She jumped backward a step, but then dropped down. He put his paws on her knees and licked her check. Squealing, laughter, and barking filled the hallway. A door opened and a man looked out. Effie apologized for the noise and stood. As we made our way, parade-like, to her boyfriend's apartment, two of the three of us kept the noise down.

She closed the doors behind us and giggled. "I'm usually pretty quiet during the day. That guy has probably never even seen me before! I hope he doesn't tell Chad."

"Effie, you sound a little afraid of him."

"He just likes things a certain way, you know?"

I did know, and I wanted to tell her to run for the hills. Effie was caught between being a girl and being a grown-up, and her recent scare had made her vulnerable. She'd turned to her boyfriend for comfort. I didn't blame her for that, but instead of stepping up to the challenge, Chad seemed to be taking advantage of her fragile nature.

I sat in the black and chrome chair. It hadn't gotten more comfortable in the last twenty-four hours.

"How are you doing? Is it better, being here with Chad?"

"It's okay, I guess. I mostly stay here. I don't like going out by myself."

"That's understandable."

"I just—I can't stop thinking about Barbie. I was with her the night she was taken."

"Effie, Barbie went to her boyfriend's house just like she planned. Whatever happened to her didn't happen at the Landing."

"I know, just like I know Lt. Allen couldn't have been the person who approached me." She pulled her knees up to her chest. "If her sister hadn't cared enough to call her boyfriend, nobody would know she was missing." She wiped tears from her eyes.

I changed the subject. "Did you tell Chad we were coming over? I'd think he'd like knowing you had a visitor."

"He knows how much I love Rocky. I even asked him if we could get our own dog." Rocky hopped onto the leather sofa and laid his paws across her thigh. She stroked his fur away from his face, showing off his round marble-like eyes. "He probably wouldn't want a Shih Tzu, even if I could convince him. He'd probably want a big dog, like a pit bull."

"Maybe you two should check out the next pet adoption day at White Rock Dog Rescue? All kinds of dogs need adoption, and I couldn't think of a person who would make a better pet owner than you."

She shrugged and slumped down on the sofa. Her shoulders sagged. "Chad thinks we're not ready for a dog. He says we have to make our own life first before bringing any crutches into it." She bent down and kissed Rocky on top of his head. "You're not a crutch, are you? No. You're Madison's perfect little guy, right? Who needs a real man when she has you?"

Ouch. After being faced with my emotional limitations with Hudson that morning, her words caught me off guard. My breath caught in my throat and my face felt warm. "Effie, can I use your restroom?" I asked.

"Sure. Down the hallway, second door on the left. If you get to Chad's office you went too far."

I left the room and hurried down the hall with Effie's words in my ear. I'd thought as much already, but hearing it from someone else was worse. Was I ignoring what Hudson offered me—an invitation to experience life with another person—because I'd convinced myself that Rocky was all I needed?

I splashed cool water on my face and wrists and looked around for something to use to dry off. Below the sink was a small cabinet, and draped over one of the doors was a pair of gray hand towels. I freed one and blotted my face and hands. When I was finished, I opened the cabinet door wide enough to drape the towel over the top. A bundle in a similar dark gray towel shifted inside and landed by the opening. I bent down to push it back in, but froze when I saw what had been wrapped inside.

It was a carpet knife. The curved metal blade matched the description of the one Effie had seen in the abductor's hand outside of the Landing. The initials "EL" were carved into the handle.

TWENTY-FOUR

The handle of the knife was wrapped in the same type of dark gray towel that I'd used on my face. It appeared to have been propped along the inside left wall of the cabinet and knocked loose when I opened the doors.

My brain spun in circles, trying to understand what this meant. What was Lyndy's carpet knife doing in Chad's apartment? Why had it been hidden under the sink in his bathroom?

I stooped down and opened both doors to the cabinet. To the right was a black plastic bin filled with bars of soap and a package of razors. A dopp kit sat against the back. Stacks of toilet paper were lined up in the middle. And the bundle with the knife was in front of it all.

I had to call the police and let them know what I'd found, but I needed a landline. I needed to convey the address for where we were, which would show up on the caller ID.

If I repositioned the knife so I could close the cabinet doors, my fingerprints might be left on it—or worse, Chad's fingerprints might be destroyed. But the knife was in Chad's house. Of course his fingerprints would be on it—it would almost be more suspicious if they weren't.

I was caught in a tug of war of indecision. Finally, I pushed the knife back into the cabinet with the toe of my shoe, closed the doors as best as I could, and snuck out into the hallway.

Effie had said that Chad's office was farther down the hall. He had to have a phone in there. I snuck from the bathroom to the office. A black laminate built-in desk filled two-thirds of the room. Three computer monitors and a handful of keyboards were scattered across the surface. I spotted the phone, a black cordless model, resting on the charger, next to a scanner/printer. Wasting no more time, I grabbed it from the base and called 911.

"Please state your emergency," said a female voice.

"This is Madison Night. I have information regarding the abductions that have been taking place in the Lakewood area. Can you connect me to Sgt. Osmond at the Lakewood Police Department?"

"What is your emergency?" she asked again.

"I'm in an apartment that I think might belong to the Lakewood Abductor. Luxury Uptown Lofts, apartment two-thirty-seven on the second floor."

I heard the sound of keys clicking. "Please—I need to speak to someone from the police force."

"Are you in need of medical assistance?" she asked.

"No—not yet, anyway. I'm here with a college girl named Effie Jones. She was one of the targets who got away."

"Help is on the way," she said. "Please stay on the line."

Out front, I heard a door slam. "Where'd that thing come from?" a male voice asked. It was Chad.

"I have to go," I said into the phone, and set it back on the cradle. I wasn't sure what I was going to do, but letting Chad discover me making phone calls to the police from his office wasn't something I thought would have a good ending. I couldn't let him know I'd made that call. I couldn't let him do anything with the knife. But I also couldn't leave him alone with Effie and Rocky.

I slipped out of the office and back to the bathroom. I double-checked that the knife was where I'd found it, and closed the cabinet doors. I washed my hands and dried them a second time, and then returned to the living room. Chad stood next to the sofa. The picture of nineties grunge, he wore a faded Nirvana T-shirt over a cream long sleeved thermal and jeans. He aimed a remote at the TV and flipped through a few screens until he landed on ESPN.

"Chad, hi. I didn't hear you," I said. He glanced at me and looked back at the screen. "I hope you don't mind that I brought

Rocky for a visit. I thought it would be nice for Effie since she's been through such a scare."

"She needs to stop acting like she's a victim. Nothing happened to her. Best thing is to move on and let life get back to normal."

That was an odd response, coming from someone who claimed to care about her. Effie sat on the sofa with her knees pulled up to her chest. She kept her eyes focused on the coffee table in front of her, like she couldn't hear that we were talking about her while she was in the room.

I forced a smile into my voice. "I'm sure Effie wants nothing more than for life to get back to normal, but speaking as someone who's had a couple of shakeups myself, I know it takes more than a few days to get over the scare of being attacked."

"Effie wasn't attacked. Nobody laid a finger on her. Paying her extra attention only makes her feel like she's a victim, and she wasn't."

In the distance, I heard the sound of sirens. I knew they were headed this way. What I didn't know was how long it would take for them to get past the buzzer in the lobby and up to the second floor to us. And what Chad was capable of doing in that same amount of time.

"Chad, I know you want me to snap out of it, but it didn't happen to you," Effie said. "You don't know what it was like. Women are getting killed by this guy and it could have been me. And you don't care!"

Effie had stood up to face Chad. Tears flowed down her red face. I had no right to watch their fight be played out in front of me, but there was no place for me to go.

Rocky sensed that Chad was threatening Effie, and his playful barks turned into bared teeth and a low growl. He jumped down to the floor and faced Chad, barking at him as if to say "Leave my friend alone." Chad kicked his foot out in Rocky's direction. I jumped in front of his foot just in time to absorb the blow that was intended for my dog. I dropped to the ground and pressed my hands against my calf where he'd kicked me.

"Madison!" Effie screamed.

Chad looked up at her and then down at me. He grabbed a blue nylon jacket from the back of a chair and shook his head. "I'm out of here," he said. He whipped the front door open and found himself facing two uniformed officers.

"Who are you?" he asked.

"Back inside," one of the men said. They entered the apartment. Behind them was Sgt. Osmond from Jumbo's parking lot the night before, and behind him was Chief Washington himself.

"Ms. Night, you made the call?" Osmond asked.

I nodded.

"What call? What's this about?" Chad asked.

"Is everybody okay? Does anybody need medical help?" Osmond asked.

"No," I said.

The chief looked at my leg, where a purplish-red bruise was forming on my shin. He looked at Effie for the first time since he'd entered. She was back on the sofa, hugging a thick black pillow close to her chest. Mascara ran down her cheeks and smudged around her eyes, giving her the appearance of having been battered.

"Did he do that to you?" one of the officers in uniform asked.

She swiped the back of her hand over her eyes and distorted the smudge of makeup even more. She sniffled twice, but didn't answer the officers.

Chief Washington turned to one of the officers. "Wait here with him while I talk to Ms. Night."

He looked at me and I pointed down the hallway. Once we were clear of the others I turned to him. "Do you usually respond to 911 calls?"

"We've got every available man out on the streets looking for this wacko. Pressure from the city is almost unbearable. This isn't the time for me to pull rank and prop my feet up on my desk."

I nodded my understanding. We reached the bathroom. He hesitated in the hallway when I went inside. "I'm not using the facilities. I need to show you something."

He stepped inside and I opened the cabinet door. I stood up and pointed at it. "I wasn't going through his things. I used the towel to dry my hands and face and the door opened up. It must have been propped along the side and it fell. The towel opened up and I saw the blade."

The chief dropped to a squat and lifted the edge of the towel until he exposed the curved blade wrapped inside. He whistled. From a pocket of his suit jacket, he pulled two folded up plastic bags. He held one open at the edge of the cabinet and used the razor to bump the knife forward until it tipped and fell in. He sealed the bag by sliding a small red clasp along the top edge, and then put the towel into the second bag. He set both bags on the sink and then stood up. Both of his knees snapped when he straightened.

"I don't like getting old," he said. "The body likes to remind me that I'm not twenty-five anymore."

"You're preaching to the choir," I said.

"I hear you got Lt. Allen swimming. That's good. He needs an outlet like that."

"Chief, what do you make of this knife being here in this apartment?"

"I don't know what to make of it. What are you doing here, anyway?"

"The young woman out front, Effie Jones, she used to live in my apartment building. She's the one who was approached out front of the Landing. She was pretty shaken up, so I called an officer she knew to come and take her statement."

His face clouded. "I thought she came in to make her statement?"

"She did, the next day. That night she talked to Nasty. Nast. Donna Nast. Officer Donna Nast."

An unexpected grin replaced the cloud. "Donna Nast is no longer on the force."

"I know. I didn't know it that night, but I know it now."

"That still doesn't tell me what you're doing here."

"My building is empty right now. It was down to Effie and myself. Her boyfriend Chad suggested she stay with him instead of remaining in the building. They both graduate college this year, and I get the feeling their on again off again relationship was in the on position."

"So you came over for a social call and found a curved knife that matched the description of a weapon that she gave. You know there's a chance she's seen this before. There's a chance her whole statement was intended to punish her boyfriend for a fight. I have two college-aged daughters. They don't play fair."

"Effie wouldn't do that."

The chief stepped out into the hallway. "Where'd you call us from?"

"There's a room with computers and a phone down the hall."

"Show me."

I left the bathroom and retraced my steps until I was back in the computer room. "The phone is on the charger by the scanner," I said. I walked behind the desk and pointed to the phone.

Chief Washington followed me behind the desk and took in the computer setup from left to right. The screens were dark, but I could hear the sound of computer fans whirring from underneath the desk. The chief reached out and tapped the space bar on the main computer and the large monitor in the center of the desk flickered to life. The screen was divided into a nine box grid that appeared to be running individual movies in each box, like the picture in picture feature on a TV, only covering the entire screen. I leaned forward to make sense of it, and then gasped when I recognized three of the video feeds: Chad's living room, the Landing parking lot, and Effie's unit in my apartment building.

In addition to a number of interiors that I didn't recognize, I understood one thing. Chad Keith had been monitoring Effie's every move.

TWENTY-FIVE

"Ms. Night, when you made the call to 911, it came up as Big Bro Security. Do you know what that is?" Chief Washington asked.

"No. Do you?"

"Ms. Night, I think you're going to have to let me take it from here."

"What about Effie?" I asked. "She's been living here."

"Can she stay with you?" he asked.

"We should leave that decision up to her."

Chief Washington and I walked back out to the living room. "Mr. Keith? We're going to need to ask you a few questions."

"Yeah? I want to ask a few questions myself. Like who gave you the right to enter my apartment?"

The chief held up the plastic bag with the knife in it. The color left from Chad's face, like a glass of Kool-Aid being drained with a straw. His complexion was left a shade of greenish beige. He doubled over and threw up on a plant in the corner. When he stood up, he wiped his mouth with the back of his hand. "Are we going to talk here or your place?"

"I think 'our place' would be better," the chief said.

Chad nodded. One of the officers cuffed his hands together and led him out of the room. Effie put her hands over her face and sobbed openly.

I put my hand on her shoulder. "Effie, I think it's best that you don't stay here tonight. Do you want to stay with me?"

"I want to go home," she said between ragged breaths.

"Home? To the apartment on Gaston?"

"No, home. To see my parents. They live in McKinney. It's

about an hour drive in traffic."

"I can take you. Do you need to pack your things?"

Effie picked up a worn teddy bear—obviously more well-loved than the one I'd seen at her apartment the night she'd been attacked—from the sofa with one hand and her handbag with the other. "I'm ready to go now."

We left the apartment behind. Effie grabbed the power cord to her phone on the way out. Rocky had calmed down from the melee, but he stayed close to Effie as if he sensed that she needed his company. When we reached my car, I found a piece of paper tucked under the front windshield wiper.

"You didn't get a ticket, did you?" Effie asked.

I glanced at the writing. *Meet me at the cemetery entrance on Oak Grove at sundown. –T*

"Advertisement," I said. I crumbled the paper into a ball and tossed it onto the floor of my car.

Effie's parents lived in a small ranch on the outer edge of McKinney, a town about thirty miles north of downtown Dallas. As soon as I saw the house, I knew why she'd wanted to live in my building.

The house was a sprawling ranch. The lines of mid-century were evident in the split of the roof, half on a slope, half flat, and the row of perfectly square windows that lined the right-hand side of the façade. Care had been taken in the form of maintenance and landscaping. Tall stalks of bamboo flanked a bright white door that contrasted nicely with the pink brick. The attached garage was on the right side of the house; a restored yellow Pontiac GTO was parked in the driveway. I pulled in behind it.

The front door opened and a woman in a long olive green linen sundress stepped out. She waved to us and Effie waved back. Even from a distance, I could see the resemblance between mother and daughter.

"Do you want to come in?" Effie asked.

"No, thank you. I need to get back. You have my number, right?" Effie nodded. "I want you to call me if you need anything."

"I'll be okay here. They've been wanting me to come visit for a while. I would have, except Chad didn't want me to leave." Her eyes went red again and filled with tears.

"Effie, it's okay. Chad's with the police now, and you're here."

"I still can't believe it was him. Why? Why would he do it?"

"I don't know." I smoothed her hair away from her face, and then stopped when I realized what a maternal gesture it was. I glanced back over at the front door and saw Effie's mom watching us. She smiled. In her arms was a black Shih Tzu as in need of a haircut as Rocky. I smiled back. It didn't take a mid-century modern interior decorator to recognize that Effie's parents were good people.

Effie gave Rocky one last hug, and then got out of the car with her teddy bear and her handbag. I waited until she was in her mother's arms before backing out of the driveway and heading back to Lakewood.

When I reached Mad for Mod, I fished my hand around the floor of the car for the wad of paper I'd thrown there and smoothed the crumpled ball open. I hadn't wanted to tell Effie that the note was from Tex, but now that I was alone again, I couldn't stop thinking about it. How had he known I was at Effie's boyfriend's apartment? He couldn't have, not unless he'd followed me there. So, did that mean he'd suspected Chad all along? I didn't know. Maybe Nasty was right. Maybe I didn't know Tex as well as I thought.

I got out of the car and walked a circle around it, looking for a tracking device, before giving in to the fact that I wouldn't know a tracking device if I sat on one. There had to be a rational explanation. I had to wait until sundown to find out what it was. That was, if I decided to meet him in the graveyard in the first place.

Rocky took a bathroom break next to the recycling. I bagged

his business and tossed it into the trash bin, and then went inside my studio. The back hallway held the Asian items that I'd accumulated for Dan and Cleo's house: extra Japanese lanterns, a coromandel screen with a painting of cherry blossoms on rice paper, and several serving sets of Asian-inspired flatware, dishes, and glassware. The resulting mix blurred the lines between Japanese, Chinese, Vietnamese, and Thai, but made a kitschy statement when combined. If things had gone as planned, Cleo Tyler would be throwing her pool party tonight. Instead, she was probably at home, struggling to get over the nightmare of having been abducted by a psycho. I almost couldn't believe it had been less than twenty-four hours since I'd found her in the Casa Linda parking lot.

I called the Tyler house. Cleo answered. "It's Madison. How are you doing?"

"I feel like an armadillo that's been hit and left by the side of the road—all kinds of banged up."

"Is Dan there with you?"

"He's been a doll. Attending to my every need since the doctors checked me out."

"Cleo, what were you doing at the paint store yesterday? That's where it happened, didn't it?"

A gruff voice replaced Cleo's lazy painkiller-induced one. "What did I tell you? My wife has been to hell and back and she doesn't need to answer to you. Don't call here again." He slammed down the phone.

I picked up my notes on the Tyler house and tapped them on the desk until the bottom edges were lined up. No need to keep them out anymore. It pained me to know I'd have to give up on the balance of their payment. Just when I'd gotten comfortable with my income, everything changed. I needed money in the bank to fund my business. The only way to get an infusion of cash was to sell the apartment building.

I pulled up the name of the realtor who had transacted the inheritance of Thelma Johnson's house to me. I was going to have to bite the bullet and do this. The building held too many bad memories. I had to let it go.

When the realtor answered, I charged ahead. "Mr. O'Hara, this is Madison Night. A few months ago I inherited a house from one of your clients, a Mr. Steve Johnson."

"Call me Dennis. I remember you—you're that Doris Day lady who busted up the counterfeiting ring, right? That kind of thing doesn't happen every day."

"You'd be surprised," I said.

"Is there some problem with the house?" he asked after an awkward pause. I was smart enough to know that even if there was, it wouldn't be his responsibility. He was only being polite.

"I'm not calling about the house. I own an apartment building on Gaston Avenue that I'd like to sell. Can you recommend someone who handles commercial real estate?"

"I'd be happy to help you with that," he said. I could almost hear the dollar signs in his voice.

"Dennis, it's not one of the fancy buildings that you might be picturing. It's a modest twelve unit mid-century building that's had only very minor updates."

"Describe 'minor.'"

"All of the bathrooms have been restored to their original pink commodes, sinks, and tubs."

Silence.

"Are you sure you wouldn't prefer to recommend someone? I know there are realtors who specialize in this sort of thing. I see their ads in *Atomic Ranch* magazine."

"I'll take a look first and see what we can do."

We made arrangements to meet for a walkthrough on Monday. I had a feeling the realtor was somewhere between determining that my building wasn't worth his while and wondering if he had somehow lucked into the easiest transaction in history.

I pulled a cold bottle of water from my mini fridge. I poured half of the contents into Rocky's bowl, and then sat back down at my desk and took a long drink for myself. I put the Tyler folder in my file cabinet and reached out for Effie's tenant application, still sitting on my desk where I'd left it. A chill swept over me as I thought about the video surveillance I'd seen on the screen at Chad's apartment. He'd been watching these women, picking out his targets, from the comfort of his own home. With his girlfriend in the next room. It sickened me.

I scanned the application a second time, looking for anything I should have picked up on. Emergency Contact: Chad Keith. Place of Employment: Big Bro Security.

Big Bro Security. Chief Washington had asked me if I'd heard of them. I'd said no, but I should have said yes. They were listed right here.

I leaned forward and picked the receiver off of my yellow donut phone. With the end of a pencil, I dialed the number listed. After four rings, a recording came on. "Thank you for calling Big Bro Security. Home and office security that feels like family."

I hung up without leaving a message. I jiggled the mouse to my computer and waited a couple of seconds for the screen to wake up. As soon as I had an internet window, I typed "Big Bro Security, Dallas, Texas" into the search field. A website popped up. The main screen of the site was black with white words. A shield, not unlike a police badge, was by the left-hand side of their header.

Our 24-hour integrated monitoring system will identify threats to you and your loved ones before they have a chance to make a move. Going out of town? We'll watch your house. Don't trust the babysitter? We're more accurate than a nanny cam. Think your kids are partying when you're not there? We'll catch them in the act. Our cameras can be viewed via remote access or smart phone so we can be there when you need us. Big Bro—home and business security that feels like family.

I surfed the rest of the site, looking for Chad's name. No names were listed. For an operation that hung its hat on feeling like family, the website was decidedly impersonal. The colors mimicked those of the Lakewood PD: black, red, blue, white. The shield on the upper corner was a clear nod to police departments everywhere. I suspected it had been used for that purpose—to instill a feeling of trust. Their contact page had a web form to be filled out with email and comments, along with the same phone number that I'd called. Instructions on the site said the phone was not monitored by a live person, but that messages would be returned within twenty-four hours.

I clicked back to the About page. Big Bro Security was a relatively new company, started six months ago, but they claimed to have a combined total of fifty years experience. Chad Keith wasn't even half that old. So who were the other bros behind Big Bro Security?

Halfway down the page I found a barely noticeable link to their management team. I clicked the text and choked on my last swig of water.

Their founder and chief executive officer was former police officer Donna Nast.

TWENTY-SIX

Nasty owned Big Bro Security? With Chad Keith? Who had a computer monitoring the residences of his girlfriend, the exterior of the Landing where she'd been approached, my apartment building, and nine other locations around town?

Something in the water did not compute.

I felt around for my phone and called Nasty. "Donna, this is Madison. I need to talk to you about Big Bro Security. It's important." I waited a few seconds, just in case she was screening her calls. "Call me on my cell." I was halfway through the number when she picked up the phone.

"Madison," she said. No hello, no what's up. After all this time, I kind of felt cheated.

"What can you tell me about Big Bro Security?"

"Nothing."

"You're listed on their website as the CEO."

"I'm impressed. You had to spend at least four minutes on the site before you found that link."

"This is important. Do you know Chad Keith?"

"When I said I couldn't tell you anything about BBS, I meant it's none of your business."

It took me a second to process that BBS meant Big Bro Security.

"Okay, how about this? Chad Keith is in police custody. A carpet knife like the one used to threaten Effie—like the one that was probably used to murder Kate Morrow and Linda Gull, was found in his apartment. And the police discovered a computer room where he was watching illegal video feed of a bunch of places around town. And every one of those places has a connection to the Lakewood Abductor case."

"If any of this was true, I would have heard about it."

"How? You're not a police officer anymore."

"How do you know about it? I can't imagine the chief gave you a badge because he likes the way you dress."

"You know how I know? Because I was there. *I* found the knife under his sink. *I* saw the TV monitor. *I* called the cops."

"Shit, Madison, are you for real?"

"I wouldn't lie about something this important. Now, can you tell me anything?"

"Not over the phone. Meet me at the new taco restaurant on Greenville."

There were dog owners who were comfortable tying their pets up outside when they frequented local Dallas eateries. I was not one of them. Rocky was more a part of my life than most people I met, and if Nasty couldn't handle a table outside to accommodate his presence, then we were just going to have to take an extra moment to make it a nonissue.

Nasty arrived shortly after I did. She pulled her Saab up to valet parking and handed over her keys. With a toss of her long, brown-streaked-with-honey hair, she headed my way. The valet attendant made no secret of the fact that he was admiring the way she walked away from him. What she lacked in female bonding skills, she made up for with sex appeal.

She lowered herself into a chair and immediately reached for the glass of ice water. Her red lips left a transfer of color on the glass.

"Have you ordered?" she asked. "The tacos here are pretty good."

"I didn't come here for food."

"Fine." She twisted around and flagged a waiter. "I'll have the taco special. Carne asada, camarones, and pollo. Cebollitas and mango jicima slaw. And a margarita." She pronounced the words with the proper Mexican pronunciation, not the Americanized way.

The waiter looked at me and I waved him off. "Not hungry," I said. He frowned and left. She waited until he was inside before she leaned in close.

"Chad Keith works for me at Big Bro. He's part of my video surveillance team," she said, all traces of another language dropped from her speech.

"He's a college student."

"Smart one, too. He's the one who suggested we go remote access. My agents don't need to sit in front of a desk anymore. They just need access to a smart phone."

"So you set Chad up with the equipment he used to single out women to abduct and it doesn't bother you?"

"Keep up here, Madison. Chad wasn't singling out women to abduct them. He was watching the locations where abductions took place so he could make sure it didn't happen again."

"He—" I looked up at a spot on the roof over Nasty's head and pictured the screens. They had included the Landing. The Casa Linda parking lot. And the apartment building where Effie and I lived until we'd both moved out.

The waiter approached with her margarita and she leaned back so he could set the glass down. She sipped at it while he fussed with the silverware on the neighboring table, then resumed our conversation after he went back inside.

"We're a relatively new business," Nasty said. "I need clients. When the first report came in that Kate Morrow was abducted from outside the organic foods store, I approached them. They weren't interested."

"You saw the abductions of women around Lakewood as a business opportunity?" I leaned in, and then caught myself. My disgust of the concept had overridden my couth. I made a conscious effort to sit straight in my chair and keep calm.

"I saw the abductions of women around Lakewood as

validation that we need more security in this area. I would think you'd appreciate that. You were attacked by a killer in your own apartment. You were shot outside of one of Dallas's oldest and most respected condominiums. You might be the only woman in Dallas who *doesn't* think additional security around town is a good idea."

Her words were cold and calculated, but in a way, accurate. And I hated that about her. Nasty had a way of cutting through the fibers that clustered around rational things and emotional bonds. It was probably what had allowed her to turn her back on Tex. She was a classic Dallas bombshell on the outside, but inside it was like she was a machine.

Except I knew she really wasn't.

In the past, Nasty and I had had more than one heated exchange about my relationship with Tex. In territorial style, she'd warned me away from him. And when I asked her to help him, she warned me off. Now I knew why.

"You're doing this to help Tex," I said suddenly. "You said you wouldn't get involved. You called me an enabler for trying to help him, but you're doing it too. Just in your own way."

She tore her gaze from my face and looked inside, as if her impatience had something to do with her tacos. I knew better. I'd hit the nail on the head.

The waiter saw her and pointed down behind the counter. He used a towel over his hand to pick up a white plate and carried it outside to our table.

"I changed my mind," I said after he cautioned her that the plate was hot. "Can I have what she's having?"

Nasty looked up from her food, surprised.

"Yes, ma'am," he said. He disappeared back inside.

"I have a feeling this conversation is going to take longer than I originally anticipated. Please, start without me." I waited until she'd taken a bite to continue. "I'm right. I know I'm right. You didn't turn your back on him."

She chewed silently, and then washed her first swallow down with a gulp of margarita. "I'm not on the force anymore, but I have ways of finding out information. I knew things were bad for him. I didn't know how bad they were until you called me." She took another bite of her shrimp taco. Juices from the salsa ran out the end and drizzled on top of the carne asada taco still sitting on the plate. She swallowed a second time and set what was left of the first taco down. "You said you found the curved knife at Chad's. Tell me about that."

Swapping stories with Nasty was about as far from normal as I could have planned my evening. I kept thinking about the note from Tex left under my windshield, and the possibility that there was something that I'd be able to report to him if I met up with him at the graveyard. Except it was no longer an if. It was a when.

"There's not much to tell. Effie moved in with Chad and when I went to visit her yesterday, she asked if I'd come back today with Rocky." Upon hearing his name, Rocky's head lifted up and he looked at me expectantly. I bent down and ran my open hand over his fur. "They were having fun getting reacquainted, so I excused myself and went to the bathroom." I left out the fact that it was an emotional need, not a biological one, that had taken me there. "I looked under the sink for a towel to dry my hands. When the cabinet door opened, the knife fell out."

She looked at me like I was making it up. "The knife had been wrapped in a towel and propped on top of some rolls of toilet paper. It fell. The towel opened up and I saw the tip of a curved blade, just like Effie described the night she was approached at the Landing."

Nasty had been reaching for her margarita, but she stopped and looked up at me. "The Landing," she repeated. "That's a new gig. That was Chad's sign-up."

I didn't like the look on her face. "Tell me how you approach businesses to hire you."

"I have a team of security agents—mostly college guys, because they're hip to computers. Gamers, you know? Security and surveillance are an easy fit for them. There's an incentive structure, like a bonus system, for anybody who signs up new clients. Chad turned out to be the best, by far. He's earned over two grand in bonuses this month."

"So what you're saying is that the screen I saw that had live feeds watching different residences and businesses in Lakewood was legit. Those companies hired Chad to monitor them."

The waiter appeared with a second plate of tacos and a margarita. When I ordered what Nasty was having, I hadn't thought much about the drink, but now, in light of everything, I was happy to have it. I took a sip, set the glass down, and bit into a taco while the waiter dropped off the check.

Nasty's phone rang with an incoming call. Before she could snatch it off the table, I saw the display: Chief Wash.

"Aren't you going to take it?" I asked. "Chief Washington has your employee in custody. Chad must have dropped your name by now."

She wiped her mouth with her napkin and answered. "Donna Nast," she said. "Hi, Chief. I hear you picked up one of my employees today." She kept her bright green eyes trained on mine while the chief said something that sounded like one of Charlie Brown's teachers. "I'm sitting here having drinks with Madison Night." Pause. "Yeah, I know." She shook her head and I knew a joke had been made at my expense. "Don't go holding your breath." She laughed.

I took another sip of my margarita and pretended I didn't care.

"Sure. I can confirm that he's on my payroll, and that the video feed in his apartment is legit, if that's what you're asking." Again with the unintelligible response, and then Nasty pushed her chair out from under the table and jumped up and cursed. She plugged a finger into one ear and walked away from me. The waiter appeared by the door. She shot him a look that told him to go back inside. He did. She walked a few feet away from the restaurant, passing a woman with two children. She said a couple of not particularly ladylike expressions and hung up.

I wasn't about to let Nasty take off after a reaction like that. I tossed enough cash on the table to cover the bill and tip and grabbed Rocky's leash. When I caught up with Nasty, she was in the parking lot waiting for the valet attendant to bring her car around.

"What was that?" I asked. "What did he tell you?"

"You're going to find out anyway." She shook her head, as if she couldn't believe what she was about to say. "There's a reason Chad's been so successful at signing up new accounts. He and a friend have been using that carpet knife to scare patrons of local businesses, and following up the next day with a boatload of charm and a sales pitch."

"He's been—it was—he what?"

"You heard me. The only person Chad Keith has managed to hurt with his actions is me."

TWENTY-SEVEN

"Let me see if I understand this. Chad was using copycat scare tactics to drum up new clients?" I asked.

"He says he needed money. When the news kept talking about an abductor in Dallas, he got the idea as a way to get paid in bonuses. It worked, too. People are scared. Nobody wants to be known as the place a woman was abducted," she said. "So they signed on the dotted line."

"Walk me through how he did it."

"He says he bought a uniform from a supply company. He still had the receipt in his wallet. Sunglasses and a sheriff's hat so nobody could recognize him."

"And the carpet knife?" I asked, though I already suspected where it had come from.

"He said he took it from some old guy who'd had too much to drink."

Lyndy. He'd told me that his regular carpet knife was missing. That's why he had a new one tucked in the loop of his painter's pants. I'd been so put off by the appearance of the new one that I hadn't stopped to think what might have happened to the original.

"But Effie said he had a badge with Tex's name on it."

"He heard the mother of the first victim accuse Tex at the press conference so he made up a name tag. Literally printed it off on a computer and slid it into a plastic sleeve that he pinned on to the uniform."

"But he went after his own girlfriend. That's not normal."

"What part of this is normal? Chief Washington said Chad

thought it would be a joke. He thought she'd recognize him, but she freaked out and took off. Knocked him down when she backed out of the space. He never expected her to go to the police about it, and after that, he couldn't tell her it was him. But she was so shaken up that he wanted to make up for it, so he invited her to move in with him."

"But he kept the knife hidden under his sink."

"Chad might be sneaky, but I wouldn't say he's the sharpest tool in the shed. He said he was going to try to find the guy he stole it from and return it."

"The guy he stole it from is Lyndy. His daughters gave him that knife because he's a carpet layer. It's the last thing they ever gave him before they were killed in a car accident. And now the police are out there looking for him because of it. And if that's not enough, Lt. Allen's practically living in seclusion because his name has been linked to the abductions twice."

"Madison, Tex isn't the victim here. He'll survive this. Those missing women might not."

We stared at each other, considering what this meant. The valet attendant pulled up with Nasty's car. She got in and drove away. I gave her a good ten minute lead before I walked Rocky the opposite direction toward my own car. It was well into date night, and Greenville Avenue had transitioned from casual daytime activities to full on restaurant and bar hopping. I drove to Thelma Johnson's house and traded my straw hat for a light blue ribbon that I tied in a bow just above my bangs. I traded my ballerina flats for navy blue Keds and turned to Rocky. "I'm going to go visit Lt. Allen in a graveyard. You're not allowed in there so you have to stay here. I'll be back before you know it. Behave, okay?" I kissed him on top of his head, filled his bowls with food and water, and left.

Traffic had let up enough that I risked taking the highway. It was a straight shot down 75 to the Lemmon Avenue exit, right on Hall Street, and then the search for parking. A brown van, still sporting the seventies paint job of amber and rust diagonal stripes on the side, pulled out of a space. I slipped the Alfa Romeo in and cut the engine. The brown van turned the corner at the end of the street and disappeared.

The temperature had dropped. Years ago, living in Pennsylvania, I would have laughed at anyone who referred to a slight change in temperature as cool, but I'd adjusted to the Dallas temps as much as the next person. I wrapped my arms around each other, rubbed the sleeves to keep me warm, and headed to the entrance gates. The first thing I noticed when I reached them was the sign that said, "No Animals Allowed." The second thing was the locked gate. I peered between the black metal bars for signs that someone was inside waiting for me.

"Psssst."

I jumped. Tex approached me from my left.

"Took you long enough," he said. "Exactly what time do you think the sun goes down?" He reached in front of me to the padlock on the gate, inserted a key, and popped the lock open.

"How do you know I haven't been driving around trying to find a parking space?"

"Because I've been sitting in that van waiting for you since seven. If you'd have driven past, I would have seen you."

"*You* were in the van?"

"Don't just stand here, Night. Go inside and let me lock the gate behind us. The last thing we need is more attention." He glanced down at my light blue dress with the white Peter Pan collar. "You couldn't just wear black, could you?"

I went inside and let him fiddle with the lock. When he turned back around, he took off his jacket and handed it to me. "You're cold. Take this."

"I don't need your coat."

"Yeah? Well, I need you to not glow in the dark. So put this on for now, okay? Besides, the last time I went on a date with a woman dressed like Doris Day, it didn't work out so well for me."

"This isn't a date."

"You know what I mean."

"I bet that line doesn't work on a lot of women, does it?" I took the jacket and draped it over my shoulders. It smelled like a pizza oven.

"Hunan Palace wouldn't deliver to the van. Joe's Pizza did," he said.

"Lieutenant, I have to tell you about something that happened tonight."

"Chad Keith, Nasty's employee. I know."

"You know? About Big Bro Security and the carpet knife and Chad impersonating you?"

He nodded. "Nasty called. When she realized what he did she thought it was best that I heard it from her."

"If you already knew about Chad, why'd you ask me to come here?"

"I asked you to come here before I knew about Chad. I want to show you something. Follow me."

He studied my face, and then headed down a paved path that ran through the middle of the cemetery. The only light came from streetlamps in the neighborhood, enough to create eerie shadows over the graves and the leaves that blew around our feet. I followed a few steps behind him. I didn't know where Tex was taking me, and I didn't ask. Something was on his mind and, especially after last night, I didn't want to push him.

The cemetery was mostly populated with nondescript tombstones that indicated the lives of parents and children, but scattered among them were graves marked off by small flags. I stopped to look at one. "Confederate Soldier" read the star emblem on the metal flagpole, though the flag wasn't the Dixie that I'd come to associate with Confederate soldiers. When I scanned the rest of the graveyard, I picked out several of the unique flags.

"Every April, the Sons of the Confederate Soldiers gather in the graveyard and honor the soldiers who died. These flags were put up then." He put his hand on the small of my back and steered me away. "That's not why I brought you here."

We walked down the paved path and turned right where the pathways intersected. To the right of us was a stretch of graves all marked off with the American Flag as I knew it. Unlike the confederate soldiers who were scattered throughout the graveyard, these graves had been relegated to the back, facing the opposite direction.

I looked closely at the closest tombstone. The outline of a shield filled the concrete. The heading just under the top of the shield was the word "Lieut.," and in a curve underneath it was "Thom. Rexford Allen." Below that was a series of letters and numbers. I stood up and looked at Tex.

"These are the Union soldiers," he said. "And that's my great grandfather. I didn't know his grave was in here until I was sixteen. Nobody in my family wanted to talk about the fact that we fought for the Union." He was silent for a second. "When I walk through this cemetery, I don't see Confederate and Union soldiers. I see men who died in battle fighting against each other. Brother fighting brother. And that's a war that nobody wins."

"You know what I think? You're the person you are today—protector of the people, fighter of bad guys—because of your grandfather. That shield on his grave? It's just like the shield you carry every day. It means something."

He picked up a twig, studied it for a few seconds, and then whipped it into the air, over the tops of the row of graves.

"My mother was a drunk," he said. "She used to have men over all the time. They weren't nice men. I had to protect my brother and sister from that."

He turned his attention from the row of tombstones to me. It was the first time I could see the vulnerability in his expression instead of his cop mask or his flirtatious side.

"She had a stroke. The hospital kept her on life support for two months. They were waiting for me to be old enough to make the decision to pull the plug."

Through everything that had happened since I'd heard Mrs. Morrow accuse Tex of abducting her daughter on TV, I'd been able to see Tex, the man, more clearly. The decisions he'd had to make that defined him: protecting his siblings, having his father leave when he was just a child, watching his mother destroy their life. It made sense that he'd been drawn to the police department. To protect and serve. To establish control.

"Night, this thing with the Lakewood Abductor. It taught me something about myself. Something I didn't want to face. I'm not just a cop for now. I'm always going to be a cop. It's my life. Even after I'm not on the force, it's not going to change. It wasn't until that whole life was threatened that I realized how much I needed it."

"You found the thing that's most important to you. Most people never do."

"This guy, this killer, he made it personal when he planted a fake badge on Kate Morrow's body. Because of that, Nasty's employee printed up a name tag with my name on it. Now I'm sitting on the sidelines because that's the only way to help. But it's killing me. Living in a camper, trying not to be seen, waiting for the phone to ring to find out if anybody has a new lead. And I can't stop thinking that whoever is doing this is inside my head. Guys on the force are looking at me differently. It's like brother fighting brother all over again."

I heard the words he'd left unspoken. *And that's a war that nobody wins.*

"It's not always going to be this way. This guy is going to get caught. Chief Washington is on it. Whoever's doing this is running out of time."

"And what if he doesn't?" He reached up and tugged the collar of his jacket that was draped over my shoulders. "Night, you put a face on the people I swore to protect. You made it personal too. I can't do my job if it's personal."

"Is that the real reason why you won't tell me where you live?"

He looked down at me, and the ambient light from a streetlamp reflected off his steel blue eyes. In the darkness, they looked soulful, like the deep end of a swimming pool that had been painted black. I'd seen Tex when he was angry, and I'd seen him when he'd been flirtatious. I'd never seen the look I saw tonight.

"You wouldn't deserve the life I'd give you," he said. He flashed a half smile. "But don't think for a second I wouldn't like to know what you wear under those dresses of yours." He hooked his index finger into the collar of my dress and stood on his tip toes. I slapped his hand away.

"Lieutenant!"

"Come here," he said. He reached a hand around the back of my neck and pulled me in for a hug. The jacket fell from my shoulders and I felt his hands against my back through the thin fabric of my dress. I wrapped my arms around his lean, muscular torso and held tight.

In the distance, the sound of sirens pierced the quiet. They grew loud, insistent as they approached. Blue and white cop cars screamed past us and swung around the corner. Tex's arms dropped from me and his head snapped in the direction the cars had driven.

"Something happened," he said. "I have to get to the van and listen in on the scanner." He took two steps away from me and stopped, turned around, and looked at me. "Show's over, Night. Let's get out of here."

I followed him to the main path and out of the cemetery. He put his hand on my elbow, urging me forward. I stumbled over the roots of a tree but mostly kept up with him, until he stopped in my way and I ran smack into him.

"Why'd you stop?" I asked. I looked over his shoulder and let out a scream.

On the path between where we'd entered and where we stood was a woman, bound and gagged and unconscious.

Vic number four.

TWENTY-EIGHT

Tex dropped to the ground and felt her neck for a pulse. A flood of policemen ran toward the entrance to the cemetery. Guns were drawn. I threw my hands up in the air.

"Allen, get away from her," said an officer I didn't know.

"She's still alive. She needs medical attention," Tex said.

"Allen, you know the drill."

Tex ignored the instructions and worked at the binding over the woman's mouth. He cast the dirty rag aside when it was untied, and turned to me. "Give me my jacket," he said.

I felt around over my shoulders. It wasn't there. I looked behind me. I didn't see it.

"I don't have it anymore," I said.

The officer held his gun at his side. "This is the last time I'm going to say this, Allen. Stand up, put your hands up, and move away from the woman."

Tex's jaw clamped shut, but he did as the officer told him. After Tex had backed up, another officer came forward and checked the woman's pulse just as Tex had done. "Wave the ambulance through," he said behind him. A white ambulance with a red stripe and a Blue Cross logo eased down the narrow one-way street. Men and women in navy blue uniforms with gold lettering hopped out and attended to the woman.

"Who is she?" I asked. Several cops looked at me as if noticing my presence for the first time.

"Who are you?" the young cop asked.

"Madison Night," I said.

Tex cut me off with a wave of his hand. "Leave her out of it."

"You know I can't do that, Allen," the officer said. "She's present at a crime scene. I have to get her name and her statement."

"I'll get her statement," said Sgt. Osmond, materializing out of the crowd. I threw a thankful glance at him, and then turned to Tex.

He leaned close and whispered, "Tell them the truth, Night."

I leaned forward and kissed him on the cheek. "Everything's going to be okay," I said, just like Hudson had told me yesterday.

"How do you know that?"

"Because the good guys always win."

Osmond cleared his throat behind me. I left Tex standing by the gates of the cemetery and followed the sergeant to the sidewalk.

"Okay, Ms. Night, what happened here tonight?"

"You know he didn't do this. You know that, right?" I said.

"Ms. Night, I know you and Lt. Allen are—have a—" He stopped talking, apparently not sure what word came next in his sentence. "Don't make this any harder than it has to be."

"Lt. Allen is my friend," I said. "He's a good cop. You know that. Chief Washington knows he didn't do any of this. The more time you waste on Lt. Allen as a suspect, the more power you're giving the real abductor."

"Ms. Night, I still need your statement."

I looked back at Tex. He was talking to a couple of officers while the woman was moved to the back of the ambulance. He didn't look particularly happy about being separated from what had to be done, but he'd lost the look of hellfire that had been on his face when he first saw the body.

"He asked me to meet him here, so I did."

"What time?"

"It was after the sun went down, maybe eight, eight thirty? Around there. He has family resting in here. We were paying our respects."

"The cemetery is supposed to be locked at night. How'd you get in?"

"Lt. Allen had a key to the lock. He let us in and locked up behind us."

Sgt Osmond made a few notes. "How long were you in there?"

"I don't know. What time is it now?"

He checked his watch. "Quarter after nine."

"Sounds about right."

"Ms. Night, are we going to find anything incriminating when we go through the cemetery?"

"Like what?" I asked, and then suddenly flushed red when I realized what he was asking me. "Sergeant, I told you. We were there to talk about Lt. Allen's family, nothing more."

"So there's no evidence to place either of you anywhere inside those gates?"

"Yes, there is. Lt. Allen's jacket. He loaned it to me because I was cold. When we ran out, it fell from my shoulders. It's inside on the ground somewhere."

He nodded and capped his pen. "Thank you, Ms. Night. If you think of anything else, give me a call."

"Who is she?" I asked.

"Who, the woman? I don't know. I sure hope she's one of the abducted women we know about."

"What do you mean?"

"We have reports of five abducted women. Kate Morrow and Linda Gull were found dead. Cleo Tyler's going to make it. I don't know yet about this woman. If she's one of the five, then we can assume the perp is only holding one more woman. If she's not, then we really don't know how many women he's got."

Sgt. Osmond walked me to my car. I shook his hand and unlocked the car. There wasn't anything I could do for Tex. It was time to go home.

Rocky and I spent the night on the sofa at Thelma Johnson's house with the local news channel on the TV. I learned nothing I didn't already know, and I woke up with a neck so stiff I could only twist my head halfway to the side.

*   *   *

Crestwood Pool was closed on Sunday. I dressed in navy and white plaid pants and a navy blue belted tunic. I packed up Rocky and drove to Mad for Mod.

We stopped off for an ottoman that someone set out by the curb and arrived at the studio shortly after nine. I locked the ottoman in the storage locker out back and then opened Mad for Mod for business, even though it was early. Never underestimate the attention of a morning walker, I say.

I distracted myself for an hour by cleaning the furniture in the display area of the studio, but eventually found myself back in the office. I pinned the photos of the abducted women back on the wall of cork. Two of them had been murdered. Two of the women had been left alive. I now discounted Effie's encounter, knowing it was Chad, but her friend Barbie fit the pattern. As far as the police knew, she was the last missing woman.

I went to the recycle bin behind the studio and dug out the newspapers that had accumulated. Inside, I stacked them by date and flipped through, looking for information on the women who'd been abducted. Each time a report had been filed, a brief bio of the woman had accompanied the article and the growing list of safety precautions that were being issued by the police.

Kate Morrow: only child, visiting her mother.

Linda Gull: passing through Dallas on her way to meet friends in Shreveport.

Cleo Tyler: recently purchased a second home in the Lakewood area.

Susan Carroll: headed to the airport after a reunion weekend where she and her brothers celebrated their parents' fiftieth wedding anniversary.

Barbie Ferrer: after living in New Mexico for several years, she was moving back for a new job.

Kate and Linda were now dead. Cleo had been left in the

grocery store parking lot, and Susan had been dropped off behind at the cemetery, barely alive. What was the criteria that determined who lived and who died? The flip of a coin? If so, then how long until that coin was flipped for Barbie Ferrer?

I'd gotten immune to the impact of Dan Tyler hanging up on me and called Cleo.

"Cleo, this is Madison Night. How are you feeling?"

"Honey, I saw the report on the news about that woman they found at the graveyard. We need to talk. How fast can you get here?"

I hopped in my car and took off for Sweetwater Drive, parking in front of the Tyler residence twenty minutes later. Another pickup truck sat in the driveway. The sound of a power saw pierced the otherwise quiet Sunday morning.

Cleo met me out front. Today she wore a red one-piece bathing suit with cutouts on the side, loosely covered with a sheer sleeveless duster printed with giant Hawaiian flowers. Heavy makeup on her face hid what was left of her fading black eye. A gold band was wound around her upper arm like a coiled snake. Flesh-colored bandages were wrapped around each wrist, hiding the welts from the handcuffs.

After an exchange of hellos, Cleo said, "Madison, I'd like to apologize for my husband."

"You don't have to apologize. I'm sure he wasn't himself from the moment you were abducted."

"That's not it. He hasn't been himself since we came to Dallas. Truth is, I thought the change of scenery would do him good. He's been more and more self-contained lately and I don't know how to draw him out. Our colleagues have started to pick up on it, and we're losing business with the studio because of him."

"Where is Dan right now?"

"I sent him out for groceries. He won't be back for a few hours."

"He spends hours at the grocery store?"

"I gave him a list that encompasses four different stores. It's going to take him awhile."

"How are you feeling, Cleo?"

"Honey, I'm not saying I like being tested, but southern women are built to last."

"I'm sorry to ask this, but is there anything you remember from when you were taken? Did the man say anything to you? Anything that can help the police find the last woman?"

"I wish I could help, honest I do. He held something up to my face and I passed out. When I came to, I was blindfolded and sitting on the floor. I don't know where we were. The only thing I remember was him asking me about my family."

"He asked you about Dan?"

"He asked if I was married, if I had brothers or sisters, and if I had any children. I wasn't going to say a word, but that's when he hit me." She put her hand to where the makeup hid her bruised cheek.

"Cleo, I'm so sorry." I put my hand on her arm.

Cleo's words were clipped, as though she'd separated herself from the nightmare and was only able to speak in mechanical terms as if it had happened to someone else. I knew she'd been over it with the police and I didn't want to make her relive it.

"I'll survive. I wish I could remember something else that would help the girl who's still missing. The reporter on the news says she's twenty-five years old." She shuddered and took a long pull on her drink. "But this isn't why I wanted to talk to you. I need something to take my mind off of what happened, and as long as we're in Dallas, this house is it. The way I see it, there's only one thing to do. Pretend Dan never fired you, and get it into shape."

"Excuse me?" I said.

"I can't entertain in a half-finished house. The pool needs landscaping, the fireplace needs refinishing, and I still want my Japanese great room."

"Cleo, are you sure you're up for this?"

"Honey, I can't let myself stop and think about what happened."

"But Dan was quite specific about firing me."

"You leave Dan to me. Now, how soon can you start back up here?"

Aside from the whiplash a yo-yo might experience, I thought it best to seize the opportunity before her husband returned and changed her mind. "How's this afternoon? I'll call my contractor and we can start to tackle that wall of glass blocks."

"Perfect."

Cleo went back inside and I called Hudson. "Hi," I said.

"Hi."

"I guess you've heard about the woman they found outside of the graveyard last night?"

"Susan Caroll. They're saying she's going to make it."

"Hudson—are we okay?" He was silent for a beat longer than was comfortable. "Okay, different question. Professionally speaking, is there any chance I can convince you to do some work today?"

"Depends what you had in mind."

"Remember I told you about Dan and Cleo Tyler?"

"The Cliff May. I thought they fired you?"

"So did I, but the wife assures me that's not the case. She wants me to tear down a partition of glass blocks that was put in during the eighties."

"And you're sure there isn't something else going on there?"

"Cleo just went through a pretty nasty scare. I don't want to do anything to upset her, but I don't trust her husband. I can't predict his reaction when he sees me here working."

"You'd like to stack the deck by bringing me in to diffuse any residual hostility on the part of the husband."

"You're good at reading between the lines, aren't you?"

"One of my specialties. That's it?"

"Well, there's one more thing. There's a chance that they're interested in more than your carpentry skills." I told Hudson what Cleo had said about wanting to meet him to talk about the film rights to "our story." His laughter told me he wasn't too concerned.

We made arrangements for Hudson to swing by Mad for Mod to pick up the elements of the Asian interior that I'd left in the hallway. As I was about to hang up, he said my name.

"Yes?"

"We're okay. See you soon."

I unhooked Rocky's leash and he took off for the backyard and the sound of Daisy barking.

I headed straight for the bathroom to check the status of the pink fixtures. It had turned out beautifully. Once we added in white tile trim to the rest of the tile work, it would be heaven. I pulled my coveralls on over my outfit, pulled my hair into a low ponytail, and stuck the hardhat on my head. When I stepped outside of the bathroom, I found Cleo standing in the great room.

"Madison honey, the last time you were here you said you might want some help," she smiled. "This here's Jake. He's been looking for work and like I always say, the more the merrier!"

A man stepped out from behind the glass brick wall. My smile wasn't nearly as genuine as Cleo's. The new contractor was Jake—Jacob—Morris, the man Tex had tried unsuccessfully to arrest all those years ago.

TWENTY-NINE

"This is quite a coincidence," I said, my voice shaking. "I don't know if you remember me, but I'm Madison. We met at the pool."

"Of course I remember you," he said. He held out his hand and I shook it. He leaned in and said, "I'm the reason you got the job back."

I straightened up. "How's that?" I asked.

"I heard her and her husband arguing about their choice of decorators. He wanted you out but she wanted you here. After what happened to her, he'd agree to just about anything to cheer her up. I took a chance that there weren't many women named Madison who specialized in mid-century modern interiors, so I told her you were the best and she should rehire you. And then I added that she should bring me on board to make sure the job got done to her specifications."

"I have my own contractor," I said. "Hudson James." Out front, Hudson pulled up behind my Alfa Romeo. "That's him now."

"Like Cleo said, the more the merrier." Jake stood in the middle of the room, shirt off, jeans on. Safety glasses were pushed up on top of his head.

"Are you sawing in here?" I kept my voice steady even though my insides were dancing like teenagers on *American Bandstand*. I didn't want to be alone with Jake. I didn't want Cleo to be alone with Jake. I didn't know what he was capable of, and I didn't want to find out.

"Why not? You're going to demo that wall, right? So the whole place is going to need to be cleaned when we're done."

"Yes, but we need a path from the front door to the great room. When we demo the glass wall, we'll partition off the rest of the house so we'll make less mess. You're going to have to go outside."

"Sure, okay." He took the glasses off the top of his head and stuck them into the back pocket of his jeans. He unplugged the saw and lugged it out back.

I went out the front door and met Hudson halfway. Before he could say anything, I told him about Jake.

"You don't like him," Hudson said when I was done.

"I don't *trust* him." I told Hudson about the verbal assault the first day I'd met Jake at the pool, and how he'd followed me to my car and checked out the board with color streaks from Paintin' Place. I didn't have to find the piece of wood to remember that Mitchell had left a sticker with his store name and address on the bottom. "Now he's taking credit for getting me back on this job, but really he used me to get work for himself."

"There's something else bothering you about him, isn't there?"

"Tex arrested him for holding a woman against her will several years ago. There was a shootout and the woman died. The district attorney couldn't make the case stick and Jake went free. He moved to Arizona," I said.

"But now he's back in Dallas. When did he show up?"

"Right around the time the first body was found. He knew about my affiliation with Paintin' Place, and Cleo was abducted in the parking lot in front of that store. And now he's here in her home. She's probably not recovered from the whole experience. I have no idea why she's so trusting, but she is." I pulled the hardhat off of my head and set it on the floor. "I need to talk to her about this. She needs to know I have no experience working with that man."

I went outside and found Cleo lounging on her chair with a fresh mimosa in her hand. The portable TV was on a small tulip table in front of her, and Rocky and Daisy were resting on the concrete next to her.

"Cleo, where's Jake?" I asked.

"He's setting up the drill in the garage. Do you need to talk to him?"

"No, I need to talk to you."

"Sure, hon, what's on your mind?" She waved toward the other chaise and I sat down.

"Jake might have misrepresented his relationship with me."

"Honey, you don't have to explain anything."

"No, Cleo, I don't think you understand. I met him three days ago, and it wasn't a particularly nice first meeting."

She tipped her head to the side and her red hair cascaded over one shoulder. "Oh?"

"This isn't about me. Jake has a history with the law. He wasn't found guilty of anything, but you went through something pretty horrible recently, and I don't think it's a good idea for you to be so agreeable about a stranger coming into your house."

Cleo leaned forward and rested one elbow on her thigh with her hand cupping her chin.

"Honey, I'm not exactly sure what happened between the two of you, but Jake is my baby brother. I know all about why he moved to Arizona, but we're the reason he's here now. After I came home from the hospital, Dan asked him to move into the spare room so I wouldn't feel so alone."

If I hadn't been about to operate heavy machinery, I would have asked Cleo to pour me one of whatever she was drinking. Instead, I forced a smile onto my face and let her have her laugh. There was no way to describe how glad I was that Jake had already been relegated to the garage. If he'd have seen that exchange, I might have to quit and refund the Tyler money out of sheer embarrassment.

I rejoined Hudson in the living room. The unasked question of how it went was written on his face. I put my hand up, palm side out. "I don't want to talk about it." I picked up the hardhat and squashed it down on my head. Before Hudson could say another word, I took a rubber mallet and swung it at a concrete block that sat on the floor. The mallet bounced off the concrete without doing any damage.

"Demoing this wall would be more of an outlet," Hudson said. He held a chisel in one hand and a hammer in the other.

"I don't think you want to let me loose on that wall right now."

"It has to come down, right?"

We took the next half hour to frame out our work space with sheets of brown butcher paper from a construction roll taped to the ceiling and floor. After we'd created temporary walls around us, we used more paper to line the floor. Once the cocoon was complete, Hudson drilled a couple of holes into the mortar around the top left glass block. Next he tapped at the mortar with a chisel and hammer.

"Your turn. Break that glass block. It's going to feel good, but if we do this the right way, it's the only one you're going to get to break. I'm not sure you can control your destructive impulses at the moment." He grinned.

"Let me at 'em, let me at 'em," I said, winding up my fists like the cowardly lion pretending to take on the Wicked Witch of the West.

"Put on your safety glasses, gloves, and ear plugs and then give it your best shot."

I climbed up on the top step of a two step ladder and tapped the hammer against the block a few times to get a feel for it. After three taps, I put a little more energy into it. The block imploded into a thousand pieces. The hammer got caught in the remaining jagged glass edges.

I tapped against those that protruded up, knocking them inside with the others. When I'd cleared most of them, I looked down at Hudson.

"Done like a pro," he said.

"Are you sure we don't need to demolish all of them?"

"I'm sure." He handed me a chisel. "Tap the mortar around the block you broke until it feels loose. Once we get that block out, we should be able to take down the rest of the wall block by block."

It was a good thing I had Hudson with me. In my current

frame of mind, I would have shattered all three hundred and sixty blocks. His calming instructions would save three hundred and fifty-nine of them that could be resold to another contractor. I tapped the end of the chisel this time, more gently than I'd smashed the glass block. Soon I felt the mortar shift. When it was loose enough, I used my gloved fingers to dig away at the joint to free it and then lifted out the remaining scraps. I handed them down to Hudson and he put it in a black industrial garbage bag.

"Now follow the mortar joint across the top row. You should be able to loosen each block and lift them out one by one."

It was slow going, but it worked. I felt the sweat pour down from under my hardhat, down my neck, and under the coveralls. Dust from the mortar stuck to me. For the first time in days, the only thing on my mind was the project in front of me, not the missing women, not Tex's troubles, not the paint names for Paintin' Place, not what to do with the apartment building. Ah, the Zen of renovation. Forget *Eat, Pray, Love.* The title of my book would be *Eat, Swim, Demolish.*

Halfway down the wall, Hudson and I traded places. I handed him the chisel and the hammer.

"It's your turn now. Take your best shot."

"I'm saving my best shot for later," he said, and smiled. I smiled back. He took the tools and picked up where I'd left off.

I'd forgotten how well Hudson and I worked in tandem. When the last of the glass blocks were down, I used the industrial vacuum to suck up the residual dust and glass that might have fallen. Hudson tore down the paper walls and balled up the drop cloth. We'd been so absorbed in the project that neither of us noticed Dan standing in the room behind us. His lips moved but I couldn't hear what he said. Hudson pulled off his headphones and I remembered the ear plugs. I pulled them out.

"Have you been standing there long?" I asked. "I didn't hear you come in."

"Long enough," he said. "You two are quite the team. When Cleo said this wall had to come down, I couldn't stop thinking about people living in glass houses and throwing stones."

"There's not a whole lot that can't be accomplished with a little TLC," I said. I cut a glance to Hudson. Dan didn't miss it.

"Madison, can I talk to you for a second?"

"Sure. Hudson...?"

"I'll start stacking these blocks in the truck."

I stepped over the pile of tools on the floor and followed Dan down the hallway and out the back door. "Is something wrong?"

"I wanted to apologize for firing you. Truth is, I was sure that police lieutenant had something to do with what happened to Cleo, and your friendship with him put me over the edge. But now Cleo tells me that you were worried about Jake being here."

"Dan, nobody would blame you for being angry about what happened."

"When Cleo was in the hospital, she said you told her Lt. Allen took a bullet for you. Maybe he is a good cop, if there is such a thing. I'll never like the police, not after how I saw my brother change after he joined the force. He was dead inside before that accident ever happened—that's why he drank so much. Couldn't deal with what he saw every day. After he died, I joined a support group for families of police officers, but considering the circumstances, they shunned me. When I heard about Cleo, I wanted blood."

I looked across the pool at Cleo, who was holding a toy above Rocky and Daisy's head. The two dogs stood on hind legs trying to get at it. She tossed the toy into the yard and flipped her long red hair over her barely covered shoulder while they raced away.

"Madison, my wife hasn't been faithful to me for our entire marriage, and she isn't the type of woman to keep her indiscretions to herself."

"Doesn't that bother you? That she's unfaithful?"

"Sure, it bothers me. It makes me damn near crazy. But I love her, and I'd do almost anything for her." He pushed his hand up through his crew cut. "I was almost happy she was abducted. That was the first time in years she needed me to come to her rescue."

The idea that Dan Tyler could think of his wife's abduction as anything other than what it was made me ill. I smiled weakly. "I'm sure it will take a while before she can fully recover."

"I'm counting on that," he said, almost more to himself than to me. He watched her talk to Hudson by the pool while Daisy and Rocky ran around their feet. "Excuse me," he said. He left me by the back doors and approached the two of them. He put his arm around Cleo in a territorial manner. Even from a distance of fifteen feet, I saw her flinch with the contact.

Something was off about Dan. What he'd said felt practiced, like he'd rehearsed a speech to deliver to me so I'd understand his animosity. I couldn't blame him for how he felt after losing his brother, but he wasn't laying any of the responsibility on George for driving under the influence or causing the death of two innocent girls. It was as if he'd absolved his brother from any ownership of the actions that had led to his death.

With Jake in the garage and Cleo, Dan, and Hudson out back, I went further into the house. The scope of my decorating job included everything in the house save for the master bedroom, but now hardly seemed the time to concern myself with floor plans and rooms off limits.

The door to the bedroom was closed. I turned the knob and eased myself inside. The bed had been made in a haphazard manner, pajamas tossed onto the pillows on top of the blanket. An iPad sat on one nightstand, a sound machine sat on the other. A small dog bed was next to the side of the bed, and I recognized Daisy's toys in the center of it.

I moved to the closet and slid the mirrored doors to the left. Diaphanous pool cover-ups and a collection of jersey wrap dresses filled that side. I slid the closet doors to the right and found Dan's business suits. Nothing unexpected. I started to slide the doors shut when something unusual caught my eye. I reopened the closet and looked at the garment hanging behind the business suits.

A dark blue policeman's uniform.

THIRTY

I closed the doors and went outside. Dan stooped down on the ground ruffling Rocky's fur. Watching him play with my dog left me feeling dizzy. I dropped the hardhat and it fell to the deck with a clatter. Hudson rushed over to me. I smiled weakly.

"What's wrong?" he said.

"We need to get out of here," I whispered.

Dan crossed the yard and put his hand on my upper arm, his grip biting into my flesh. He spun me around and forced me to the front of the house. "What's the rush, Madison? Why are you in such a hurry to leave?"

I flung his hand off of my arm. "I saw the uniform, Dan. In the closet. It's you. You kidnapped your own wife and set it up so you could rescue her. Why are you doing this? Where are you hiding the other women?"

Hudson stepped between us. "Madison, what's this all about?"

"We need to call Chief Washington. Dan has a policeman's uniform hanging in his closet. He could be the Lakewood Abductor. He said he went out of town the day Cleo was taken, and he could have left her stranded in the Casa Linda parking lot so she'd be found. He wants her to need him. He set it up so he could rescue her."

By now, Cleo had joined us. Rocky and Daisy came with her. Rocky, in tune with my emotions, stood by my feet and faced Cleo and Dan in a show of solidarity.

"Dan? Is any of this true?" she asked.

Dan ran his hand over his short buzz cut hair and then turned to her, his back to us. "Cleo, baby, don't listen to her."

"But the uniform? And you being out of town when I was abducted. Does it mean what she said?"

Dan turned halfway toward us and stared me in the face. Hudson had moved closer to me. Dan looked at him for a second, and then at Cleo, and then back at me.

"That's my brother George's uniform. I've had it in storage for a long time. Being back here, having all of this drug up again, the anger came flooding back." He turned to Cleo. "I know you want this house, and I know you wanted to work with Madison and Hudson because of their past, but I don't know if I can do this."

"Our past?" Hudson said to me. I put my arm out and shook my head, silently telling him not to bring that up now.

"Where did you go when you left town on Wednesday?" Cleo asked.

Dan hung his head. "There's a support group in Austin. For families who've lost someone in law enforcement. I can't attend the meetings around here. These cops—they took George long before he died in that crash. But I needed to talk to somebody. I had to find a way to deal with the anger."

Cleo put her hand on her husband's arm. "You could have talked to me," Cleo said. "We're supposed to be a team."

"When's the last time we felt like a team, Cleo? When's the last time we turned to each other instead of turning to someone else?"

She ran her hand up and down his arm. "Maybe we should try to change that," she said softly.

He wrapped his arms around her and she nestled into him and hugged back. I stood there, awkward, wanting to leave but still feeling like something had to be said. Moments later, their embrace ended. Dan turned to me.

"All things considered, I think it's best if you hire another decorator," I said. "I'll put together a list of recommendations and refund the balance of your deposit."

"No," he said. "This is your job. I need to get over my demons. I promise I'll stay out of your hair until you're finished."

With the confession of what it was he'd been trying to hide came a visible change in Dan's appearance. His eyes looked wider, his shoulders looked softer, his smile looked more genuine. Was it the act of a psychopath who plays for the audience in front of him? Uncomfortable as I was, I needed to leave their property to process what had just happened.

"I think it's best that we call it a night," I said. I went inside, clipped Rocky's leash to his collar, and collected my belongings. Hudson stood by the front door waiting for me. Dan caught up with us after I'd rolled the coveralls up and shoved them into my hardhat.

"Madison," he called. "This whole Asian room is Cleo's idea and I want to give it to her. How soon can it be done?"

"It's going to take time to do it right." I calculated the time frame. I was thinking silver walls with a gold hand-painted pattern, like custom wall paper. To achieve the level of depth I wanted on the walls, it would take about four coats of silver paint, which would take a day to dry. Add in the time it would take Hudson to hand paint the detail on top of the undercoat, another day. We wouldn't even start on lighting until later in the week. Furniture and accessorizing would happen last.

"We could be done sometime next week," I said.

"I want it done on Friday."

"There's no way I can do that. It'll take twenty-four hours to do the basecoats and let them dry before Hudson starts on the hand painting. I haven't even picked out the paint yet."

"I thought you said silver and gold?"

"There's more than one shade of silver and gold," I said quickly.

"I'll have Jake pick something up tonight."

"No," I said with more finality than I'd planned. "I have an account at Paintin' Place, and I have some outstanding business to discuss with the owner. You know the store, don't you?" I studied his face for signs of a tell, but he didn't react.

"Jake can meet you at the paint store tonight," Dan said.

"That'll shave some time off the job."

"But—"

"Madison, either you can pick the paint tonight or Jake can pick the paint tonight. What time do you want him to meet you?"

There were few things I wanted less than to meet up with Jake at the paint store that night, but one thing I wanted more was to get out of there.

"Let's play it by ear."

"I'll wait to hear from you."

Hudson and I walked out together but climbed into separate cars and went opposite directions. I drove to the end of the street and called Tex. He didn't answer. "Meet me at Thelma Johnson's house," I said. "It's urgent."

The first thing I did after arriving was to check for evidence that Tex had been there. The same number of beers were in the fridge; the same number of soup cans were in the cupboard. The sheets, pillows, and towels were as I'd left them that morning. As far as I could tell, Tex had moved out. I left him a just-checking-in message and headed upstairs for a shower.

It took three rounds of lather and a washcloth to get the dirt from the construction site off of my skin and two rounds of conditioner to detangle my hair. After the sudsing, I stood under the nozzle and let the hot water pelt me. The release of working demo on Cleo and Dan's living room had been what I needed in order to think clearly.

And then, a color name popped into my head. One that I liked. And then another. Using my index finger, I wrote them in the condensation on the wall. When I got out of the shower, my normally fair skin was a bright shade of pink. I wrapped my head and body in towels and wrote the names on my mirror in a stubby pink lipstick.

They worked. I could hand them over to Mitchell tonight and cross something off of my list. Better yet, it was a something that had nothing to do with abducted women, cheating spouses, or police impersonators. It was something that represented Mad for

Mod and me.

As a counterpoint to the coveralls and hardhat look, I dressed in a fitted black and white checked cotton dress that belted at the waist and ended just below my knees. The dress had a matching blazer lined in yellow silk. I added a yellow flower pin to the lapel and buckled a pair of black patent leather T-strap shoes on my feet. Even though there was a matching checkered hat on the shelf of my closet, I rooted around in a bin of ribbons until I found one that matched the lining of the jacket. I placed it under the back of my hair and tied it in a bow on top.

When I went downstairs, I found Tex in my kitchen. Rocky sat by his feet, and an open bottle of beer sat by his right hand on the countertop.

"I came by to return your keys," he said.

"Keep them."

He tapped his finger on top of a set of keys on the table and then slid them toward me. I made no move to take them. Behind me, the clock ticked off the passing seconds.

"Lieutenant, I think the abductions have to do with family. According to the newspaper, Susan Carroll was here to celebrate her parents' anniversary with her brothers, and I found out today that Cleo Tyler's brother is Jacob Morris."

Tex registered surprise at this, but I continued. "Kate Morrow was an only child and she was killed."

"What about Linda Gull?"

"I don't know. The paper only said she was on her way to meet friends in Shreveport. If it turns out she's an only child, then that could be the determining factor in whether these women live or die. Can you call the chief and ask him?"

Tex shook his head.

I didn't understand his reticence. "You don't think this is worth investigating?"

"I quit the force today. Effective immediately." He held a hand out to stop me from interrupting him.

"But last night you said—"

"Last night I was a cop with orders to stay out of an open investigation. Today I'm not."

"No!" I said, slamming my closed fist down on the kitchen table. Tex stood up and walked around behind me, looking out the window at the property next to mine.

"Somebody is destroying everything I stand for, and as long as I'm on the force, I have to sit on the sidelines and give up control. I can't do it. There's still one vic out there but we have no way of knowing this guy's next move."

"You have to trust the system."

He picked up his beer bottle and threw it at the backsplash over the sink. The glass shattered and beer sprayed the counter. He put his hands down on the edge of the sink and stared at the drain. "The system's not working, Night. I *was* the system. Now I'm just a guy."

"Damn it, Lieutenant, you're not just a guy. You're the person who swore to protect the rest of us from whatever threats are out there. You're the person who's supposed to make it okay for the rest of us to sleep tonight."

"Not anymore."

"I don't believe this for a second. Last night you told me you were a cop. You were always going to be a cop. You said even after you retired, it was who you were. What happened in the past twenty-four hours to make all that change?"

He yanked several paper towels from the roll, pushed the broken glass into a pile, and dumped it into a plastic bag. He wiped down the counter with the sponge from the sink, making sure the beer and the residual shards were gone. He was holding something back. His ability to turn off, to block me from his world when I was trying so hard to help him, infuriated me, and I raised my voice in a desperate attempt to get his attention.

"Don't shut me out, Tex. I know what it feels like to be alone. I know what it feels like to think you have nobody."

"Night, if I'd have met you twenty years ago when your parents died, I would have made sure you never felt like you were alone."

"But I'm not alone anymore and that's what matters. We all get to make choices."

"And I made my choice today. Finding this guy is something I have to do. Now I don't have to answer to the chief or to the city. I can't risk anybody else getting hurt. That's *my* choice."

He stood up and let himself out the front door. The spare set of keys remained behind on the kitchen table.

THIRTY-ONE

If Tex had expected me to follow him outside or beg him to reconsider, he'd be let down.

I couldn't force him into seeing things differently than he did. I could only hope that after this was over, he could return to the job that defined his life.

Just like I needed to return to mine. I made my color name choices slightly more official by writing them on Mad for Mod letterhead, smiled at all four names, and folded the paper in thirds. I slipped it into an envelope and into my handbag.

Next, I called the police department. Officer Iverson answered. I identified myself and asked to speak to Chief Washington.

"He's in a meeting. You want to leave a message?"

"No, thanks," I said.

"You heard about Lt. Allen didn't you? That's why you're calling."

"Does it make sense to you?" I asked.

"He was a couple months shy of retirement eligibility. I have a good twenty years before I'm at that point, but I can't see throwing it all away in the last couple of weeks. I didn't figure him for the type to quit, but a case like this messes with a cop's head."

"Are you guys any closer to finding Barbie?"

"I'm sorry, Ms. Night. You know I can't talk about the investigation. Did you get that tail light fixed yet?"

"Yes."

"Good. I'll tell the chief you called."

I thanked him and hung up.

*   *   *

Paintin' Place was due to close by six. I made a quick phone call and told Mitchell I had what he wanted but would only deliver those paint names in person. He agreed to stick around until I arrived. I told him my shopping list, and he said he'd start pulling the supplies needed for the job so all that would be left for me was the selection of the paint. I collected Rocky and we headed to the store.

The lot was close to empty. I swung my car around in an arc and backed into a space in front of the paint store. Mitchell met me by the front door.

"Hey, Madison, you're finally going to deliver? You weren't pulling my leg, were you?"

"Not pulling your leg." I pulled the envelope out of my handbag and gave it to him.

He unfolded the sheet of paper. "Beach Party, Lemon Twist, Cherry Rocket, and Cool Cat." A smile crept over his face. "Gotta admit, I was expecting something more along the lines of Yellow Yikes and Retro Red. But these," he flapped the sheet of paper back and forth, "these have style."

"So we're good?"

"Better than good. I'll drop the names onto the labels and send them to the printer. We'll go into production with the paints within a week. If these sell, maybe we can talk about carpet samples."

I held my hands up in surrender. "One thing at a time, Mitchell. You wouldn't want this collaboration to go to my head."

We consulted about gold and silver paint swatches for a couple minutes, and I narrowed the decision down to two. He suggested adding crushed mother of pearl to the paint for added luminosity and rolled out a sample on a piece of scrap wood. I called Hudson while I waited for the paint to dry.

"Are you busy?" I asked. "I'm at the paint store, and I'm caught between gold number twelve and gold number seventeen."

"I thought they closed at six."

"I promised Mitchell a product endorsement if he'd wait for

me."

"Tell you what. I'll meet you there in a couple of minutes if you'll agree to come over for dinner when we're done."

"Sounds good."

The store's front door chimes rang after I hung up. Mitchell was using a blow drier on the paint samples and didn't hear it. I turned around. Jake stood in the doorway. In a flash I was enveloped in hot fear that prickled my skin from my ankles to my hairline.

"Jake. I told Dan I'd call you when the supplies were ready."

He came closer. "I wanted to talk to you. Alone."

I looked at Mitchell, and then back at Jake. "Hudson—you met him today—is on his way over to help with the final decision."

"It'll only take a minute to say what I need to say."

Mitchell set the plank of wood down and moved to the register, where I'd stacked a package of drop clothes, a dozen paint trays and liners, and several rollers and brushes. As long as he stayed in the store, we wouldn't be alone.

"What's on your mind?" I asked.

"Your friend at the pool, he's a cop, isn't he?"

"Yes."

"Sgt. Allen."

"It's lieutenant now," I said, ignoring the fact that for the past several hours, Tex didn't have a title that connected him to the force.

"He made a lot of trouble for me a few years ago."

"From what I heard, you made that trouble for yourself."

"Did he tell you about Stephanie? About how she died?"

Even though I hadn't heard the name before, I knew immediately that Stephanie was the woman who had been behind the sofa, the woman who had been killed by the stray bullet fired from Tex's gun.

"Yes."

Jake looked away. "I made a lot of mistakes back then. I never thought anybody would die. But when that bullet went through the sofa, I was more scared than I'd ever been. Her little brother came after me. He couldn't have been more than fourteen. He said I'd pay for getting her killed and I split."

"Who was he?"

"I don't know. She told me she came from an abusive family. She never mentioned a brother. I think that's why she was willing to run away with me. She liked the idea of a fresh start. At least she did at the beginning."

"You kept her there against her will."

He looked down at the toes of his shoes. "She wanted to leave and I wouldn't let her. We had a fight. Her death was an accident, but I'm more to blame for what happened to her than your friend the cop."

"After the case went to trial, you left Dallas. Why'd you come back?"

"Cleo tracked me down when our parents died. She said she was buying a place in Texas and I could stay here when they were in Los Angeles. After years of having nobody, of staying away from this area because of what happened, I wanted to have a sister." He studied me for a moment. "Madison, I can't bring Stephanie back. I can't change any of that. But I put it all behind me. I'm just a guy looking for a break. You know what that feels like?"

Hudson's truck pulled into the lot and parked next to my car. Mitchell pointed to the door and Hudson nodded and came inside. He looked at Jake and then at me.

"Perfect timing," I said. I raced to him and pulled him outside. I didn't say another word until we were in his truck.

"You want to tell me why you just ran away from Jake?"

"I'll tell you over dinner."

"What about the silver paint?"

I pulled two swatches from my pocket. "Pick one and we'll call it in."

Hudson drove out of the parking lot to Brick House, a small brick oven pizza place down the road. I didn't miss the way he scanned my outfit as we walked inside.

"There aren't many women who can look as good in coveralls and a hardhat as they do in a 1960s power suit."

"You have a preference?"

"Yes, but I'm keeping it to myself."

We decided on silver number seventeen. I called Mitchell while Hudson ordered a pizza. Mitchell said he'd have the paint ready in an hour and would stack the cans in the back of my car while Hudson and I ate.

We sat in a booth across from each other, waiting for our food. Hudson fiddled with the wooden napkin dispenser that sat on the side of the table, straightening the rods that jutted up and leveling the piece of wood that ran between them, holding down the pile of napkins.

"You want to talk about why you left Paintin' Place so suddenly?"

"Not right now."

I took a swig of water. *I'm just a guy looking for a break.* Jake's words rang in my ears. That had been Hudson when I first met him. Was I guilty of letting Jake's past mistakes color my opinion of him now? A woman was dead because of him. But I knew he was on Tex's radar. I knew the whole force was aware that he was back in town, and if Jake Morris came close to breaking a law, they'd catch him.

"Okay, new subject. Are you still thinking about selling the apartment building?" he asked.

I welcomed the shift in conversation. "I'm leaning toward it. The memories—they're not all good."

"So why haven't you?"

"They're not all bad, either."

He reached his hands across the table and set them on top of mine, their warmth squashing the last of my nervousness from seeing Jake at the paint store. If there were other people in Brick House, I didn't notice.

As Hudson and I stared into each other's eyes, the rest of the world dropped away, which only became an issue when the waiter cleared his throat to let us know he was next to our table with the pizza.

I enjoyed the company and the change of pace from Chinese food and dug in. For the first time in a week, I relaxed. We took what we didn't eat, and Hudson drove me back to the paint store. We both got out of the truck, and he walked around the back of the car while I counted the number of paint cans in the back seat. Alongside the cans of silver and gold that we'd phoned in sat cans of the taupe Beach Party, red Cherry Rocket, yellow Lemon Twist, and turquoise Cool Cat. Mitchell must have blended them after we left as a thank you.

"Your tail light is out," Hudson said.

"No, it's not. It was fixed on Thursday." I joined him at the back of the car. The red plastic tail light cover was snapped in half, part of it missing.

Hudson bent down and found the broken piece of plastic on the ground. "Must not have been put back on properly. The light here's no good. You want to leave your car? I'll take you home tonight and fix this in the morning."

"Not necessary. You go ahead, I'll be right behind you."

I climbed in and started the car. Hudson pulled out of the lot and I followed. Seconds after I backed out of my space, the engine sputtered and died. I disengaged the key and then started the car again. This time the engine wouldn't even turn over. I pumped the gas pedal, but nothing happened. I fished my phone out and called Hudson. He didn't answer. I left a message and called AAA. The operator took my name and location and listened as I described the problem.

"Sounds like you're out of gas," she said.

"That doesn't make sense. I just filled the tank yesterday."

"I'll send a service truck out. He should be there in about thirty minutes. You'll receive a courtesy call on this number when he's close."

"Thank you." I hung up. The car was close enough to being in a parking space that I didn't have to worry about pushing it, but I didn't like being alone in the Casa Linda parking lot. The next call I made was to Hudson's home phone. "I'm going to be late. The engine died and AAA is on their way," I said to his answering service.

In the corner of the lot, I saw Tex's Jeep. I got out of the car and headed there on foot. A uniformed police officer stood by the driver's side window, leaning against the car. As I got closer, I recognized Officer Iverson. He looked up at me and I waved. He said something to Tex, nodded, and met me halfway.

"Madison, what are you doing here?"

"Car trouble. I'm waiting for AAA."

He put his arm up to block me, and then turned me around the other direction. "Tex doesn't want to talk to you."

"I'm not going to lecture him. I just want to make sure he's okay."

"Take my word for it. He's okay. It's been a rough day and he wants to be left alone."

My phone rang. I excused myself and answered. The AAA operator said my driver would be arriving within the next few minutes. I thanked her and hung up.

"They're close. I should be getting back over there," I said to Officer Iverson.

He escorted me back to my car. "I thought you said you fixed that tail light."

"I did. Thursday."

He pulled on a pair of gloves and snapped what was left of the light off the car. "So this happened recently?"

"It probably happened tonight. The other half was sitting under the bumper." I pointed to the piece of plastic that sat inside the car on the back seat. He picked it up and held the two pieces together. They made a perfect fit.

Iverson pursed his lips and tipped his head to one side, and then the other, as if he was weighing what I'd said. He held up the broken plastic. "These should be dusted for prints. Maybe our guy is getting sloppy."

"Officer, you're keeping an eye on Jake Morris, aren't you? He was here tonight. He might have been alone with my car."

"We're aware of Mr. Morris's return to Dallas. Now, about this tail light, don't think I'm going to go easy on you."

"It'll be fixed tomorrow. I promise."

"I'm going to make it my personal agenda to make sure you're not lying to me."

The AAA truck pulled into the lot. I said goodbye to Iverson and he left us. I showed my membership card and the driver ran a couple of tests on my car. "Out of gas," he said.

"I just filled it yesterday."

"How long have you had this car?"

"A couple of weeks."

"I'd take it in to the shop. Seems to me you might have a leak." He pulled a red gas can out of the back of his van and poured its contents into my tank. "That'll get you to the nearest station," he said. "If you have a leak, I wouldn't try to go much farther than that."

When he was finished, I drove out of the lot to the gas station on Buckner. I pulled up to the pump and reached into my handbag for my wallet. It wasn't there. I looked on the floor, and behind the seat. No wallet. Had I left it in the paint store? I leaned back and thought about it. No, I had a standing account with Paintin' Place. There'd been no need to use a credit card. And Hudson had paid for dinner.

I moved my car to a space near the air pump. I felt between the side of the passenger seat and the door. No wallet by the door. I felt under the seat. A police car pulled up behind me and Iverson got out.

"What's the problem now?" he said with a smile.

"I can't find my wallet," I said.

"Doesn't seem like it's your night."

"No, it doesn't."

"Looks to me like somebody cut your fuel line."

"What?"

"Come take a look," he said.

I got out and shut the door behind me, and then, too late, realized my mistake.

He'd gotten me out of the car.

THIRTY-TWO

Iverson stood by the back tail lights. His police cruiser was parked catty-corner behind me, leaving me nowhere to go. He pointed to the ground where a puddle was forming from a drip underneath my car.

"I'd loan you money for gas, but there's no telling how much good it'll do you. How about you hop in and I'll give you a ride?"

He acted cool—too cool. It was like he was detached from what was happening—aloof and calm and emotionally bereft. Conversely, adrenaline coursed through my arms and legs. In that moment, I saw the pair of handcuffs that dangled from his left hand, a hand that he kept close to his side so I wouldn't see it. And I knew. We were alone in the parking lot to the side of a Mini Mart. He'd cut my fuel line, so even if his car hadn't parked me in, I couldn't get far. My handbag with my phone was on the floor of the passenger side of my car—too far to reach.

"Get in my car, Ms. Night." His voice was dead, like it had been programmed.

"No," I said. "I'm not going voluntarily." I had to keep calm. I had to figure out something before Iverson got me into his car. I looked over his head. I couldn't see inside the shop from where we were, and any cars on the road wouldn't be able to see me.

"You were one of the lucky ones," he said quietly. He reached into the back seat of my car and pulled out a black plastic trash bag that had been stashed behind the cans of Cool Cat and Beach Party. I hadn't put it there. He must have anticipated this very encounter from the minute Hudson and I left the paint store. "You could say

Lt. Allen saved you. When I pulled you over, you were just another woman to me. Then you mentioned his name. Ironic, isn't it? That the same man who killed my sister is the one who saved your life." He fed his arm into the trash bag and then pulled his gun from the holster.

"Your sister? The woman Jake Morris was hiding in his apartment was your sister?"

"Stephanie." His voice hitched, and he stepped toward me. I stepped back. "She left me alone when she went off with him. And now she's dead and I'm alone again."

He didn't have to explain what he meant. Jake had said that Stephanie came from an abusive family. She ran away and left Iverson to fend for himself. He'd been fourteen at the time. Whatever he'd lived through in those fourteen years had turned him into a killer.

"Lt. Allen was at that house to save your sister. He heard her call for help."

"I've heard his story," he said. "His shift was over. He should have walked past. I kept a watch on her. I would have saved her. He had no business going inside."

"But you're a police officer now. You know he only went inside because he thought she needed help. Just like he's trying to find Barbie Ferrer—" I stopped. "Where is she? Where are you keeping her?"

"It ends where it started," he said. His voice remained flat, lifeless. He pulled a rolled up wool blanket from the back seat and folded it around the gun.

"You abducted women. You killed at least two. It couldn't all be to frame Lt. Allen."

"My sister was abducted. The police didn't save her, they killed her. That's what I relive over and over."

Realization dawned on me. "You kill the women who have no siblings. You release the ones who have brothers and sisters." He was tortured by his own sister's death when he was fourteen. He protected the sisters of families from living through the nightmare of loss he'd dealt with, but murdered the women he thought no one would miss.

"Your sister wasn't abducted. She left with Jake voluntarily. She wanted to get away. She would have come back for you."

"You know your fate, Ms. Night."

He spoke my name with the same detachment he spoke of life and death. I remembered his words in front of Jumbos. *When will this end? When justice is served.* He saw himself as justice.

Without warning, Iverson lunged at me. The handcuffs snapped onto my wrists. I pulled away. He was faster than I was. He jerked on the links between bracelets. I fell forward. He pushed me back. My thigh bounced off the side of the car.

Fear clouded my mind. My hands were cuffed together and I couldn't think. A car appeared on the road. I turned to look at it and heard a faint gunshot. I looked back at Iverson. He'd shot out my right rear tire. He moved to the right and fired at my front tire, and then tossed the blanket in the front seat of my car.

"You almost spoiled everything, you know that? I marked your car like I marked the rest of them—broken tail light, out-of-state plates. Single woman in her late forties. No family. No anybody. You would have been perfect. Who would have come looking for you?"

Inside, a rage bubbled up to the surface. I stood perfectly still. The only thing within reach were the paint cans stacked in the backseat of my car. A bullet would tear through the aluminum like a hot knife cutting through butter.

"What about Tex?" I asked.

He laughed. "Your precious lieutenant isn't available to save your life tonight."

"Where is he?"

"Two women missing. Which life is more valuable? You? Or Barbie Ferrer? He knows about her. He'll find out about you on the news."

He spoke Barbie's name with a quiet reverence. Barbie, I knew, had a sister. She had a family. In Iverson's world, she was going to live and I was going to die.

Time stood still. I grabbed the handle to the can of Lemon Twist. Iverson aimed. I swung the paint can at him. It clipped his elbow. The lid came loose and bright yellow paint flooded the ground. The gun fired past me. I grabbed a second paint can and threw it. He fired again. Beach Party exploded on impact, sending taupe paint through the air.

I ran to his police cruiser. He tackled me. I clawed at the ground, trying to get away from him. The handcuffs made it difficult. His fingernails bit into my calves and yanked me backward. The flesh of my knees and thighs burned as I was pulled over the loose gravel. I twisted and kicked wildly, terrified.

"We both know how this is going to end, Ms. Night. Don't make it harder than it has to be."

I hated the way he said my name, how he maintained the professionalism of the police force while his hand moved up my leg and gripped the back of my thigh. My stomach turned. I relaxed for a moment, and then shot my foot out at him. My patent leather shoe connected with his head. He screamed. I scrambled back up and ran to his cruiser.

The keys were still in the ignition. I threw the gear shift into reverse. A gun fired. The car rocked to the right. In the rearview mirror I saw Iverson stand and approach. He was grotesque, his face bloodied and his uniform now covered in taupe paint. I stomped on the pedal but my shoe, slick with my own coating of paint, slipped off the surface. Iverson fired at the left tire. The car shuddered and stalled.

I twisted the key and pumped the gas. "Come on, come on, come on," I said. The car jerked to life. Iverson was directly behind me. I threw the car in reverse and slammed into him. Even after I felt the collision, I kept my foot on the pedal. The tires jumped the curb in front of the Mini Mart and plowed through the corner of the building. The airbag deployed and smacked me in the face and that's the last thing I remembered.

THIRTY-THREE

To count among my least favorite experiences was waking up in a hospital bed. I left as soon as the staff was comfortable that I could manage my pain at home. The physical injuries I sustained would heal in time. The emotional ones would too. Iverson had called me one of the lucky ones. I couldn't help but be reminded of those who hadn't been as lucky: Kate Morrow and Linda Gull, now dead. And those who had lived: Cleo Tyler, Susan Carroll.

Barbie Ferrer had been found chained to the back of the sofa in the same house where Iverson's sister had died. He'd bought the house years ago but had left it unattended. If Tex had noticed anything unusual about it on his drive-bys, lives might have been saved. But Iverson had been hip to what people would notice and what they wouldn't, and he used that knowledge to stay under the radar while keeping hostages. Each woman would be forever scarred by the memories of their imprisonment. I suspected feelings of paranoia and mistrust would haunt them far longer than they'd been held captive.

I had an odd pair of caretakers: Hudson and Lyndy. It seems that while on painkillers, I'd refused Hudson's offer to stay with him until I was well, so instead, he brought me to my apartment building. Lyndy joined him. Something about me reminding him of his daughters. The thought was both heartbreaking and touching at the same time, so I accepted his kindness.

I knew from the news that ran on the small television set in my hospital room that Officer Iverson—just Iverson now—had been pronounced dead on arrival. Chief Washington and Sgt. Osmond had visited me and I'd told them what I'd learned in that parking lot. Iverson's sister had been abducted when he was fourteen. Tex had worked the case. Iverson had been drawn to the force to protect and serve to try to avenge her death, but he couldn't handle what he saw on the job. Tex had predicted it when he said he didn't know what the job would do to Iverson in the long run, but he'd been blind to the fact that the long run was also the here and now.

Any consolation I could have taken from knowing the abductions were over was trumped by the knowledge that I'd killed a man. That's what *I'd* have to live with for the rest of my life. It made me a different person than the one I thought I was, and it made me rethink a whole lot of things about what it meant to be an independent forty-eight-year-old woman.

The sun streaming through the bedroom curtains told me it was afternoon, and the empty feeling in my stomach told me I was hungry. I was in a pair of yellow cotton PJs, and I pulled a lightweight robe on top of them and went to the living room. Rocky bounded into the hallway and almost knocked me over.

"Well, look who's awake," Hudson said. He sat at my dining room table with Tex, Lyndy, and Dennis O'Hara, the realtor I'd called to list the building. A pile of poker chips sat in the middle of the table. Hudson set his hand of cards face down. I recognized the deck; the cards were printed with orange and green daisies.

"You never have a camera when you need one," I said. My legs collapsed under me and I caught myself on the turquoise sofa. Three of the four men jumped up to help me. Tex remained seated.

"Lt. Allen, can I see you outside for a moment?"

He pushed his hand over his dark blond hair and leaned back in his chair. His eyes connected with Hudson's, who nodded once. Tex stood and left the room.

"I'll be right back," I said to the remaining men. I followed Tex out of the apartment and into the hallway. It smelled vaguely of paint. Tex descended the stairs faster than I did, and I caught up with him in the parking lot. A mist hung in the air, indicating that rain had either happened while I was asleep or was on its way.

"Night, I don't know what to say," Tex said.

"You don't have to say anything."

"I bought into Iverson's act. He fed me just enough information to keep me distracted. I knew the job was taking its toll on him but I didn't know why. I didn't even see that every time a body showed up, he was there. I should have seen the rest. I should have been there."

"No, you shouldn't have been. It was not your investigation. You should have been anywhere *but* there. So I don't see what the problem is."

He turned to me, and I saw loss in his eyes. "Because of his vendetta against me and the force, women died. Blood was shed. You almost died. I trusted him and that put you in danger."

"He would have gotten to me no matter what you did, Lieutenant. He kept a watch on me because I kept a watch on you. I'm as much to blame for my part in this as anybody."

He put his hands on my upper arms and faced me head-on. We were six inches apart. "You're not to blame. You were a victim."

"No, I wasn't," I said quietly. "I fought back. Iverson's dead because I wouldn't let him make me a victim."

He put his arms around me and held me close. I felt his heartbeat against my ear. There was no heat in the embrace, no passion, no lust. Only consolation. And I hugged him back to reciprocate.

Tears filled my eyes. In the past week, Tex and I had traded in the commodity of personal experience. We knew each other's vulnerabilities; we'd shared secrets that we might both have preferred to keep to ourselves. Things between us would never be the same.

"When I moved to Dallas, I put up walls. I built myself a glass house and you came along and threw a rock at it." I said. "Before that, I didn't know what I was shutting out of my life."

"Night, I've seen things I never want you to see. I've seen bugs digesting a corpse. Victims of knife wounds. Women who have been beaten to the point of concussions."

"You didn't put those things in the world. They were already there."

"But if I can keep you from seeing them, then I'm doing my job."

"Your job?"

"My job. To protect and serve."

He reached his hand out and hooked his finger over mine. We stood there, index finger to index finger, with the scent of cut grass and burning mesquite in the air. While I could feel things falling into place, I felt other things shifting. I looked down and blinked a few times to stave off the tears of good-bye.

"Hey," Tex said. He raised his knuckle to my chin and tipped my head up. "You're in good hands," he said. He bent down and kissed me lightly.

We pulled apart. "You know there's no way we would work as a couple, right?" I said.

"I've played a couple of scenarios out in my head and—while I wouldn't mind reenacting a few of them—I came to the same conclusion."

I stepped away and held up a hand in a wave. "See ya around, cowboy," I said.

He walked to his Jeep, but turned back when he reached it. "Hey, Night," he said. "No matter what, we'll always have Hunan Palace."

I walked backward toward the building. The mist had turned to a light rain that bounced off his shoulders like a halo of pixie dust. He flashed me a bright white smile that, coupled with his crisp, clear, blue eyes, would have stolen the heart of a lesser women. Who was I kidding? No matter what happened, there would always be a place in my heart for Tex.

When I went back inside, I ventured into the downstairs hall. The walls glowed with a soft shade of aqua, and the casing around each door frame had been refreshed with a coat of bright white. The vintage lighting fixtures mounted to the hall ceiling cast off a soft, pinkish light. There wasn't a burned out bulb in sight.

I climbed the stairs and found Hudson alone at the table. The poker chips sat in a pile in the center. I raised an eyebrow and sat in one of the empty seats.

"Who won?" I asked.

"Lyndy," Hudson said.

"Too bad for you."

"You win some, you lose some."

"Where'd he go?"

"I think Tex made him nervous. When you guys went out the back door, he collected his winnings and left out the front."

I laughed. "What about Dennis?"

"Outside having a smoke."

"How do you know him?"

"You had a meeting scheduled for this past Monday. When you didn't show, he tried to track you down. He probably would have figured things out from the news, but I called him back and told him what was going on."

"I asked him to list the apartment building for sale. We were going to do a walk-through. Did you paint the hallway?"

He tipped his head to the side. "Lyndy thought it would be a nice touch to spruce the place up before you sold it."

"A buyer might not want aqua walls in the hallway."

"The realtor found an interested buyer and it turns out, that's exactly what he wants."

"Already?"

"Madison, I know you have some bad memories of this place, but it's a good investment. Somebody was bound to snatch it up."

"I guess so. I didn't expect anything to happen so quickly."

"Nothing's going to happen if you don't want it to. You're the owner and technically it's not even listed for sale."

The clock on the wall read two thirty. "What day is it?" I asked.

"You don't know?" He looked amused. "It's Wednesday. The doctor gave you some pretty heavy medicine. You don't remember me coming up to check on you? Bringing Rocky to visit? Putting *Pillow Talk* into your DVD player?"

I looked away and tried to remember details from the last

couple of days. Fragmented images ran together like a pileup of cars in a highway accident. I didn't remember Hudson checking on me. I didn't remember Rocky or *Pillow Talk* or day turning to night or night turning to day. The only thing I remembered was feeling safe.

He reached his hand across the table and held mine. His amber eyes stood out against his tanned face and black hair. I stood and pulled him to his feet. "I'm going to shower and get dressed. When I come back out, do you think we could get dinner?"

"I can't. Dan and Cleo Tyler are expecting me to come over. They want to talk to me about optioning the rights to my story."

"That's okay with you?"

He shrugged. "I'm willing to listen to what they have to say. Besides, I think we'd make a pretty attractive on-screen couple, don't you?"

I laughed.

"Why don't you and Dennis go on that walk-through?"

"Sure," I said. After all that had happened, I was less certain about selling the apartment complex than I'd been, but the ball had been set into motion. "Give me ten minutes and I'll be ready. Come on, Rocky," I said.

Rocky sat on the bathroom rug while I showered and dressed in a turquoise and white eyelet dress that belted at the waist and swirled out in a full skirt. I slipped on lime green ballet flats and knotted a white ribbon in my hair. Dennis was waiting in my living room.

I hooked Rocky's leash onto his collar and we walked out the back door, around the perimeter of the property, and up the sidewalk to the front. We entered the lobby. I hit the switch on and off a few times, but the light didn't go on.

"Blown fuse," Dennis said. "Happens in these old buildings."

He walked further into the hallway and looked at the newly painted aqua walls. He ran the toe of his shoe over a spot where the carpet had been pulled away from the wall, exposing unfinished hardwood floors underneath. As we walked into and out of the vacant units, I tried to see what Dennis must have seen, a running list of upgrades needed to get top dollar. Instead, all I could see were aqua walls and Mamie Eisenhower-pink bathrooms. Memories and opportunities.

"I heard you have a buyer," I said as we walked up the stairs to the second floor.

"I have an interested party," he corrected. "Technically you haven't created a listing. Technically, I haven't said I'm going to handle the sale."

I looked down the vacant hallway and tried to picture what an investor might do. Chrome lamps, textured walls, generic art from the big DIY home décor stores. High traffic carpet, sterile white bathrooms, and big ugly ceiling fans. And then an overwhelming sense of being in the right place at the right time rooted me to the torn carpet. It was like the last five minutes of every Doris Day movie when the music swelled before "The End" hit the screen. When the characters' eyes are suddenly open wide and they realize what's been in front of them all along.

"This interested party, do you know what he plans to do with the building?"

It was Hudson's voice that answered. "I thought I'd pull up the carpet, maybe install a Nelson Bubble lamp in the foyer. Nothing major," he said.

"You're the interested party?"

He leaned down to my ear and dropped his voice. "It was Mortiboy's idea."

"Mortiboy's a smart cat," I said.

"Hasn't steered me wrong yet."

Hudson rescheduled his meeting with Cleo and Dan and I followed him to his house for dinner. The mist had turned into a steady shower. It was too hot to stand over a grill, too late to plan an elaborate menu. Hudson prepared a picnic of pitas, hummus, and fresh vegetables, and I poured us two glasses of Chablis. Dinner conversation steered clear of recent events involving the abductions and decorating jobs. Hudson told me stories about driving out west with Mortiboy as his copilot and Rocky and I listened with rapt attention.

As the night grew to a close, Hudson turned to me. "You don't have to leave." He brushed a few stray blond hairs out of my face. "Stay here with me."

"Okay," I said, surprising him by not thinking it over. "Which do you want? The sofa or the bed?"

His eyes moved from my mouth to my eyes and back to my mouth. "You pick," he said.

I reached forward and hooked my index finger into the waistband of his jeans, tugging him closer to me. "I thought maybe we could start on the sofa and then move to the bed."

He scooped me up in his arms and we kissed. And just like that, I was back in the game.

READER'S DISCUSSION GUIDE

1. By the end of the first chapter, Madison hears a woman accuse Tex of being responsible for the abduction and subsequent murder of her daughter. Did the accusation surprise you? Do you think it is possible for a police officer to use his role to commit horrible crimes?

2. Officer Nasty cautions Madison from blindly believing in Tex. She warns that he is not the man Madison thinks he is. Do you think Nasty's advice is rooted in jealousy? Do you think she still has feelings for Tex?

3. Madison is experiencing a mild bit of celebrity now that she's been involved in two high-profile cases. Do you think she is wise to try to help Tex, or do you think she should lay low and let him handle things himself?

4. In addition to spending time with Tex, Madison works with new clients and has the opportunity to endorse a collection of mid-century modern paint colors. In this sense, she seems to be keeping her business as a top priority. Do you think it helps her or hinders her to be a smart businesswoman in the middle of everything going on around her? Do you think she should close the doors to Mad for Mod and move out of Dallas?

5. What does it say about Madison that she is willing to risk her own safety to spend time with Tex? Would you have done the same thing? Or would you have distanced yourself from the abductions?

6. Throughout this book, Madison is expected to trust law enforcement and independent security companies, even though there is a constant threat that the people hired to protect her might

be the same people behind the abductions and killings. Do you think it was easier for Madison to trust the police because of her previous involvement with them?

7. Hudson returns to Dallas at a time when Madison least expects it. If he hadn't come back, do you think Madison would have made different decisions at the end of the book? Or do you think the events with both Tex and Hudson shook her up enough to push her forward?

8. Do you think Madison's self-inflicted emotional isolation is entirely behind her now, or do you think she will have trouble getting past what happened in this book? If you'd been through what she's been through, how do you think it would affect you? Would it change how you interacted with your current loved ones? Would you try to move on, or would you seek out people who might understand what you felt?

9. Do you think Madison and Tex could make it as a couple? Do you think Madison and Hudson could?

10. At the book's end, Madison is a forty-eight-year-old independent woman about to embark on a new relationship. Despite personal tragedy, she appears to be moving on. Do you think she can? Do you think this will lead to her happily ever after, or do you think there is more turmoil ahead for her?

FROM THE AUTHOR

I have always felt that something special happened when I first wrote *Pillow Stalk*, and it's been important to me to honor those characters who first sprang off the page in 2012. As much as each book is a mystery, it is also about personal growth, learning about ourselves, and taking chances. *With Vics You Get Eggroll* asks the question: how well do we know the people we think we know? Over the course of three books, I've fallen a bit in love with Madison, Tex, and Hudson, and I hope you have as well.

Diane Vallere

After two decades working for a top luxury retailer, Diane Vallere traded fashion accessories for accessories to murder. She is a Lefty Best Humorous Mystery Nominee and, in addition to the Madison Night series, writes the Material Witness and Style & Error mysteries. Diane started her own detective agency at age ten and has maintained a passion for shoes, clues, and clothes ever since. Visit her at www.dianevallere.com.

In Case You Missed the 1st Book in the Series

PILLOW STALK

Diane Vallere

A Madison Night Mystery (#1)

Interior Decorator Madison Night might look like a throwback to the sixties, but as business owner and landlord, she proves that independent women can have it all. But when a killer targets women dressed in her signature style—estate sale vintage to play up her resemblance to fave actress Doris Day—what makes her unique might make her dead.

The local detective connects the new crime to a twenty-year old cold case, and Madison's long-trusted contractor emerges as the leading suspect. As the body count piles up, Madison uncovers a Soviet spy, a campaign to destroy all Doris Day movies, and six minutes of film that will change her life forever.

Available at booksellers nationwide and online

Visit www.henerypress.com for details

Don't Miss the 2nd Book in the Series

THAT TOUCH OF INK

Diane Vallere

A Madison Night Mystery (#2)

When a rare five thousand dollar bill arrives in the mail, interior decorator Madison Night knows it's a message from her past. In happier times, she once joked that she could be bought for $5000—how could she deny a bill with her name on it? Suspecting the bill indicates trouble, she consults a numismatist. They set up a meet, but upon arrival she finds an abandoned office, a scared dog...and a dead body in the kitchen. The twist? The victim isn't the numismatist; it's a John Doe.

The police—led by Lt. Tex Allen—are on the case, but it's Madison who discovers the victim's identity. But where's the numismatist? Before long, she uncovers a kidnapping plot, a unique counterfeit operation, and the true price of her own independence.

Available at booksellers nationwide and online

Visit www.henerypress.com for details

Be sure to check out Madison's prequel novella
MIDNIGHT ICE featured in

OTHER PEOPLE'S BAGGAGE

Kendel Lynn, Gigi Pandian, Diane Vallere

Baggage claim can be terminal. These are the stories of what happened after three women with a knack for solving mysteries each grabbed the wrong bag.

MIDNIGHT ICE by Diane Vallere: When interior decorator Madison Night crosses the country to distance herself from a recent breakup, she learns it's harder to escape her past than she thought, and diamonds are rarely a girl's best friend.

SWITCH BACK by Kendel Lynn: Ballantyne Foundation director Elliott Lisbon travels to Texas after inheriting an entire town, but when she learns the benefactor was murdered, she must unlock the small town's big secrets or she'll never get out alive.

FOOL'S GOLD by Gigi Pandian: When a world-famous chess set is stolen from a locked room during the Edinburgh Fringe Festival, historian Jaya Jones and her magician best friend must outwit actresses and alchemists to solve the baffling crime.

Available at booksellers nationwide and online

Visit www.henerypress.com for details

Henery Press Mystery Books

And finally, before you go...
Here are a few other mysteries
you might enjoy:

THE DEEP END
Julie Mulhern

A Country Club Murders Mystery

Swimming into the lifeless body of her husband's mistress tends to ruin a woman's day, but becoming a murder suspect can ruin her whole life.

It's 1974 and Ellison Russell's life revolves around her daughter and her art. She's long since stopped caring about her cheating husband, Henry, and the women with whom he entertains himself. That is, until she becomes a suspect in Madeline Harper's death. The murder forces Ellison to confront her husband's proclivities and his crimes—kinky sex, petty cruelties and blackmail.

As the body count approaches par on the seventh hole, Ellison knows she has to catch a killer. But with an interfering mother, an adoring father, a teenage daughter, and a cadre of well-meaning friends demanding her attention, can Ellison find the killer before he finds her?

Available at booksellers nationwide and online

Visit www.henerypress.com for details

ARTIFACT

Gigi Pandian

A Jaya Jones Treasure Hunt Mystery (#1)

Historian Jaya Jones discovers the secrets of a lost Indian treasure may be hidden in a Scottish legend from the days of the British Raj. But she's not the only one on the trail...

From San Francisco to London to the Highlands of Scotland, Jaya must evade a shadowy stalker as she follows hints from the hastily scrawled note of her dead lover to a remote archaeological dig. Helping her decipher the cryptic clues are her magician best friend, a devastatingly handsome art historian with something to hide, and a charming archaeologist running for his life.

Available at booksellers nationwide and online

Visit www.henerypress.com for details

BOARD STIFF

Kendel Lynn

An Elliott Lisbon Mystery (#1)

As director of the Ballantyne Foundation on Sea Pine Island, SC, Elliott Lisbon scratches her detective itch by performing discreet inquiries for Foundation donors. Usually nothing more serious than retrieving a pilfered Pomeranian. Until Jane Hatting, Ballantyne board chair, is accused of murder. The Ballantyne's reputation tanks, Jane's headed to a jail cell, and Elliott's sexy ex is the new lieutenant in town.

Armed with moxie and her Mini Coop, Elliott uncovers a trail of blackmail schemes, gambling debts, illicit affairs, and investment scams. But the deeper she digs to clear Jane's name, the guiltier Jane looks. The closer she gets to the truth, the more treacherous her investigation becomes. With victims piling up faster than shells at a clambake, Elliott realizes she's next on the killer's list.

Available at booksellers nationwide and online

Visit www.henerypress.com for details

DINERS, DIVES & DEAD ENDS

Terri L. Austin

A Rose Strickland Mystery (#1)

As a struggling waitress and part-time college student, Rose Strickland's life is stalled in the slow lane. But when her close friend, Axton, disappears, Rose suddenly finds herself serving up more than hot coffee and flapjacks. Now she's hashing it out with sexy bad guys and scrambling to find clues in a race to save Axton before his time runs out.

With her anime-loving bestie, her septuagenarian boss, and a pair of IT wise men along for the ride, Rose discovers political corruption, illegal gambling, and shady corporations. She's gone from zero to sixty and quickly learns when you're speeding down the fast lane, it's easy to crash and burn.

Available at booksellers nationwide and online

Visit www.henerypress.com for details

MACDEATH

Cindy Brown

An Ivy Meadows Mystery (#1)

Like every actor, Ivy Meadows knows that *Macbeth* is cursed. But she's finally scored her big break, cast as an acrobatic witch in a circus-themed production of *Macbeth* in Phoenix, Arizona. And though it may not be Broadway, nothing can dampen her enthusiasm—not her flying caldron, too-tight leotard, or carrot-wielding dictator of a director.

But when one of the cast dies on opening night, Ivy is sure the seeming accident is "murder most foul" and that she's the perfect person to solve the crime (after all, she does work part-time in her uncle's detective agency). Undeterred by a poisoned Big Gulp, the threat of being blackballed, and the suddenly too-real curse, Ivy pursues the truth at the risk of her hard-won career—and her life.

Available at booksellers nationwide and online

Visit www.henerypress.com for details

16040329R00147

Printed in Great Britain
by Amazon